The Trial c

By William Cooper

About the Author

William Cooper is an attorney, journalist, and the award-winning author of *How America Works ... And Why It Doesn't*. His writings have appeared in hundreds of publications globally including *The New York Times, San Francisco Chronicle, CNN, Newsweek, Toronto Star,* and *Jerusalem Post. Publishers Weekly* calls his commentary about American politics "a compelling rallying cry for democratic institutions under threat in America." Visit him online at will-cooper.com.

© 2025 by William Cooper

All rights reserved.

No portion of this book may be reproduced in any form without written permission from the publisher or author, except as permitted by U.S. copyright law. This is a novel. Some characters are real people, and some are not. All dialogue was invented and certain historical events have been imagined or reimagined. The story is one of fiction and should be read and understood accordingly.

Published by Laughing Nuisance Productions LLC.

ISBN: 979-8-9999029-0-0

Available as an electronic book; ISBN 979-8-9999029-1-7

Cover design: Zeljka Vukojević

Author's Note

This story is a mix of things that were said and things that weren't; things that happened and things that didn't; people who changed the world and characters devised from scratch. It is therefore a work of fiction. All *Rumsfeld's Rules* are quoted verbatim from the book of the same name written by Donald H. Rumsfeld.

Rumsfeld Rule: "The two most important rules in Washington, D.C., are: Rule One: The cover-up is worse than the event. Rule Two: No one ever remembers the first rule."

Prologue

Part One: Cross-Examination

(October 14, 2018)

Part Two: Rummy's Rise

(June 29, 1963 – September 10, 2001)

Part Three: The Tape

(September 11, 2001 – June 31, 2005)

Part Four: Iran

(July 20, 2005 – October 24, 2005)

Part Five: Taos

(January 8, 2010 – September 19, 2018)

Part Six: The Trial

(September 23, 2018 – October 19, 2018)

Prologue

I knew Donald Rumsfeld well. His friends all called him Rummy. So did his enemies. Born outside of Chicago in 1933, Rummy entered Congress at the tender age of 29. After a few years in the Nixon administration, he became President Jerry Ford's chief of staff and later his secretary of defense. Years later, after making millions in the private sector, President George W. Bush selected him to run the Pentagon again, where he prosecuted the wars in Afghanistan and Iraq.

Not a bad resume for an ambitious fellow like Rummy. But this was all just prelude to the real drama.

A series of unfortunate events in 2005 led to Rummy becoming president of the United States. While the path there was twisted and scandalous, he made it to the top, like he always dreamed he would. His first order as commander in chief—to invade Iran—was a disaster. And Barack Obama came along a few years later and walloped him at the polls. Rummy had big plans for a second term that never came to be.

His story, however, didn't end there. While his rise was stratospheric—from an unknown kid in the Chicago suburbs to the president of the United States—his fall was just as extreme. Rummy ultimately became the most prominent victim of Donald J. Trump's presidential wrath.

What follows is all this in detail, plus much more. It's Rummy's life story: the ups, the downs, the shock, the awe. The big parts—the ones that mattered most to him and to the world. A great deal has been told before, in newspapers, classrooms, and history books. But much is revealed here for the first time. I've included some words of wisdom (and, in retrospect, irony) from Rummy himself, which are plucked from his famous book of axioms, *Rumsfeld's Rules*.

Whether you love Rummy or hate him (few are in between) it's one heck of a story.

How do I fit in? Well, that will eventually become clear. Let's just say, for now, that I had a little bone to pick with Rummy, and shedding some light on his life isn't just good for the world. It's good for me, too.

Part One: Cross-Examination
October 14, 2018

Rumsfeld Rule: "Don't do or say things you would not like to see on the front page of *The Washington Post*."

Chapter 1
October 14, 2018

Rummy could feel his heartbeat throbbing through his fingertips as his right hand rested on the mahogany paneling of the witness box. He had always liked public speaking, but this was different.

"Please be seated," Judge Sullivan said to the packed courtroom gallery—hundreds strong—in a thick Irish accent. In his early sixties, the judge's body was draped neck to toe in a black robe. He had slicked-back silver hair, a red complexion, and a wide double chin. Turning to Rummy, on his right, a now-familiar look of disdain formed on his face. "It is now time to start the afternoon session, which will consist of further cross-examination of the defendant," Sullivan said. Then his face relaxed as he turned forward to the prosecutor and nodded. "Mr. Perche, you may resume cross-examination."

"Mr. Rumsfeld," Patrice Perche said, standing tall at the podium in an all-black suit and tie. He was tan and had the body of an athlete. "This morning you testified that you honestly believed that Iraq had weapons of mass destruction in early 2003, before the United States invaded the country, is that right?"

"Yes, that is correct," Rummy replied, fidgeting in his hard chair. His tailbone ached from the four hours he'd spent on the stand that morning. He looked uncomfortable and worn—physically and psychologically—and I felt bad for what I had done. This whole thing wouldn't have happened if it wasn't for me. But it was too late for me to do anything about it now.

"Your Honor," Perche said, looking up at Sullivan, who was presiding over the proceedings in his giant, throne-like chair at least ten feet above everyone else, "the prosecution moves Exhibit 62 into evidence." His French accent made Rummy's blood curdle.

Sullivan looked from Perche over to Rummy's lawyer. Everyone in the gallery did too. "Any objection, Mr. Clement?"

"No objection, Your Honor."

Perche walked up to the witness box and placed the document on the dark wood. "Mr. Rumsfeld, please familiarize yourself with this document."

Rummy gave Perche a sharp stare. Thirty-five years his junior, Perche had run this prosecution from the beginning. It was clear to Rummy that he had no clue how the highest echelons of the United States government actually worked. Yet thanks to the president of the United States—Donald Trump—Perche had the power to upend, and potentially destroy, Rummy's life.

Rummy looked down at the document for a few seconds. Then he picked it up and began reading. The cavernous room was so quiet that everyone in the crowd—the international press, foreign dignitaries, interested observers from around the world, Joyce—heard a thump when Rummy placed the paper on the wood after he was done reading. He looked back up at Perche.

"What is this, Mr. Rumsfeld?" Perche said, tapping the paper.

"It's a memorandum from Colin Powell to Richard Armitage."

"What's the date?" Perche asked as he slowly walked across the courtroom floor. The clank of his shiny, black shoes echoed softly throughout the room.

"October 29, 2003."

"And who are these two men?"

"At the time, Colin Powell was the United States secretary of state and Richard Armitage was his deputy."

"Please read the text into the record."

Rummy sneered. "The whole thing?"

"Yes, the whole thing."

From: Secretary of State Powell
To: Deputy Secretary of State Armitage

Date: October 29, 2003
Subject: Rogue Intelligence Operation in DOD

"And what does DOD stand for?" Perche interrupted.
"Department of Defense."
"And you were its leader at the time?"
"Yes, I was secretary of defense."
"Please continue."

> *Further to our discussion yesterday, I have definitively confirmed that DOD Chief of Staff Jenkins' off-the-books, rogue intelligence shop obtained an audio recording of a conversation between Iraqi Ambassador Tariq Aziz and Saddam's son Qusay. On the October 5, 2002 tape, both men affirmatively and expressly said that Iraq DID NOT have weapons of mass destruction. In fact, they discussed whether to recommend Saddam restart the dormant WMD program. Cheney and Rumsfeld found out about this in October 2002—months before my speech to the United Nations—and buried it and never told the President, me, Condi, or anyone else about it. They tried to erase the tape from history. Please be prepared to discuss this during our one-on-one meeting tomorrow.*

Rummy then put the paper down and looked up at Perche. Palpable disdain flowed in both directions. After a few seconds, Perche resumed the cross-examination:

"Have you seen this memorandum before Mr. Rumsfeld?"
"Only this week, in preparing for my testimony."
"Did you see it while you were secretary of defense?"
"No ... no I did not."
"Who is Jenkins?"

"James Jenkins. I worked with him for many years in the public and private sectors. At the time he was my chief of staff at DOD."

"Do you know what intelligence shop Secretary Powell is referring to?"

"Yes, I do."

"Please explain."

Rummy paused a few seconds before answering. "We asked Mr. Jenkins to sanity check the intelligence community's conclusions regarding Iraq's weapons-of-mass-destruction program with his own team of agents in the field. We did this because—"

"Excuse me Mr. Rumsfeld," Perche said. "I did not ask *why* you did this. I simply asked what the intelligence shop was."

"Well, Mr. Perche, I would like to provide context for the—"

"Mr. Rumsfeld," Judge Sullivan intervened in his deep, authoritative voice, "you've answered the question already."

"Thank you, Your Honor," Perche said, smiling at Rummy deviously. "Mr. Rumsfeld, you said '*we* asked Jenkins…' Who are *we*?"

"Well, me, actually. If I remember correctly, it was just me."

"So, you set up a rogue unit of your underlings to manufacture intelligence in order to justify the United States' impending, inevitable, disastrous invasion of Iraq?"

Rummy looked over at the jury and then back at Perche. "No, no, I wouldn't characterize it like that at all."

"How would you characterize it then?"

"How I just did. We needed a sanity check on the intelligence community, which was failing to do its job in numerous—"

"Why didn't you tell the president or anyone else about this tape?"

"Objection, Your Honor," Rummy's lawyer Paul Clement said, standing up from counsels' table. "Assumes facts not in evidence."

"Overruled," Sullivan said immediately.

"Your Honor ... may I ... may I please speak with my attorney?" Rummy said, looking up at Sullivan. Rummy thought that Sullivan didn't like him, that the judge believed Perche's lies. He felt a sharp pain piercing his midsection when his eyes met the judge's.

"No," Sullivan said. "No, you may not. You may speak with your attorney *after* today's proceedings. And he will have an opportunity to question you before the jury on redirect examination."

Rummy fidgeted again in his chair. "Mr. Perche, can you please repeat the question?"

"Why didn't you tell President Bush or anyone else about this tape?"

"Well, I thought it was very likely the conversation took place with Aziz and Qusay knowing full well they were on tape, that they knew we had bugged them, and that their conversation was all a lie, was calculated misinformation. I thought Iraq really did have weapons of mass destruction, Mr. Perche. Saddam had used WMDs on his own people repeatedly. And his regime lied about everything, all the time."

"But why not share with the president the tape and also your thoughts about it? Why hide it?"

"We didn't hide it from the president, Mr. Perche. We simply chose not to affirmatively share it with him. We thought it would be more confusing than helpful."

"Who's we?"

"Cheney, Jenkins, myself."

"Did anyone else know about this tape before the US invaded Iraq in March 2003?"

"Not in the leadership, no. There were Jenkins' agents in the field, but they merely reported up the chain what they found."

"So you buried it?"

"No, we … we … we concluded that it was misleading and that it would be counterproductive to share it with other members of the administration."

"Including the president of the United States?"

"Yes."

"The commander in chief?"

"The president is the commander in chief."

Perche shook his head several times before continuing. "Mr. Rumsfeld, you didn't tell the president of the United States about the tape before he made the momentous decision to preemptively invade Iraq and start a war that killed thousands of innocent people?"

"I wouldn't characterize it that way."

"But that's true, isn't it? Yes or no."

"I wouldn't put it that way."

"Answer the question, Mr. Rumsfeld," Sullivan commanded. "Say whether it's true. Yes or no."

Rummy picked up the Powell Memorandum in front of him, his hands shaking, looked at it for a few seconds, and then put it back down. He licked his parched lips. "Can you repeat the question Mr. Perche?"

"You didn't tell the president of the United States about the tape before he made the momentous decision to invade Iraq?"

"Your Honor, may I speak with my lawyer privately? I'm not sure I can answer this question yes or no." Rummy's mouth was dry. His heartbeat dangerously fast. Perche was twisting everything into an unrecognizable cartoon, he thought, a farce that was radically at odds with the truth. But since Perche's narrative had a logical coherence, his deceit before the jury seemed to be working.

"Mr. Rumsfeld," Sullivan said, "no you may not. Take the question at face value, don't play games, and answer it. I do not want to have to hold you in contempt of court for refusing to answer."

"Can you please repeat the question?" Rummy asked Perche.

Perche sighed loudly. "You didn't trust the president of the United States with the tape before he made the momentous decision to invade Iraq?"

Rummy looked at Clement, who nodded at him. Then he responded: "Yes."

"And, of course, it turned out that Iraq did *not* have weapons of mass destruction, did it?"

"We never found conclusive evidence they did."

"So, the tape wasn't misleading but rather accurate, correct?"

"I can't ... I can't vouch for the accuracy of the tape, but we never did find weapons of mass destruction in Iraq."

"To the best of your knowledge, Mr. Rumsfeld, sitting here today, the statements on the tape that Iraq didn't have weapons of mass destruction were accurate, correct?"

"We still don't know."

Perche looked at Sullivan and raised his eyebrows.

The judge's baritone voice exploded as he leaned toward Rummy: "Mr. Rumsfeld! You need to answer the question with a yes or a no. You are under oath. This is not a press conference with reporters asking you questions. Or a business meeting with your underlings. This is a criminal trial before the International Criminal Court, and you are the defendant. Stop playing games and answer the question."

"Understood, Your Honor," Rummy responded. A wave of despondency coursed through his body. He knew his only option now was complete and utter submission. To Judge Sullivan. To Perche. To this trial. For a man who had been in control of the conversation his entire life, the dissonance was searing. "Can you please repeat the question Mr. Perche?"

"To the best of your knowledge, the statements on the tape of Qusay and Aziz, that Iraq didn't have weapons of mass destruction, were accurate, correct?"

Rummy looked at his lawyer again. Clement nodded back.

Rummy answered. "Yes."

Perche exhaled. "Yet the belief that Iraq had weapons of mass destruction was why President Bush authorized the war in Iraq, correct?"

"It was one of the reasons."

"It was one of the *main* reasons, correct?"

Rummy looked at Clement who this time gave him a blank stare and a soft shrug.

"Answer the question, Mr. Rumsfeld," Sullivan said.

"Yes."

"And as a result of the war, Iraq's national infrastructure was largely destroyed?"

"Yes."

"And as a result of the war, Iraq's economy was decimated?"

"No, that's just … this just isn't fair …." Rummy said, leaning forward. He looked out into the gallery at Joyce, who had started crying a few minutes earlier. She wiped her eyes with a yellow scarf. He turned from Perche up to Sullivan, then to Clement. He could feel the stares of everyone in the room watching his life's work—his hard-earned reputation as a leader and statesman with uncompromising integrity—swirl violently down the drain.

"That's just … that's just …" He looked up at the judge, whose mouth was starting to open. "Oh, never mind," Rummy said, slumping back in his chair, capitulating. Judge Sullivan simply wasn't going to allow him to explain himself. "My answer is yes."

"And as a result of the war, tens of thousands of innocent Iraqis were injured by US bombs, correct?"

"Yes."

"And as a result of the war, tens of thousands more innocent Iraqis were killed by US bombs, correct?"

"Yes."

Perche looked over at the jury, eight people (four men, four women) from eight different countries in Europe and Africa. All their eyes were fixed on him, enraptured. He noticed that several of them were nodding. So did Rummy. Then Perche looked up to Sullivan. "No further questions Your Honor."

"Thank you, Counsel," Sullivan said, fighting back a smile. "That will conclude today's hearing. Tomorrow the defendant's counsel will have the opportunity to examine him. Closing arguments from both sides will commence in the afternoon. The guards shall now escort Mr. Rumsfeld to his cell." He banged the gavel hard two times on the slab of mahogany in front of him. *Thwack, thwack.* The sound reverberated throughout the courtroom.

As Rummy walked through the center aisle toward the courtroom door he surveyed the crowd. His eyes danced from one spectator to the next. Then our eyes met. He squinted and scowled. My pulse quickened.

Part Two: Rummy's Rise
June 29, 1963 – September 10, 2001

Rumsfeld Rule: "Trust your instincts. Success depends, at least in part, on the ability to carry it off."

Chapter 2
June 29, 1963

"There are known knowns, you see," Rummy said, leaning back as everyone else at the table leaned in, enchanted. His small, muscular hands moved with confidence and vigor. He was smiling as he spoke. "These are the things you know that you know. You know how much milk is in your fridge. You know how much gasoline is in your car. You know that the Cubs won yesterday at Wrigley Field."

He paused and adjusted the glasses perched on his pointy nose. "Then there are known unknowns. This is the category of human knowledge where you know that something exists generally, but you don't know the details. You know that the Yankees played yesterday, but you don't know whether they won or lost cause you haven't checked the paper yet. You know that General Electric has already made millions this year, but you don't know how many millions because they haven't released their financial statements yet."

As the waitress at this Washington D.C. restaurant poured water into his glass he looked up into her eyes. "Thank you," he said. The waitress smiled and blushed. Joyce smiled too, slightly embarrassed, and glanced around the table at all the people admiring her husband. She was used to Rummy being the center of attention wherever he went. But she was shy and reserved by nature and over many decades had never quite got comfortable with it.

Then Rummy's face took on a more serious expression. "And you know people all around the world are plotting to attack the United States of America. But you don't know exactly *who*, exactly *where*, or exactly *how*." The chandelier glistened overhead. So did Rummy's eyes. His meal was untouched. He hadn't eaten since breakfast and the savory scent of his food made him salivate. But he was busy holding court, and the food could wait. "Then there is the third category of human knowledge ... the unknown unknowns. These are the things that you don't even know you don't know."

A woman in her early forties wearing a purple dress and sitting across the table, to his left, gently put her right hand over her mouth. She was tall and slender, with long, dark hair. Her lips were full and her facial features youthful and vibrant. He hadn't met her before that evening, but Rummy had noticed her looking at him frequently from across the table. Their eyes had met twice in the previous 15 minutes. Rummy had forgotten her name and was trying to remember it while he spoke.

"But they are out there. *Lurking.* These unknown unknowns. Some of them you will never consider; they will never enter your consciousness. Most of them, even. But some of them will arrive quickly and without warning." Then he simultaneously hit the table hard with his open right palm and said: "Boom! Without warning." The water danced in his glass. Several people in his audience gasped softly. A few smiles grew bigger.

"Some unknown unknowns introduce themselves to us without warning but are innocuous. Like a bird flying into the living room window. We don't expect them but they cause little trouble. While others are ferocious. Pearl Harbor was an unknown unknown to most people. Every American was focused on Europe and Asia. That's where the war was being fought. Hawaii was merely where we kept our ships and trained our troops. It wasn't on the radar screen at all. And that's what made us vulnerable."

He leaned back into his chair and crossed his arms, smiling, satisfied, and looked around the table. His suit jacket was tight around his bulging forearm muscles. Then he uncrossed his arms and picked up his fork and finally took a bite of salmon. Joyce put her hand on his knee.

"That's fascinating Rummy," said Ned Janetta, Rummy's childhood friend and former campaign manager. Janetta was sitting on the other side of the table to Rummy's right. His thick brown mustache stretched out well past his mouth and into his cheeks. "But isn't it a little esoteric? Don't we have to live life day-to-day doing the best we can with what's before us, not thinking about various tiers of knowledge but rather just reacting to what comes our way?"

Rummy looked at Janetta and squinted. "What do you mean 'just reacting'? We do some things affirmatively don't we?"

"I mean we can't always slow down and think deeply about tiers of human knowledge ... in a practical sense."

Refusing, as always, to go easy on his longtime friend, Rummy pushed back, injecting more authority into his voice with a louder sound and deeper tone. "I don't think we're so limited, *Ned*. Not always. What you say might be true in some contexts, like when you're going grocery shopping or having dinner with friends. Sure, in those settings it's fine to be on autopilot. But we live in a dangerous world with lots of threats and lots of things that can bite us if we're complacent. We must account for this part of the world too. We need to be aware of what we know and what we don't know, so we can act intelligently."

The woman in the purple dress started to bring her hands together to clap but stopped herself. The man to her right, her date, looked at her with raised eyebrows before turning back to Rummy.

"Well then, Rummy," said the gentleman immediately to his right in a soft voice. "What are some unknown unknowns you've been thinking about lately?"

"That question doesn't make sense, Bob," Rummy said with a smile. "Unknown unknowns are the things we don't think about at all." He raised his voice: "If I had been thinking about them, well, then they wouldn't be unknown unknowns, would they?" He hit the table with his fist right after he said it and the whole table laughed.

Even Bob.

The next morning Rummy was on Capitol Hill, in the spacious office of Gerald R. Ford, a veteran Republican Congressman from Michigan. The office smelled like many others in the building: a mix of stale cigar smoke and cheap aftershave. It was a crisp winter day in Washington D.C., with cold, sharp wind and a cloudless turquoise sky.

Rummy was new to Congress, having been elected—at age 29—to a seat representing his home district in Illinois. *Not bad for a middle-class kid from the Chicago suburbs*, Rummy thought on election night. His biggest fear in life was that he would always be anonymous, just another faceless person in the crowd. He worried that his intellectual talents would go unrecognized by the world. When he won the Congressional seat, the accomplishment alleviated this fear, to a limited extent and for a little while. But it would never be totally conquered. Even as president of the United States four decades later—when he had become a household name—he still harbored this fear that people wouldn't fully appreciate how extraordinary he was.

Joyce was happy for Rummy when he entered Congress, but a little nervous about raising the kids in Washington D.C., a city she'd never been to before the election. She wanted to stay in Illinois, but Rummy insisted they live in Washington. She knew that stifling his ambition was far worse for both of them than going along with it. Rummy loved Joyce for many reasons, and one of the biggest was that she accepted the fundamental truth that he couldn't function as a human being unless he was feverishly ascending some professional ladder. The status quo—no matter what it was—was never enough. That was exactly what had brought him into Ford's office on Capitol Hill.

"Jerry, we need you," Rummy said to Ford. "You're the only person in the Republican Party with the respect and support to oust Halleck. The party needs to change, and to change, we need *you*."

Ford was sitting at the large wooden desk in his office; his left leg draped over his right. A blue-and-yellow University of Michigan football helmet was on the desk to his left. Pictures of his family glittered in the morning sunlight on the cabinet behind him. Tall and athletic, the former college football star had thinning light-brown hair and handsome, genuine features. He was smoking a pipe.

Rummy sat in front of Ford, his left leg draped over his right knee, too. His thick brown hair was combed from left to right. Rummy's pipe was bigger than Ford's, but his puffs were smaller and less frequent. He still didn't like smoking cigars. They made his throat hurt and his clothes stink. But all the big boys in Congress smoked, so there was no way he wasn't going to, too. He even practiced in the mirror how to take a puff like a pro. Joyce had caught him practicing a few months earlier and still teased him about it when no one else was around.

His eyes were fixed hard on Ford.

"Well, thank you, Rummy. That's awfully nice of you to say. But I'm really not interested. I'm a loyal Republican, and Charlie, well, he's my friend. Been so for years. He's doing fine as leader. And I'm happy where I'm at. Chairman of the conference ain't too shabby." He turned and looked out the window. "I don't need … I just don't need to be atop the leadership right now. One day, yes. But I've got lots of time and don't need to betray a friend on the way up the ladder."

Rummy sighed. "I hear what you're saying, Jerry."

"But?" Ford said with a smile.

"But the status quo just isn't working. Charlie is decent a decent man, but he can't run a gas station, let alone a national political party. Just look at the results! The Democrats dominate this town. We have all the right ideas and only 140 seats out of 435 to show for it. 140! Goldwater got shellacked. We've lost the courts. We need to *do* something. We can't let conservative ideas in this country—the intellectual underpinnings of the American experiment itself—wither into historical novelties. I know you don't want to offend your friend, but we can't keep losing all the time."

Ford slowly shook his head back and forth. Rummy could tell his sales pitch wasn't working. So he did what he always did: push harder. I saw this side of Rummy consistently years later when he was secretary of defense. If he didn't like how something was going, he would simply push harder. He was self-aware enough to recognize this trait in himself, and once told me, "My dad used to joke when I was a kid that my operating principle was, 'if it doesn't go easy, force it.'"

"Now is our opening, Jerry, especially with sentiment for the war continuing to get worse. Inaction is just as much a choice as action and we can't abdicate responsibility to the party—to the country—to change things, to stir things up, to make things better. We need to go back to limited government. A stronger military. Bigger police forces. Better judges. We need someone with the ability to get things done. We need you, Jerry."

Rummy was a little nervous talking to Ford, but his face didn't show it. He was new to Congress and wouldn't stand for being just another suit and tie in the Republican minority. He wanted to stand out, and Ford was his ticket. Being Ford's ally was an important step toward achieving his ultimate goal: to be president of the United States.

"Well, I don't know, Rummy. I just don't know," Ford said, taking a deep puff of his pipe. Thick smoke scampered out of his mouth and formed a cloud that hovered between them.

"We can change things. We need you to run."

"Okay, okay, let me think about it some more."

"Great! That's all I can ask for," Rummy said, peering deeply into Ford's eyes and flexing his cheek muscles into a huge smile. Then he took a puff of his pipe and coughed in a way that made Ford smirk.

Late that night, Rummy arrived home at the Rumsfelds' two-bedroom, second-floor apartment several blocks from the Capitol. He and Joyce didn't have much money (yet), and the apartment was small. The furniture was used and the paint faded. The old brown carpets emitted a slightly nauseating stench. While home, Rummy was consumed with being present for his family and, when they were sleeping, his work. His meager surroundings bothered him little. Joyce was another story, though. While she was proud of Rummy's accomplishments, she wanted a nicer home and was looking forward to his promised entry into the private sector within a few years. "If he's gonna work 18 hours a day," she once vented to a friend, "it'd be nice if he actually made some money."

It was just after 11 p.m. and Joyce and their three kids (two girls and a boy) were asleep. They'd left him a note on the fridge: *We love you Daddy! Dinner's in the Tupperware. Don't stay up too late. We need hugs before school!*

Rummy smiled. Right next to Joyce's note was Rummy's favorite poem, *If*, by Rudyard Kipling. He read it aloud to the family once or twice a week—though no one really paid attention when he did. His favorite line: *If you can trust yourself when all men doubt you, but make allowance for their doubting too.* It summed up his intellectual self-image: a confident but open-minded thinker, unburdened by hubris or ideology.

Then he walked slowly and quietly into the bedroom and sat on the bed next to Joyce. *Still as beautiful as ever*, he thought, admiring her soft, thin features and wavy light brown hair. Whenever he saw her sleeping, he yearned to see her eyes, those stunning green eyes he'd been staring into since they were kids. He kissed her gently on the cheek. She was sleeping deeply after another long day with the kids in a town without close friends or real support. Rummy's guilt about uprooting his family nagged at him but was nonetheless outweighed by his ambition to make a name for himself in Washington.

He got up and walked back into the kitchen and placed his briefcase on the gray plastic table in the middle of the oval-shaped room. He took off his jacket and, grimacing at the cigar odor, hung it up by the door. *Needs to be dry-cleaned soon*, he thought to himself. Then he sat down and pulled out a thick stack of paper from his briefcase along with a yellow notepad. He pulled a pen from his shirt pocket and composed a list:

- *Stay on top of Jerry, Halleck must go!*
- *Get Dole's support on Halleck too.*
- *Call Searle again re: contributions, plant seeds about CEO job.*
- *Get lighter tobacco and a bigger pipe.*
- *Don't forget haircut.*

At the top of his stack of papers was a memorandum entitled *US Involvement in Vietnam: Pros and Cons*, written by the Republican National Committee. Pen in hand, he started to read it. A few minutes later he added two bullets to his list:

- *Plan visit to Vietnam, need foreign policy experience on resume.*
- *Need show of force on the ground in Vietnam. Weakness is provocative!*

After two more hours of working under the dank kitchen light, he finally went to bed. His alarm was set for 5:30 a.m. He put his pen, notepad, and glasses on the bedside table next to the clock and crawled under the blankets. He was asleep seconds after his head hit the pillow.

When the alarm went off a few hours later Joyce grabbed his arm and said, "Snooze, please." Rummy smiled. This meant that instead of waiting for her alarm an hour later, she'd be up when he got out of the shower. He hit the snooze button, excited to savor a few minutes with Joyce before heading to the Capitol.

When he emerged from the shower Joyce was sitting up in bed with a cup of coffee in her hands. Two pillows were perched behind her. She was wearing a blue robe and her long brown hair hung over her shoulders.

"Hi there, handsome," she said, handing him his coffee and admiring his chiseled physique as water dripped down his chest. Rummy was a wrestler in high school and college and still worked out at least five times most weeks. While only 5'7 and very lean, he weighed 157 pounds.

"Thank you, darling," he said, taking the coffee, feeling it warm in his hands. He leaned in and kissed her on the lips. "How are you?"

She could feel the heat emanating from his body after the hot shower. "Better now that I'm with you. Feels like it's been weeks."

"Months, I'd say. It's always too long when we're not together." He sat down next to her on the bed and took a sip of coffee. "Anyone call yesterday?"

"Just Ned. Said it was something about Searle—didn't specify but said it wasn't urgent."

"Okay, I will call him back at the office."

"Gotta keep those campaign contributions flowing," she said.

He chuckled. "Can't argue with that!"

"I have an idea," Joyce said, sitting up straight with a bounce and turning towards him.

"Oh yeah, what's that," Rummy said, raising his eyebrows.

"Take the day off from work, play hooky. Ditch all those boring old Congressmen and their stinky cigars. They're no fun. We'll get the kids to school and then do whatever we want all day. Brunch. Shopping. A movie." She put her hand on his knee and smiled. "We can come back home for a while, too." Knowing the answer already, she asked, "What do you think?"

Rummy's heart sank and he gave her a guilty grin. "Ah, I wish I could, hun. I really do. But I need my boots on the ground today at the Capitol. Lots of drama about who will be the next leader of the party." He kissed her again before standing up and looking over at the clothes closet.

"Oh yeah? Let me guess. Donald H. Rumsfeld, the new kid from Illinois?"

"Ha! Not yet!"

She put her coffee down and reached up and grabbed his right arm and pulled him back close to her. Her hair bounced up and down. She stared at him intently, saying plenty without a single word.

He wrapped his arms around her and said, "I wish we could. I really do. I'm sorry. It's important that I'm there today." She looked down and he kissed her on top of the head.

She sighed and looked back up at him. "It's okay. I understand."

"Can I take a rain check? Next week maybe?"

"You know where to find me."

Rummy stepped back and walked over to the closet to get his suit pants. He looked at her as he put them on. "You sure you're okay, hun? I know this is hard on you, being here and all."

"Yeah, I'm fine. I know this is temporary and what you're doing is important work."

Rummy knew Joyce's version of "temporary" wasn't necessarily the same as his, and a jolt of anxiety pierced his stomach. He reached into the closet to grab a shirt. "Date night Saturday will be fun. We like the sitter, right?"

"Yeah, Mrs. Smith, she's an old pro."

"Okay, great. Will be just me and you. No one else. I'm already craving the raviolis."

Joyce smiled. "I'm already craving the merlot."

Chapter 3
January 18, 1973

Rummy did indeed make a name for himself in Congress. So much so that after seven years in the House, in 1969 President Richard Nixon appointed him to a cabinet position as Director of the Office of Economic Opportunity. He was a little hesitant to take the job. "Not exactly secretary of state," he quipped to Ford after getting the offer. But he said yes and made the most of it. *Quite boring but a platform for something better*, he often thought. Then, in 1971, Nixon made him Director of the Economic Stabilization Program.

Also cabinet-level.

Also boring.

Rummy wasn't satisfied. He needed more responsibility, more power, more prestige. A *lot* more. He would aim for nothing less than secretary of defense. Leading the US military would not only be a worthwhile use of his time, it would also be a nice steppingstone to the presidency. A long-time reservist naval pilot, he loved the idea of going to the Pentagon every day, exercising civilian control over the military, and shaping America's posture in the Cold War. He'd hinted to Nixon his desire to run the Pentagon, but it hadn't gotten any traction.

By early 1973, he sensed a storm brewing, one that could damage what he prized most: his reputation. He wasn't going to let that happen.

"Mr. President!" Rummy said, with a huge smile, walking across the thick blue carpet in the Oval Office toward Richard Nixon. His right hand rose toward the president.

"Good to see you, Rummy," Nixon replied, extending his right elbow out awkwardly and then stretching his large hand down towards Rummy's.

"Thank you," Rummy said, squeezing Nixon's hand firmly. Nixon squeezed back even harder, and Rummy relaxed his grip, letting the president have the edge. Nixon's hand was cold and sweaty and Rummy discretely wiped his hand on the side of his pants. Nixon gestured towards the bright yellow couch in the middle of the room and Rummy took a seat. Nixon sat down in a large chair to Rummy's right.

"Nice suit," Nixon said, looking Rummy up and down. "Though I still think you should drop the glasses. The future senator from Illinois shouldn't wear glasses."

Rummy chuckled. *Here he goes again*, Rummy thought, *obsessing over my career when his is the one in trouble. No wonder this place is in shambles.* "Still considering it, Mr. President," he said, beaming his big, bright smile.

"Okay, okay. How can I help you? You requested this meeting, right?" Nixon asked.

"Yes, thank you for taking the time to see me, Mr. President."

Nixon looked him in the eyes and nodded in an awkward, forceful way, apparently intended to make Rummy start explaining why he was there. The drooping skin dangling from his chin danced around like jelly as his head jerked up and down. His black hair was strikingly devoid of gray. The bags under Nixon's eyes had grown since the last time Rummy had seen him just a few weeks earlier. They seemed darker, too.

"Well, let me get right to it. There's an opening at NATO, as you know, Mr. President, and I would like to go to Brussels and be the US Ambassador."

Nixon's head lurched back violently. "What ... fuck ... Don ... why?"

"It's an important role and I think the country needs strong leadership. With the trouble in Vietnam and the growing sentiment against the war, we need competence in important foreign-policy positions. And Russia is only getting stronger and more emboldened. We need to force our NATO allies to be firm and contribute their fair share and project strength ... and I just don't think that's happening right now, Mr. President."

Nixon fidgeted in his chair and crossed his legs. "But things are really picking up domestically, Don, here at home. We may need your sharp acumen in the coming weeks and months. You see all the shit that's happening around here. You read the papers. The vultures are circling. They want blood. You know what I'm talking about."

"I understand, Mr. President, but you have a very sound domestic team with Bob and Chuck and others. You don't need me here. But the country does need me in Brussels. To be honest, Mr. President, this is something I would like to do for my own future as well," Rummy said, speaking the language of careerism that Nixon welcomed and respected. "As you know, foreign policy is my true passion. I'd like to serve your administration in the years ahead in national security and international diplomacy. It will help a possible Senate candidacy. This is a way to start that journey."

"Fuck ... Don ... I don't know. I just don't know. How long do you want to be there?"

"No set timeframe. But I would like to get the wheels in motion on this now."

Nixon scratched his cheek hard enough that a pink line appeared. "I'm just not sure," he said. Rummy thought the look of distress on his face was oddly disproportionate to the subject at hand. Why did Nixon care this much if the head of the Economic Stabilization Program—far from a central player in his administration—went to Brussels? While their relationship was cordial and he knew Nixon respected him, they only saw each other a few times a month.

"You will be just fine here without me, Mr. President. This is nothing you can't handle and certainly nothing you and your team can't overcome. I would—"

"One moment," Nixon said, holding his index finger up into the air as he looked Rummy in the eyes. Then he got up and walked to his desk and sat down. Without Rummy noticing (he was admiring the portrait of Teddy Roosevelt on the wall) Nixon pressed a red button under the desk to stop the recording of their conversation. After pretending to jot down a note on a yellow pad on the desk, he stood up and walked back to his chair next to the couch.

"Can I confide in you, Rummy?" he said, looking at Rummy. He was squinting, his bottom lip quivering.

"Of course, Mr. President."

Nixon's voice lowered into a scratchy whisper. "Well, these accusations flying about, about what I knew and what I didn't know. What I was involved in and what I wasn't."

Rummy leaned toward Nixon so he could hear him better. "Yes."

"Well, and don't repeat this to anyone, you hear me."

"Yes, understood. I hear you."

"*Anyone.*"

"Understood."

"Well, most of them are total bullshit, either invented out of thin air or grotesque exaggerations. Horrific lies, really. You wouldn't believe the viciousness of my enemies."

Rummy's face was expressionless as he looked Nixon in the eyes, but his stomach was boiling with anxiety. He learned as a teenager that for some reason when he got nervous, even really nervous, his face didn't show it. It wasn't a conscious effort, it just worked that way—like a duck floating quietly atop a pond, but underneath the tranquil water, out of view, its legs paddling at warp speed.

He knew where Nixon was headed.

"But some of them, a small subset, well, they aren't total bullshit. We made some mistakes. Our intentions were sound. The Democrats simply can't get back into power. No fucking way. The country won't survive. We barely survived Johnson. We can't let them get control again. The ends justified the means, clear as day, Rummy."

Rummy was nodding gently, trying to appear sympathetic and understanding, all the while thinking, *Run away ... run as far away from this mess as you can. You cannot go down with this ship.*

"So, we did some things," Nixon went on. "Some of them worked well and you'll never hear about. But this Watergate mess has legs. Don't tell anyone. You understand?"

"Yes, I understand."

"It has legs. And so we need you to help us. The country needs your help. It would be disastrous for the party, for the country, for the world, for this to get traction, for the Democrats and the press to twist this into a real scandal. We need brains on this. We need competence. We need you, Rummy."

Run, thought Rummy. *Run. Run. Run. Run. Get as far away from this man as you possibly can.*

"I appreciate that, Mr. President. I really do." Nixon was frowning awkwardly, his head tilted to his right and his bulging, bloodshot eyes fixed on Rummy. "But I'm a policy guy, not a political guy. The team you have in place already, here with you at the White House, they know what they're doing. You're in good hands. You'll be fine."

Nixon just stared at him.

"Look at your poll numbers," Rummy continued. "You're still popular. You are a strong president. You have achieved great things already and will achieve more. I think sending me to Brussels is best." Then Rummy closed the deal: "And ... Mr.

President ... that way no one will ask me what I know and what I don't know. I'm no good at answering questions like that. Sending me to Brussels is safer, for you even more than for me. It's best for everyone."

Nixon stared at him for several seconds without speaking.

Chapter 4
August 10, 1974

"Rummy," Ford said, his voice hoarse and urgent. "I need you in Washington. Tomorrow. Get on the first flight you can find."

Rummy held the phone hard against his ear. He was at his desk at NATO headquarters in Brussels. The sound of the new president of the United States needing him at an urgent hour was music to his ears. He smiled and his eyes got moist. He even felt a little dizzy. This wasn't the kind of call you made so someone could run some marginal cabinet department. The only explanation was that Ford wanted him to be a central player in the new administration. Rummy had been craving something like this for years. "I don't know if I can make it to Washington in a day, Mr. President, but I will do my best."

"Things are all over the place right now. I need you to run my transition, so get over here ASAP. We can discuss the right position for you after that."

Two powerful questions collided in Rummy's mind at the same time: One: *What position should I angle for?* Two: *How on earth am I going to tell Joyce that we have to move* back *to Washington?* "Understood, Mr. President. I'm on my way."

Rummy thought Ford sounded tired and frazzled. Understandably so. The Watergate scandal was making front page headlines across the globe. He'd read about a new damning revelation nearly every other day. None of it surprised him. He felt sorry for Nixon, whom he liked personally. Had he been advising Nixon, he would have told him not to resign, to fight harder, to take a chance in the Senate. The House was going to impeach him—no doubt—but the Senate was up for grabs. A two-thirds vote to remove him from office was a high hurdle. And even if he was convicted by the Senate, that wouldn't be much worse than resigning. Fighting gave him materially better odds of survival with only a slightly worse downside. Decades later, when Rummy observed President Donald Trump fight off the Democrats trying to impeach him for withholding Congressionally authorized aid to Ukraine, Rummy recalled Nixon's resignation. *Trump is unfit to be president*, Rummy thought, *but he does get one thing right: never give an inch when being attacked by your enemies.*

But Rummy hadn't been advising Nixon on Watergate. He had very intentionally been in Brussels as the US Ambassador to NATO, a million miles away from that mess.

Rummy's ability to see trouble brewing and leave Washington before the Watergate scandal broke added to his great confidence that he could navigate around virtually anything. When I raised concerns with him years later that he was being too aggressive in foreign policy, he cast aside my concerns as being too timid, too risk averse. "We need to lean forward," he would always say. He under-weighed the potential downsides of big decisions because he had never experienced them. He'd always been able to move the chess pieces around in just the right way to win—so he thought he could never lose. This blind spot would eventually seal his fate.

Chapter 5
September 22, 1975

Rummy woke up at 3:45 a.m. He'd been Ford's chief of staff for more than a year now. He spent a few hours in his room at the Saint Francis Hotel in San Francisco getting things done, including editing President Ford's speech, which was going to be delivered that evening. It hit the usual points: restoring trust with the American public after Nixon; getting inflation under control; maintaining a strong defense in the Cold War. Rummy had to rewrite several passages about Vietnam after Secretary of State Henry Kissinger's edits made the president sound weak.

"Weakness is provocative!" Rummy wrote in the margins.

Then Rummy pulled out a blank sheet of paper and wrote a letter to Joyce. It was something he did often while traveling.

> *Dearest Joyce,*
>
> *I write to you from the Saint Francis Hotel, here in San Francisco. As is true every time I travel, it's very hard being away from you and the kids. Washington feels so far away. I'm already looking forward to the private sector where, as a CEO, I'll be able to control my own schedule. I haven't forgotten my promise, either: my office will be in (or near) Chicago.*
>
> *For now, I continue to serve President Ford each day. But my thoughts, as ever, are with you, the love of my life. There's a diner near the hotel and as the motorcade drove past it last night, I remembered how much fun we used to have at Davey's, those Friday nights filled with burgers, milkshakes, and laughter. I can still see your dazzling smile lighting up the whole room. Every teenage boy in town had their eye on you, yet somehow you chose me.*
>
> *How did I get so lucky?*
>
> *I will be home in four days, not long after this letter reaches your hands. After San Francisco, we have a stop in Denver (to meet with*

business leaders) and Kansas City (for a speech to the Chamber of Commerce). Then we fly back to Washington.

This is important work for the administration; we need to meet key constituents face-to-face to build trust after Watergate. As you know, what the American people need now more than anything else is trust in their president. President Ford is the right man at the right time, and I'm proud to be helping him in this important mission.

I cannot wait to walk through our door soon and be in my favorite place in the world, my only true home: with you.

Thank you for everything.
I love you,
Don

A few hours later, Rummy stood in an elevator. He, President Ford, and three Secret Service agents rode from the sixth floor to the ground floor at the Saint Francis. No one spoke. As the elevator clunked and burped its way down, Rummy stood behind Ford and looked closely at his head. There it was on the left side of his skull: the red spot where Ford's head smacked the ground earlier that day after tripping and falling on his morning run.

All we need is for another physical blunder to get out to the press, Rummy thought, shaking his head. *Chevy Chase will have a field day if he finds out about Ford's latest trip-and-fall. I should be thinking about the Cold War and the economy, how to get our legislation through Congress. But instead, half my time is spent trying to prevent another Jerry Ford skit on Saturday Night Live.*

The group of five men in suits walked out of the elevator and turned left toward the lobby. The rustle of a crowd grew louder as they approached. As they turned the corner into the lobby, a group of several dozen people stood behind a thick red divider. Men, women, and children with big smiles and bright eyes.

Several of them were waving small American flags. They started yelling:

"Mr. President!"

"Mr. President!"

"Thank you. Thank you," Ford said, smiling and waving as he walked by. A natural people-pleaser, Ford started to veer toward them to shake some hands, but Rummy put his hand on Ford's shoulder and said softly: "Not today, Mr. President." Ford turned and walked toward the exit.

The Secret Service men all had blinking electronics in their ears. One of them, with short fire-engine-red hair and darting green eyes, was speaking softly into his wrist. Rummy noticed this and was glad to see them focused on protecting the president, given his paranoia over Ford's safety. In meetings with the head of the agency Rummy urged him to be more proactive, more forward-leaning, more decisive in identifying and responding to threats.

"The country can't handle another presidential assassination," he said. "We'll get through a controversy if you get too aggressive. That's fine. But we can't have another Dallas. Don't let it happen. Lean forward. Always err on the side of action."

Rummy was a young Congressman when JFK was assassinated. It shook him deeply. He ran to the bathroom and vomited after hearing the news. Years later he still remembered the feeling of holding the porcelain toilet in his hands, vomit coming out of his mouth and nose, images of the president getting shot flashing in his head. It wasn't just a national tragedy; it was a powerful personal wake-up call. His primary goal in life— the only thing that might truly satisfy his ambition—was to be president, and Dallas was a reminder that if he ever did achieve his goal, it wouldn't be fun and games from there. Being president was dangerous.

The group turned right and walked down a short flight of steps. A Secret Service agent opened the door. Two agents walked out first. Then the president. Then another agent. Then Rummy. As the group walked out of the hotel onto the sidewalk the bright sun scolded their eyes. Rummy inhaled the cold fresh air. Ford squinted as he waved to the cheering crowd, several hundred strong.

"Mr. President!"

"Mr. President, over here!"

"We love you, Jerry!"

A long motorcade with eight vehicles, including the presidential limousine, was waiting. The cars' engines purred. San Francisco police officers stood to the entourage's left and right, intermixing with Secret Service agents. The cop closest to the president, on his right, had a sturdy build and a thick, brown, handlebar mustache. Rummy squinted as the sunlight beamed down on the people and pavement. He was the only member of the administration with the president. Just the way he liked it.

Ford was a few feet ahead of him as the group approached the sleek black limousine. Suddenly Rummy heard the chilling, thundering cadence of gunshots:

Thwack, thwack, thwack.

Screams erupted. There was violent commotion in the crowd. Policemen and Secret Service agents started tackling people. A man in blue jeans and a T-shirt—an innocent bystander—was thrown to the ground like a rag doll. His shoulder hit the ground hard and he howled in pain. A Secret Service agent grabbed Ford and hurled him into the limo. Rummy jumped in after them, headfirst, landing awkwardly and painfully on his side. Then another agent jumped in. The doors slammed shut behind them. As the car sped away its tires screeched and thick, black, rubber-stenched smoke rose from the hot gray pavement. And four terrified grown men with racing heartbeats wearing fancy 1970s suits and ties wiggled and squirmed on the floor of the accelerating limousine. The driver squeezed the wheel with both hands and clenched his teeth.

"Are you okay Mr. President?" Rummy asked frantically, as they took a turn sharp enough to throw him back to the ground as he fought to right himself.

"Yes ... yes, I'm fine," Ford said, flustered and shaken.

One of the agents told both men to stay on the floor of the car, to stay down. He put one hand on each of them. "Do not sit up!" The other agent reinforced the point: "Don't move!" They didn't have time to wait for a police escort, so the driver just zigged and zagged around cars and pedestrians as he made his way toward the freeway several blocks away. "Don't move a muscle." Rummy was a little perturbed at the lack of deference being paid to the president of the United States and his chief of staff but nonetheless complied.

Later they would learn that a San Francisco political activist named Sarah Jane Moore had pointed a .38 special revolver at Ford. A policeman named Joseph Curry struck her arm as she pulled the trigger twice. The bullets went between Ford's head and Rummy's head before hitting the wall of the Saint Francis.

"Where should I go?" the driver asked as the car approached the freeway on-ramp.

"We need to fly back to Washington!" Rummy shouted, lying on the cramped floor of the limousine in a contorted two-man pretzel with Ford. "Drive to the airport," he commanded. His right shoulder was throbbing.

Ford was still grimacing with closed eyes. He was squeezing the shoe of the Secret Service agent lying next to him. His heartbeat racing, Rummy's eyes were wide open, staring at the door to the limousine. The left side of his head was pressed against the floor and he felt the engine accelerate as the car sped onto the freeway. He winced as the scent of Ford's aftershave seeped into his nostrils.

As they made their way to the airport—still lying on the floor—Rummy smiled ever so slightly. Now that he spent so much time with the sitting president, he lived in fear of dangerous events and yet, to his surprise, he found himself relishing the triumphant dopamine explosion of surviving the attack. He couldn't help but like the dangerous side of making history.

About two months later, on November 18, 1975, Rummy was sworn in as United States secretary of defense. Dick Cheney became Ford's chief of staff the same day. After a few weeks in his new job, Rummy was lying in bed on his back with his hands interlocked behind his neck. His biceps bulged out of his T-shirt and his wedding ring pressed on the back of his head. The heavy gel in his hair produced a thick layer of oily residue on the white pillow. As usual. Joyce thought it was gross but never complained when she washed the pillowcases and Rummy never even noticed it.

He couldn't sleep. He was running the Pentagon now. The president had indulged his desire to add a foreign-policy trophy to his resume. One big reason was that Ford liked and trusted Rummy's 35-year-old protégé, Cheney, and was comfortable with him taking over as chief of staff.

"This kid has ice in his veins, Rummy," Ford said about Cheney from behind his desk in the Oval Office. "And smart as a whistle. Where'd you find him?"

Rummy smiled. "Plucked him right out of the teeming intellectual hotbed of Casper, Wyoming."

Ford chuckled. "Well done."

"Yes, and he isn't just smart. He's loyal. We can trust him."

The Cold War and Vietnam were Rummy's biggest challenges in his new job. A close third: the Pentagon bureaucracy. The Department of Defense was a large, complicated, nebulous animal he had quickly come to loathe. Special interests had run amok. The bureaucracy was already disrupting Rummy's goals and thereby, he thought, endangering the country. He was angry much more as defense secretary than in his other jobs. He was cursing about three times as much at home, Joyce noticed. She tried to help him keep perspective: "The bigger the job, the higher the stakes. Don't take bureaucratic fighting personally, Don. It's how people are and always will be."

"I know, I know," he replied. "You're right."

"This is what you've wanted. It's a privilege to have this job."

"You're right, hun. I know. It's just that it really does hurt the country when it's *this* hard to get things done and make change. I didn't put in all that work to get the job—years and years of studying and striving—so a bunch of bureaucrats could thwart my every move."

She put her hand on his cheek and smiled. "I understand, I do. Just keep it all in perspective. You've come a long way since Congress and the Economic Stabilization Program. This is what the major leagues are like. A big part of succeeding is not letting things get to you and staying focused on what you can control."

Joyce's words didn't stop him from tossing and turning that night. It was about 2 a.m. He was remembering something that for multiple decades crept into his mind when he couldn't sleep. He was a sophomore at Princeton, wrestling against some muscular Ivy Leaguer (Harvard, or maybe Yale) with a brown buzz cut, flaring nostrils, and over-sized triceps. It was the league championship match, the biggest of his life. His folks were there. So was Joyce.

His opponent was good: strong, quick, nasty. Though a wrestler since high school, Rummy hadn't faced anyone like this before. A few minutes into the match, but before any points were scored, his opponent flashed a cocky smile at Rummy and said confidently: "I own you." The way he said it scared Rummy and he felt his expression subtly reveal this fear to his opponent. His face typically didn't reveal his emotions, but this time the fear was so pronounced that it did. And it made his opponent smile even wider. Rummy's teeth clenched and his abs tightened. Once they clashed again, Rummy hung in there for a while, but his opponent eventually pinned him, handing him the most devastating loss of his wrestling career. After the match, Rummy sat in the locker room for over an hour, staring at the floor with a towel over his head, sweat and tears dripping into a puddle on the floor. To this day Rummy could still smell the guy's breath, still feel those hard, vicious hands wrap around his arms and throw him to the ground.

The experience taught Rummy a searing lesson he would internalize deeply: showing weakness strengthens one's opponent. He'd sharpened this formulation over the years into one of his most frequently uttered sentences: weakness is provocative.

"Weakness is provocative," he said out loud, softly, as he switched again from lying on his back to his side. He felt his opponent forcing him down on the hard wrestling mat, unable to escape. He felt the guy's warm exhales press against his skin. Joyce stirred and rolled over toward Rummy. She put her hand on his shoulder. "Everything okay Don?"

"Yes, hun. Everything is just fine. Please go back to sleep."

Accustomed to her husband randomly saying things to himself while lost in thought, she rolled back over and fell back asleep. He switched again to his back. Then he thought about Kissinger's détente policy with Russia—the attempted relaxation of tension between the two countries—and clenched his fists. *We are showing the Russians weakness*, he thought. *We need to show strength, we must be forward-leaning, make them fear us.* He whispered it again very softly: "Weakness is provocative."

He sat up and grabbed the pen and notepad on the bedside table. He added another bullet to his long list of notes: *Articulate to Jerry one-on-one (no Kissinger) the full dangers of détente.* Often worried he'd forget something if he didn't write it down, he could feel the stress seeping out of his pores with each stroke of the pen.

Fiercely intelligent in a way Rummy couldn't match, Henry Kissinger was Rummy's main rival in the Ford administration. Rummy knew Kissinger wasn't the only member of the administration who was smarter than he was. Alan Greenspan and Paul O'Neill—the two main economists—were also geniuses. But Kissinger was the one person who Rummy worried could convince Ford to make a big mistake, over his own objection. Rummy was convinced that being too soft on the Soviet Union would be a huge unforced error. He added to his note: *Keep Kissinger at State and away from WH as much as possible.*

Then he lay back down and rolled onto his side and, a few minutes later, finally fell asleep.

Chapter 6
November 15, 1982

"Paul! How are you?" Rummy said, holding a bulky phone to his head with his right hand and the cord with his left. He was standing at the desk in his corner office at G.D. Searle's headquarters in Skokie, Illinois. A giant pharmaceutical company, Searle was famous for inventing and producing NutraSweet, an artificial sweetener.

Nearly fifty now, Rummy had been using standing desks since entering the private sector as Searle's CEO in 1977, after Ford lost the presidential election to Jimmy Carter. Sitting at a desk made him feel sluggish while standing made him feel more productive. It was essential to his mental health to feel productive, to move away from the status quo toward something bigger and better. Not an angry person by nature, he could feel his blood pressure rise whenever someone wasted his time. In government, there was often little he could do about it. *Few things are more inherent to the federal government than wasted time*, he once thought while testifying before Congress. But now that he was CEO—king of the show—he painstakingly structured his time to avoid having it wasted. His subordinates knew better than to keep droning on if Rummy started getting restless. Sometimes he would just get up and leave in the middle of slow-moving meetings without saying a word. That was preferable to the times he felt compelled to ... voice his displeasure.

On the other end of the line was Paul O'Neill, one of President Ford's top budgetary gurus and—they both enthusiastically agreed—the smartest person either he or Cheney had ever met. O'Neill could crunch numbers like a calculator yet also had impeccable judgment. A rare combination. As CEO of steel giant Alcoa, he'd helped the company's stock rise tenfold in just a few years. It was almost as impressive as Searle's stock under Rummy.

"I'm great, Rummy, how are you? Sounds like you're doing very well from what I'm reading in the papers." O'Neill replied. Born and raised in Indiana, he spoke confidently and with a strong lisp.

They were good pals at the time. I had a front-row seat years later when their relationship imploded over the Iraq war. It was painful to watch, though far from the only friendship Rummy lost during the Bush administration.

"Top of the world, Paul. Can you believe it's been seven years since the American people threw us out for Jimmy Carter?"

"He was even worse than we said he'd be!"

"Yes indeed. He promised change and he delivered: more dysfunction, higher gas prices, less security. Oh, and your favorite: a bigger deficit."

O'Neill chuckled.

"But the private sector's been good to both of us, huh?" Rummy said.

"No doubt about it. Congratulations on the NutraSweet FDA clearance. The wind is in your sails now."

"Thank you, thank you. The government is finally off our back. Holding up the approval for no damn reason all those years was tough. The fate of the company was at stake. Those government bureaucrats are nasty. But we got it done and no more excuses."

"My Diet Pepsi already tastes much better. What's the secret sauce you have in NutraSweet anyway?"

A grin spread across Rummy's face. "Ah, if only I could tell you and not have the board fire me!"

Rummy laughed audibly into his phone. Since he couldn't show his big smile while talking to people on the phone he would laugh extra loudly and hold the phone close to his mouth.

"How's Dick?" O'Neill asked.

"He's great. Serving the people of Wyoming. Living the dream. Spending most of his time protecting Reagan, trying to prevent Congress from reducing the presidency to a nullity."

"Dick always loved doing the people's work."

"Ha! Yes. So ... down to business Paul ... when can I get you in here? You've promised me a visit to Skokie a few times and with all our momentum our managers are ripe for a visit from my old friend who happens to be the smartest CEO in America."

"I don't know about that Rummy, but I appreciate the sentiment. Let me check my calendar with Nancy and see when it might work."

"I've heard that before Paul. I'm not gonna let you get away with it anymore. We need to pick your brain on operations, get some feedback, learn from you. Even if it's only an hour or two. With the FDA approval now official we're bringing on thousands of new employees. We're scaling up big time. We'd love to hear from you in person."

"Understood. I'll make it happen this time. And soon. I promise."

"Fantastic!" Rummy said, pressing the phone hard against his mouth as he stood at his desk.

Rummy gave a speech that night at the downtown Chicago Hilton hosted by the local Chamber of Commerce. The topic: supply-chain management, one of his favorite subjects. He'd spent hundreds of hours poring over every dimension of Searle's supply chain—how the company purchased and used the ingredients that went into its products—and had made the whole thing exponentially more efficient, even though he'd had to rip up and rebuild some of Searle's internal systems in the process. It was classic Rummy: making an inefficient process better through brains and sheer force of will. He loved public speaking and savored the opportunity to share his expertise and talk about his success. Bulbs flashed as he spoke, and he wondered which newspapers were there to cover the speech. He crossed his fingers behind the podium that *The Chicago Tribune* was one of them.

After the speech, dinner followed. The grand ballroom teemed with business leaders, politicians, and other local dignitaries. Diamond-studded chandeliers hung from the high ceiling and servers in black dresses and tuxedos crisscrossed the room holding plates, trays, and pitchers. Silverware clanked endlessly on plates and the aroma from the food mixed with cigar smoke, leaving Rummy craving fresh air.

He stayed late, speaking with friends, planting seeds with donors for his then-top-secret 1988 Presidential run. He was excited about the campaign and his prospects: he knew Reagan's Vice President George Bush from the Ford days and considered him a political and substantive lightweight.

"If he's my competition," Rummy told his old friend and campaign manager Ned Janetta, "then this president thing might just happen."

Rummy didn't exit the ballroom until after 10 p.m., long after most of the crowd had left. Joyce was going to come but their sitter cancelled at the last minute. She knew it would be a late night.

The ballroom was on the eleventh floor of the hotel. His briefcase in hand, he got on the elevator alone. But just as the doors started closing a woman in her mid-forties squeezed herself through the gap. She was in a dark business suit and had a purple scarf wrapped around her neck. She had big green eyes, full lips, and a friendly smile. She took several steps in, stood right next to Rummy, her right shoulder grazing up against his.

The door to the elevator closed and it started to go down.

"Nice speech Mr. Secretary," she said.

Rummy was taken aback when she stood so close to him, but he liked her reference to his days as secretary of defense.

"Well, thank you." Her fresh perfume seeped into his nostrils, and while a little too potent, he thought it smelled nice.

"I'm Karen Schmidt, VP of Marketing at Pritzker." She took a small step back and stuck out her hand. Rummy shook it. When he tried to release his grip, she squeezed harder. Rummy smiled awkwardly and pulled his hand away.

"You sure do know an awful lot about supply chains, Mr. Secretary."

"Thank you. It's a fun subject."

"We have lots of companies at Pritzker, lots of different supply chains."

"So I've heard."

"You'd have a ton fun making them better, I'm sure."

"It's a great company, Pritzker. I've heard plenty about it. VP of Marketing you said?"

"That's right. Been with the company almost ten years now."

"Congratulations. That's great."

She paused for a few seconds. "Um, are you staying here, Mr. Secretary," she said with a smile, gazing into his eyes. She softly bit her bottom lip. As their eyes met, Rummy noticed how attractive and confident she was. He felt a flutter in his stomach. Her eyes were wide open and she didn't blink once.

"No, no, I'm going home," he said.

"That must be far."

"Well, no, it's not too long a drive."

"Oh, that's too bad."

Rummy wasn't quite sure how to interpret that statement.

"You can stay here if you'd like," she said. "My room's plenty big."

Rummy raised his eyebrows. The elevator kept making its way down. She wasn't the first woman to be this forward with him, especially after the local papers reported that he made over a million dollars a year at Searle. "Oh, no ... I need to head home and sleep in my own bed. My wife and kids are at home."

"Are you ... are you sure?"

"Yes, I'm sure."

"Do you need to go now or do you wanna come see my room for just a little while first?"

The elevator stopped and the door started opening.

"Oh ... well ... I need to go now," he said as they both stepped into the lobby. "But thank you."

"But Mr. Secretary ... there's no one here," she said, stepping close to him and gesturing toward the empty lobby with her hand. "No one would ever know."

Rummy paused, looking her in the eyes. "That's not true," he said. "I'd know."

And he turned around and walked away.

Chapter 7
December 20, 1983

Saddam Hussein walked into the dimly lit room inside his Baghdad palace and reached down toward Rummy's outstretched hand. Their hands clasped and they both squeezed hard. Saddam tried to overtake Rummy's hand with the force of his shake, but Rummy wouldn't let him. Both men grimaced and squeezed for three solid seconds.

It was a draw. They released their grips.

Rummy was surprised how shiny and black Saddam's hair was. He thought Saddam, nearing fifty, must have used hair dye for his hair and mustache. *Why bother?* Rummy mused to himself. *You've terrorized your entire country into utter submission, and you kill anyone who criticizes you. Who cares if a little gray creeps in.*

Saddam was above average height with an impressive, sturdy build. He stood tall, proud, defiant. He was wearing green military fatigues with red and yellow patches on his shoulders. His skin was tan, his jaw strong, his face serious.

Armed guards from Saddam's military were all around. A menacing pack of at least a dozen followed him everywhere he went. Rummy thought they outnumbered his own military detail at least two-to-one. He also noticed that the Iraqi soldiers' guns were bigger than the US soldiers' were.

Camera bulbs flashed as the two men sized each other up. Rummy's endorphins danced in his bloodstream. He liked the attention. *The pictures in the papers will get my right side*, he thought. *Much better than my left.* He did not, however, like how much taller Saddam was than him, which would be reflected on the front pages. Rummy's diminutive height was a source of frustration and disappointment. It was the one thing about himself he didn't like. And he knew it hurt his presidential prospects. *No one wants a short President*, he'd thought to himself more than once.

As they talked, Rummy felt a surprising kinship with Saddam. All business, just like himself. *Would have been a senator if he was born in the United States,* Rummy thought. *An influential senator, not one of those schmucks who talk a big game but have no pull in the chamber.* Rummy listened as his interpreter relayed to Saddam that he liked Baghdad's impressive architectural landscape.

After a few more minutes of pleasantries, Rummy, Saddam, and their entourages ditched the press and started walking down a long straight hallway deep in the bowels of Saddam's palace. The light was dim, the ceiling low. Everywhere Rummy looked he saw guns in people's hands. *Loaded guns, no doubt.* That thought and scent of stale body odor in the air combined to make Rummy feel queasy.

Big colorful paintings of Saddam wrapped in golden frames adorned the walls. After a few minutes they came upon two thick gold doors at the end of the hallway and two men dressed in military fatigues with rifles hanging on their shoulders opened the doors. Rummy squinted as he entered the bright room. It was filled with lavish furniture and artwork, sparkling gold and glittering jewels everywhere he looked. Intricately carved wooden doors and marble walls surrounded a long mahogany table in the middle of the room. Rummy counted at least five more portraits of Saddam. *Progressives in America complain about our inequality,* he thought. *What a joke! This is inequality: an iron-fisted king hoarding his nation's scarce resources to decorate his palaces while his people starve in the streets.*

There was no air conditioning. Two large fans were on full blast, rotating loudly and spraying thick plumes of warm, stale air in all directions, doing nothing to alleviate the heat. Sweat was building on Rummy's neck around his collar, the moisture seeping into his tie. Saddam wasn't sweating at all, Rummy noticed. He was calm and confident.

"President Reagan sends his greetings," Rummy said after sitting down on one side of a long, gold and burgundy couch pressed against the wall. Saddam was on the other side of the couch. Each man's interpreter took a nearby chair.

A few weeks earlier, Secretary of State George Schultz—Nixon's treasury secretary and someone Rummy respected and admired—had called Rummy. Schultz had asked Rummy to be Reagan's Special Envoy to the Middle East after terrorists bombed a US marine barracks in Beirut, Lebanon, killing over two hundred American servicemen. Searle was excelling under Rummy's iron fist, its profits skyrocketing thanks to sales of NutraSweet. And while he had some reluctance to loan the reins there, even temporarily, he still had strong views about foreign policy and was eager to participate in the Reagan administration. He also missed seeing his name in *The Washington Post*. So he said yes to Schultz.

"Please tell President Reagan that we appreciate his attention to our concerns," Saddam replied, his voice deep and authoritative. "And we appreciate your visit, Mr. Secretary."

Rummy nodded, still fixated on Saddam's black hair, which he could see shining from the other side of the couch. The Iraqi dictator's green army uniform seemed faded compared to his glistening hair.

"Please also tell President Reagan that we are focused on our survival," Saddam continued. "The battle with Iran and hostilities with Syria require our full attention. I cannot turn to broader international concerns until the blood stops flowing. Baghdad is only one hundred miles from the Iranian border and I don't have to explain to you how close that is in the context of war."

Rummy thought he would feel the same way if he were in Saddam's shoes. Appeasing Western sensibilities just wasn't worth much in the midst of a brutal war with your neighbor.

Rummy's opinion was that the stupidity of recent US foreign policy, especially under President Carter, was directly responsible for this conflict. The only explanation for the United States having terrible relations with all three countries involved in the war—Iraq, Iran, Syria—was rank incompetence. Rummy held a special disdain for Carter, whose weakness on the world stage, he thought, had been dangerously provocative.

"For now," Saddam continued, "we merely ask President Reagan to help stop other nations from assisting Iran in the economic sphere. They are getting war supplies from numerous countries whose trading relationship with the US is central to their economies. Ambassador Aziz will provide you with a memorandum detailing the particulars of our request."

"Very well," responded Rummy. "We will do what we can on that front. Do you have any other requests or messages for President Reagan?"

Without waiting for his interpreter to speak, Saddam shook his head.

"Okay, well, we have one request," Rummy said. "We want you to start funneling Iraqi oil through the pipeline into Jordan."

"I will consider that," Saddam said. Then he raised his index finger in the air. "Under one condition." Rummy leaned in. "We need explicit assurances from the United States that Israel will not attack the pipeline."

Rummy smiled softly. "Understood," he said. He always appreciated how Arab nations refused to publicly acknowledge Israel's existence as a sovereign nation yet deeply respected and feared the small nation's military. To Rummy, Israel was a shining example of how strength was essential to success in international relations. This tiny little nation surrounded by its enemies had somehow created an environment where its people flourished. The biggest reason: its enemies knew that if they attacked Israel, it would respond ferociously. Rummy and Cheney would often talk about how the United States needed to be more like Israel, how global peace and stability depended on it.

As the meeting adjourned Rummy was surprised that Saddam didn't ask for more from the United States. *That's it?* he thought. *Just try to restrain trade with Iran's allies?* Rummy knew that Saddam didn't trust the US, that he thought America was playing all sides in the Middle East. The dictator wasn't wrong about that. This lack of trust meant Iraq under Saddam would never get too close to the US. While Rummy understood and respected that impulse, he thought Saddam was leaving too much on the table. *No requests for weapons? He doesn't want to use any American military bases in the region? He doesn't want to share intelligence?* As Saddam knew, Reagan and Schultz were eager to help Iraq defeat Iran.

The two men rose and shook hands. They looked each other in the eyes and again squeezed hard to a draw. As Rummy walked out of the palace, he thought about how he would frame the meeting to Reagan and Schultz to sound as successful as possible. He had learned long ago that the right framing could make even a bad meeting sound good. And vice versa: a good meeting could sound like a failure if described poorly. Rummy desperately wanted to be Schultz's successor as secretary of state. It was an ideal steppingstone to the presidency. Making his visit to Iraq a success—making it *sound* like a success—was important.

He also thought he was unlikely to deal much with Saddam Hussein in the future. *Just another Middle East dictator who will surely come and go without much consequence to the United States, or to me*, Rummy thought.

Chapter 8
May 5, 1999

Rummy clanked his wine glass with a knife as he rose from his chair. His blue suit was fresh and bright under the light from the hovering chandelier. He looked trim and fit. His morning weight hadn't dipped below 154 pounds or gone above 159 pounds since the Ford administration. He was emotional this evening, thinking about Joyce and how thankful he was that she'd put up with him all these years.

"Thank you all for being here to celebrate our anniversary," he said, smiling and looking around the table of familiar faces. "This is a momentous occasion and one that fills my heart ... one that fills my heart with joy. No man could be more blessed than I have been to spend 45 years with Joyce Rumsfeld, the best mother, the best wife, the best friend in the whole wide world."

"Hear, hear!" someone said.

About twenty people had joined the Rumsfelds for dinner at Smith & Wollensky's in Chicago. The Chicago River glistened under the moonlight outside, and several candles glowed on the long rectangular table. All eyes were fixed on Rummy, just the way he liked it. "When I met Joyce in junior high school we were both 14. It was 1947. She was dazzling. The prettiest and smartest girl in school. As for me, I was, shall we say, less refined than I was to become in adulthood." Rummy turned to Ned Janetta who was sitting to his left. "Not long after we met, she became my best friend, swiftly unseating Ned from the top spot."

That got a nice chuckle from the group.

"Our Friday evenings at Davey's, the local diner, were filled with burgers, milkshakes, the juke box, and laughter. Then I went to Princeton with Ned while Joyce went to the University of Colorado. It wasn't easy being so far away from her, but we stayed in touch. She even came to one of my wrestling matches and saw me get walloped and lose the championship in the worst loss of my career. And she still wanted to date me after that!"

A little uncomfortable with all the attention, Joyce blushed. The smiles around the table got bigger.

"By the time I graduated college I knew that I wanted to spend the rest of my life with Joyce." Rummy held his wine with his right hand as his left hand gestured confidently. He paused, letting the silence build, enjoying the focused attention of his guests. "But I was slated to begin my tour with the Navy just a few days after graduation. Two days before I was set to leave, while having breakfast with my parents, it hit me like a bolt of lightning—I need to propose *right now* or Joyce might go off with one of her many other suitors. So being the impetuous romantic that I am, I dropped my fork and got up from the table and went straight to Joyce's house and asked her to marry me—at 10 in the morning ... with no wedding ring."

Everyone laughed.

"Swept away by this romantic proposal, she said yes. And my life has been exponentially better ever since. Indeed, Joyce has stuck with me through many challenges. To name a few: The Nixon administration ..."

Everyone laughed again.

"... getting thrown out of the White House by Jimmy Carter ..."

Everyone laughed louder.

"... my long hours getting Searle off the ground; my short and anything but sweet Presidential run in the 80s; my grueling effort running Bob Dole's Presidential run in 96; oh, and all these decades dealing with my grumpy demeanor and inability to sit still."

The laughter gave way to claps and whistles. Rummy paused. Then he looked down at Joyce and started to choke up. "I've had a life filled with challenges … many of which I've no doubt invited. But with you, my dear, most everything has been easy. You somehow make even the hardest things in life easy. My troubles simply disintegrate when you smile."

Rummy took a deep breath and looked back up at his dinner guests. Like a seasoned trial lawyer, his eyes danced from one person to the next. "Joyce and I are thankful to have so many wonderful familiar faces here with us tonight. Susan Walton, who went to high school with us," he said, gesturing with his wine glass. "Thank you for coming, Susan."

"Dick and Lynne, thank you both for being here." The Cheneys smiled and nodded. "Dick, I remember when we first met, for your interview. A strapping young man you were." Dick opened his mouth wide and laughed. "But not quite what we needed at the Office of Economic Opportunity. Sorry you didn't get the offer. We needed an aggressive lawyer, not a dreamy academic. Things turned out okay for you … for us … though … didn't they?"

"Yes indeed," Cheney said loudly from his chair.

"Though I have a feeling we might be just getting started," Rummy said.

Cheney gave him a knowing nod.

"Paul and Nancy, so, so glad you could make it." Paul O'Neill and his wife smiled and nodded as Rummy said their names. They were seated next to the Cheneys. "It's not every day you get to have dinner with the smartest CEO in America."

"I second that one," Cheney said, raising his glass high toward the ceiling.

"Please, Rummy, come on now," O'Neill said, shaking his head.

"And Ned, our dear friend for many years, and the campaign manager on my first campaign." Janetta smiled and lifted his drink up and winked at Rummy. He was short and squat, with a thick mustache and ready grin. Rummy winked back. "Wouldn't ever have gotten elected if you hadn't talked some sense into me about our campaign strategy."

Rummy slowly looked up and down the table. "All of you, thank you, thank you, thank you. It means the world to us to have you here." He then returned to Joyce. He leaned down and kissed her gently on the lips. Then he raised his glass: "Please join me in raising your glasses to Joyce Rumsfeld on this wonderful anniversary day. I love you my dear."

Smiles burst. Eyes widened. Glasses clinked. Joyce's eyes were sparkling in the light. His eyes moist, Rummy was grinning ear to ear.

Chapter 9
December 24, 2000

"Rummy, the president-elect would like to see you at the Madison Hotel tomorrow afternoon," Cheney said. "That's the transition team's headquarters, for now."

Rummy's stomach fluttered as he held the phone to his ear. He smiled. "I can be there after lunch. That work?"

"Yes indeed."

Rummy knew that if George W. Bush wanted to see him in person that meant he didn't just want Rummy's advice on potential cabinet secretaries. It meant he wanted to interview Rummy *to be* a cabinet secretary. Reading between the lines of his recent conversations with Cheney, Rummy thought this was for either Director of the CIA or secretary of defense. If he got the latter job, he'd have been both the youngest secretary of defense in American history *and* the oldest. While in his late sixties, he thought there was still a possibility—however remote—of a successful Presidential run. Reagan, after all, was in his seventies most of his presidency. And Rummy knew he was way smarter than Reagan.

When his head hit the pillow that night Rummy rehearsed all the things he'd say to Bush about foreign policy. About Russia, China, the Middle East. About seizing control of the Pentagon bureaucracy. About all the lessons he'd learned over the decades as a statesman and business leader. He was nervous. Excited. "Don't seem too eager," he whispered softly to himself while staring at the ceiling. Joyce stirred. After about an hour of restless thought he finally fell asleep.

The next day, Rummy walked into the president-elect's suite at the Madison hotel only a block from the White House. It was frigid in Washington and Rummy appreciated the hotel's warm air blanketing his face the instant he stepped inside. He'd met

Bush a few times already. While his intellect resembled Gerald Ford's (and perhaps was inferior), the younger Bush was solid and confident. He asked good questions. And Rummy thought he'd make tough decisions when necessary and not simply fold under the pressure of Washington's establishment or the whims of public opinion. This was a quality Rummy valued and thought the country desperately needed after eight years of Clinton's mischief and deceit. He also thought Cheney held a lot of sway over Bush, and that Dick would be a significant asset to the administration and the country. Rummy had come to admire Cheney, especially after his successful tenure as secretary of defense guiding the defense establishment through the end of the Cold War and the Gulf War. While Cheney was once Rummy's deputy, they were now coequals.

Rummy also liked that Bush was considering him despite Rummy's tense relationship with Bush's father. During the Ford administration, Rummy and George Herbert Walker Bush—Ford's China envoy and CIA director—hadn't got along. Rummy thought Bush was an intellectual lightweight more focused on politics than substance. Bush thought Rummy was a Machiavellian insider, always jockeying for the president's attention. In my opinion, neither man was far from the mark.

"Mr. President-elect," Rummy said with a big smile, reaching out his right hand and walking past two Secret Service agents and into the large suite. "Congratulations."

"Thank you, Rummy," Bush said, smiling too, as their hands clasped. Bush's shake was firm, and Rummy carefully calibrated his shake to be just as strong, but not more so.

Bush wore a thick maroon sweater over his white button-up shirt and blue slacks. Rummy wore his finest suit, dark blue, and a red tie that Ford gave him during his 1988 presidential run. Andrew Card, Bush's soon-to-be chief of staff, was the only other person in the room. Bush looked at Card and nodded curtly without saying anything. Card responded, "Yes sir," and walked out.

The drapes were drawn in the fancy suite. The lighting was dim. Rummy was surprised not to see what he expected in a transition office: binders, briefing papers, computers, printers. There were some personal belongings and a few cups and plates, the leftovers of lunch perhaps. But that was about it.

"It's great to see you again," Bush said. He was a few inches taller than Rummy, and 15 years younger, but they were both lean and trim. "Take a seat," he said, motioning towards a small table and two chairs near the window. As Rummy walked towards the table he grimaced. He had to go to the bathroom. His flight to Washington from New Mexico arrived just an hour before and, not wanting to be late, he hadn't found a moment to take care of business.

They took their seats and Rummy crossed his legs. Bush didn't cross his. "Allow me to cut to the chase, Rummy," Bush said, his eyes focused on Rummy's, his Texas accent thick. "As Dick may have told you, we're strongly considering you for either CIA director or defense secretary. Whadduya think?"

Rummy uncrossed his legs and settled into his chair. He stared closer at Bush and thought he looked more tired than the last time they'd met, at Bush's ranch in Crawford, Texas about six months earlier. His skin was a little paler, the bags under his eyes a little bigger. *Not surprising*, Rummy thought. *The campaign was grueling, and the Florida recount fiasco couldn't have helped.*

"Well, Mr. President-elect, I am not inclined to serve in either position. Joyce and I have finally reached a phase in life where we can relax at our home in Taos, New Mexico and spend time with our children and grandchildren. She's taken to calling it our 'rural period.' I've been sprinting for many decades now and we were planning to relax a little."

Bush tilted his head to the left and squinted. He looked a little surprised.

"That said," Rummy continued, quickly pivoting and leaning forward in his chair, "of course, if you want me to serve it's something that we will consider very strongly. My devotion to this country is unqualified and you are putting together a very strong cabinet."

Rummy was surprised how nervous he felt as the conversation got underway. It wasn't Bush personally that made him uneasy but being this close to the man who would soon be president. Rummy felt his ambition stirring.

"Appreciate that," Bush said. "Makes good sense. All I ask for is a quick and firm response if I do make the offer."

"Understood," Rummy said. His full bladder was making him increasingly uncomfortable.

"Okay now. Answer me this Rummy, what are the three biggest threats to our country right now?"

Answer me this? Odd phrasing there George, Rummy thought before responding. "Well, I would start by saying that there are not merely three threats but many, and the top three may or may not be more important than the others combined."

Bush nodded.

"With that qualification, I would put Russia at the top of the list." Rummy's eyes stayed laser focused on Bush. His voice was crisp and authoritative. "Russia has a huge arsenal of weapons, including nuclear weapons. And this is a time of dramatic upheaval and instability for them. Their entire system of government collapsed just a decade ago, making predicting their moves, especially into the medium-term, difficult. But it's also an opportunity for us. While it's essential that we show strength, we should try to integrate them into the community of nations … primarily from a commercial standpoint. A stable Russia that grows in strength but stays consistent with the international system of rules and commerce is ideal. If they plummet and fall into disarray, they are more likely to be antagonistic toward our interests, more likely to be a problem."

Bush just stared at him and nodded every few seconds. He didn't interject with questions like he did during the campaign. Rummy thought he was listening carefully, but he wasn't sure.

"Next on the list is China. They are smart and patient, far more patient than we are. This is a potent combination." Rummy's heartbeat was picking up and dopamine was swirling through his bloodstream. He was passionate about foreign policy and talking about these issues with Bush felt good. "They are taking the blueprint that Lee Kuan Yew laid out in Singapore and applying it on a grand scale. Strength. Discipline. Order. It's inevitable that China will succeed and grow and be a major player on the international stage. No question. Just look at the growth rate of their economy and extrapolate it conservatively for a decade or two. While, again, we must project strength, it's important that, as they ascend in international influence, we recognize China is a global player and that we align our strategic interests with them so we can coexist peacefully and cooperatively."

Bush nodded again.

"Mr. President-elect, I'm sorry to do this, but do you mind ... do you mind if I use your restroom?" Rummy said. His bladder was screaming. "I came straight from the airport and haven't had an opportunity to—"

"Of course, Rummy," Bush said with a chuckle. He looked to the bathroom on the other side of the room and gestured his hand toward it. "By all means."

Rummy resisted running for the bathroom, but was barely able to wait for Bush to stop speaking before he leapt up. As he washed his hands, he looked down to the left of the sink and saw an empty wine bottle on the floor, up against the wall by the door.

The bottle was tall and dark, and the cork had been put back in. Rummy picked it up just to confirm that it was empty. It was. He recalled that Bush had an alcohol problem many years before but given his success as governor in Texas and on the campaign trail Rummy was confident he had overcome it. "Hm," he whispered. He filed it away in his mind, but it didn't alarm him. Maybe Bush had shared it with someone over dinner.

Rummy sat back down in his chair, feeling relieved. He picked up where he left off: "There's nothing we can do to stop China's emergence. Nothing. They are going to grow; they are going to be more influential. The key is for us to try to harness their power in a direction we like, showing strength but keeping friction to a minimum."

Rummy stopped for a few seconds. The more he talked to Bush, the more he wanted to join the administration. He wanted to come back to government; he wanted to put his hands all over the military and shape it and mold it—just like he had done to Ford's political career and the supply chain at Searle. The more he looked at the president-elect of the United States the more he remembered the feeling of being in power. And being a cabinet official gave him so much more power than being a CEO ever did. Being a CEO paid a lot more, but he already had his millions. More money didn't mean anything to him. More power did.

But was he telling Bush what he wanted to hear? He wasn't sure.

"Finally, third, there are a slew of asymmetric threats that we face from terrorists around the world, primarily in the Middle East."

Without saying a word, Bush stood up and walked to a nearby dresser and grabbed a cigar out of a box. Romeo y Julietas, Cubans. "Do you mind?" he asked.

"No, not at all."

"Do you want one?" Bush asked, holding out the box towards Rummy.

"No thank you, I'm fine." Rummy quit smoking a pipe in the 80s after studying the health effects and never got started with cigars.

Bush cut the tip off the cigar with fluency and ease. Then he pulled a lighter out of his pocket. A silver zippo. He lit the flame and raised it slowly to the cigar, as Rummy sat there and watched, anxious to get started talking again. The tip of the cigar became hot and flashed red and crackled and smoke wafted out from it. The smell of the smoke made Rummy slightly nauseous. Bush took a few puffs, and a cloud rose and formed between the two men. Bush put the lighter back in his pocket.

Now looking at Bush through this hazy veil, Rummy at last felt like he could continue. "There are a lot of desperate men waking up every day in the Middle East who have nothing to lose and want to harm America. They've done some damage already … but their ambitions are much greater. Combine this with a region filled with unstable dictatorships and the risks are amplified. The possibility, for example, that Saddam Hussein gets weapons of mass destruction—if he doesn't have them already— and deploys them against the United States, or sells them to terrorists who in turn do the same, is significant. Clinton made a major mistake being weak on terrorism."

Rummy paused to see if Bush had anything to say. He didn't. Instead, he took another deep puff of his cigar.

"The common thread across all three of these threats, and those outside of the top three, is that to protect ourselves we must be strong. Even where we seek peace, we must show strength. Weaknesses is provocative."

Bush seemed to perk up at the sound of that phrase. His eyes widened. "Weakness is provocative," he said with a smile.

"Yes indeed … it is," Rummy continued. "We need to lean forward, we need to deter bad actors through strength and action.

Inaction is just as big a choice as action. Again, weakness is provocative."

"It is, I agree," said Bush, sitting up straight and taking a puff of his cigar. "We shoulda gone right into Baghdad in '91 and taken out Saddam. We showed weakness by not doing so. Dick agrees. He advocated for it at the time but got shut down. So now Saddam thinks he can do anything and stay in power."

Impressed that Bush would criticize his father's foreign policy so openly, Rummy nodded. "Precisely my point. Inaction is every bit as consequential as action in world affairs. Failing to remove Saddam is a great example of that fact." Bush smiled and it made Rummy feel good. He seemed to appreciate Rummy's perspective. "Moreover, the United States—"

"Well, thank you Rummy," Bush said, cutting him off and starting to get up from his chair. "Those thoughts are most appreciated."

Rummy raised his index finger. "I'd like to add one more thing, if I may ... if you don't mind."

Bush relaxed back into his chair and nodded. "Alright."

"When Dick was before the Senate for his confirmation as secretary of defense, he didn't receive a single question about Iraq, the subject that would define his tenure. Not a single question. It shows how hard it is to predict what will happen on the world stage, what will ultimately be most important. I think about it like this. There are known knowns, the things we know we know. Saddam has used weapons of mass destruction on his own people, for example. We know that's true. Then there are known unknowns. The things we know we don't know. We know terrorists all around the world want to harm the United States—right now, today—but we don't know their specific plans to do so. And, finally, there are unknown unknowns, the things we don't know that we don't know. And it's this last category, the things not even on our radar, that tend to cause the most trouble."

Bush tilted his head to the left without changing his blank expression. Rummy thought he might have missed the point. He looked like he might say something. Then, instead, he savored a long puff of his cigar and slowly exhaled a huge plume of smoke.

Chapter 10
January 24, 2001

I knew Rummy before he became George W. Bush's secretary of defense. But not well. We'd met a few times at business and foreign policy events and had several mutual friends. I initially found him incredibly smart and likable. He had a fantastic reputation as the man who effectively ran the Ford administration in his early forties and then turned a flailing pharmaceutical company into an industry powerhouse. I called to congratulate him on his confirmation.

"Congratulations Mr. Secretary," I said. "Must feel good to have the confirmation process behind you."

"Yes, it sure does, thank you. Excited to roll up my sleeves and get started." He sounded as passionate and energetic as ever. I enjoyed talking to him back then. Our conversations were always positive and stimulating.

"Youngest *and* oldest defense secretary in American history? Not too shabby."

"Well, I'd prefer to still be the youngest, but what can I do?" We both chuckled.

"A lot's changed since you first ran the Pentagon," I said.

"Yes, for better and for worse."

"Feels like a totally different world now from the days of the Cold War. It was simpler back then; still dangerous but simpler. We had a better handle on our threats than we do now."

"Agreed."

"What's on your agenda when you get there? You've never been one to be happy with the status quo."

"Yes indeed. Lots to learn; lots to fix. Obviously, Russia and China are vitally important. We need to align their behavior to our interests as much as we can. I don't think Clinton did a good job at that."

"I agree."

"Showing strength to both countries will be key."

"True, but don't forget about the Middle East," I said. "It's a big challenge too."

"True, very true. The asymmetric threats involving terrorism coming out of the Middle East are very serious. Iran, Iraq, Al-Qaeda, and so on. There are numerous important global flashpoints. It's a long list, to be sure. But my first order of business will be to wrestle the bureaucracy to the ground. We simply *must* gain control of the building. The waste, fraud, and abuse is rampant."

"Makes sense."

"If you can't control the Pentagon, it doesn't matter as much what your foreign policy goals are—cause you can't get things done the way you want to. So I need to dive right into the belly of the beast and seize control."

"Yes, good point," I said, knowing you couldn't stop Rummy once he got rolling.

"Did you know there's over a trillion dollars—a trillion!—that the DOD can't track? Doesn't even know where it is?" Rummy said. "Lost. Gone. Thousands of auditors in the building and no one knows where it is. Can you believe that?"

"I've heard something along those lines. Mind boggling."

"That's the taxpayers money. So step one is wrapping my head and my arms around all this and getting the Pentagon functioning like a modern organization should. Or at least moving in that direction."

"I like it. Spoken like a man who's turned around a business before."

"Ha! Yes, that was small potatoes compared to this. But that's the idea."

"I know Dick has similar views," I said.

"He does, yes. Lots of unfinished business from his tenure. I should add that an essential part of gaining control over the building will be to reclaim the chain of command. As you know well, civilian control of the military is essential to our constitutional system. This seems to have been forgotten in recent years."

"It sure has been. Clinton and his folks let the military walk all over them."

"Exactly! When do you think this dynamic—where the military just rebuffs the civilian leadership—really started?" Rummy asked.

It felt good that Rummy wanted my opinion on this important topic. "Well, I think the trend started under Carter," I said. "The presidency had weakened after Watergate and while you and Ford had things moving in the right direction, Carter let it all backslide. He was weak and the generals knew it."

"Good point," Rummy said.

"This all accelerated dramatically under Clinton," I continued. "It really took off and got out of control. He was too busy watching his poll numbers and fending off impeachment to assert civilian control. And he never really felt comfortable with the military to begin with. The generals took advantage of him and his administration from the outset."

"Absolutely true. That won't happen with me. No way. The Clinton era of civilian abdication is over."

I was glad to hear Rummy was ready to fight. "The chiefs are nasty SOBs, though," I said. "Set in their ways. Dick knows this as well as anyone. You really want to tangle with them?"

Rummy chuckled. "I don't mind a good fight as long as I'm on the right side of history."

Looking back on this conversation, it's incredible how cordial and friendly we were before the Bush administration got underway. Little did either of us know that our relationship would go down as one of the most controversial and explosive in US political history.

Chapter 11
September 10, 2001

Rummy was standing at his large brown desk in the middle of his office at the Pentagon. The carpets in the vast room were dark blue, the walls and ceiling bright white. His glasses were perched high up his nose, and he was focused on his work.

While some meetings took place sitting down, there were often ad hoc meetings at the standing desk with gray-haired military leaders awkwardly standing and writing on their notepads, trying (and failing) not to look like they really just wanted a chair.

Rummy was dictating a short memorandum into his voice recorder. Throughout the day his secretary would transcribe these recordings and have them distributed to recipients throughout the Pentagon and other government agencies. There were so many of these notes that they earned the nickname "snowflakes," as they constantly fell down upon every nook and cranny of the federal government. I received my fair share.

This one was to his chief of staff, James Jenkins:

> *From: Secretary Rumsfeld*
> *To: Chief of Staff Jenkins*
> *Date: September 10, 2001*
> *Subject: Security Detail*
>
> *I'm growing weary of the mob of security following me around everywhere. I'm not some Middle East dictator. If the Pentagon isn't safe for everyone in the building equally, including the secretary, then we've got a host of problems. Going forward my security detail shall have no more than two people.*

There was a knock on the door as he finished and placed the dictation device on his desk.

"Come in."

It was Jenkins. "Mr. Secretary?"

"Yes. I was just drafting you a note James."

"If I could grab five minutes of your time before the chiefs arrive for our 12:30?" Jenkins said in his nervous, eager voice. Tall, awkward, and pale, with a pot belly and skinny legs, Jenkins had the unmistakable look of a man who worked too much and slept too little. Rummy liked and trusted him and found him particularly good at what he prized most in his underlings: getting things done.

Jenkins had been a young bureaucrat at the Pentagon during Rummy's first tenure as secretary of defense. They clicked and Rummy brought Jenkins along with him to Searle, where he worked his way up to being Rummy's chief operating officer and right-hand man. While they were anything but coequals—Rummy was the boss—they had a strong bond rooted in years of intense collaboration.

"What's up?" Rummy asked.

"The pushback from the chiefs on personnel continues to be fierce. They keep telling me it's none of our business and not our domain to get involved in who is recommended to POTUS for promotion." Rummy shook his head. Jenkins continued: "General Shinseki said we need to stay in our lane."

"Well ... that's just too darn bad for General Shinseki. The people elected the president and the president nominated me, the Senate confirmed me, and I hired you. We're in charge. The personal preferences of the generals will not override the Constitution of the United States. Not on my watch."

Jenkins nodded. "Understood."

Fifteen minutes later, Rummy was seated at a big conference table in his office. The entire Joint Chiefs of Staff were sitting on the other side of the table. All eight of them. In full uniform.

Sixty-four stars on sixteen shoulders; hundreds of combined years of military experience. The room was tense, quiet; the only sound was of papers ruffling. Rummy was nervous but, as always, didn't show it. His goal for this meeting was simple: assert his authority.

"Allow me to go ahead and get to the point," he said. "As I have said many times before, civilians control the military—not the generals. I may have uttered that sentence more than any other these first eight months. It's vitally important that America's military leadership be the best and the brightest. I won't allow overrated candidates to be promoted just because they happen to be in the right club in the military, the preferred clan, who happen to have been the roommate of a current chief or the cousin of some influential figure in the ruling guard. That kind of thing might be good enough at a university, but this has to be a meritocracy, a pure meritocracy. It's just too important not to be. We need the right people to get promoted, the right people to set strategy, the right people to give sound advice to me and to the president so we can exercise civilian control under the Constitution and make the right decisions."

Rummy paused and looked around the table. His heartbeat thumped in his chest. The chiefs stared at him with blank faces. He continued: "So I welcome your opinions about who the right people should be. And I want to hear the pros and cons of every candidate. But the idea that this is your purview and not mine is flat out wrong."

Nobody said anything for several seconds. Rummy and Jenkins wondered if anyone would respond at all. Then Eric Shinseki, a decorated four-star general, spoke: "But Mr. Secretary ... this is ... this is how it has always worked. The military knows the military. How can you make decisions about people you don't even know?" His black hair was combed neatly to the side and his dark eyes glared at Rummy through his glasses. His hands were on the table, and his fingers were trembling, though from nervousness or anger, Rummy couldn't quite tell. "You're gonna look at their resume and spend 30 minutes interviewing them. We've been in the trenches with them, known them for decades, we know the true fiber of these people. Respectfully, you don't."

Rummy didn't hide his contempt. His tone was dismissive and angry. "And I should hear about all that so that I can factor it into my decision on who to recommend to the president. I want that information, General." He looked across the table at each member of the Joint Chiefs. "I want your opinions. And I will give them the weight they deserve. But the ultimate decision will not be yours. You're mistaking what is relevant with what is determinative."

It was pretty clear by the expression on his face that General Shinseki didn't know what Rummy meant by that.

"Excuse me, Mr. Secretary," said General Aaron Bergstrom, sitting to Shinseki's right, holding up his hand. "I think this has profound implications. You are going to lose a lot of support in the forces if you hijack this process and change things from the way they have always been done."

"Hijack ... *hijack*? I'm doing no such thing. I'm sorry General but the fact that it's always been done this way just doesn't matter. The Constitution of the United States—"

"We know, we know—"

"Let me finish," Rummy said as several chiefs rolled their eyes. "The Constitution of the United States vests control over the military in the president of the United States and the secretary of defense. *Not* the generals. I won't allow people who are better, who are more qualified, who are smarter, not get their fair shake because they don't run in the right clique."

"You need to trust us to sort that out, to separate the wheat from the chaff," Shinseki said.

Rummy smiled. These guys just didn't get it. No way would he trust them with this. He moved both his hands from his lap onto the table and squeezed them hard into fists. "The answer is no. The Clinton era is over. Civilians are in charge. There are no longer a bunch of commanders in chief. There's one. And I report to him. And you report to me." He paused for a few seconds before ending the discussion. "Next subject."

Several hours later Rummy was standing at his desk thinking about the meeting with the generals earlier that day. He had Bush's and Cheney's strong support for reclaiming civil control over the military—and the generals' negative personal feelings toward him weren't going to get in the way. According to Rummy, Bill Clinton's desire to be liked by the generals diminished his authority and harmed the country. Trying to be popular in government was a fool's errand anyway. It often backfired.

He pulled an index card out of his pocket and wrote: *RR: If you try to please everybody, somebody's not going to like it.*

It was something he had done for decades—keep an index card on him and write down his thoughts and the best axioms he heard. He kept the cards in a shoe box. Jerry Ford heard about this habit early in his presidency and had Rummy compile the best lines into a collection and distribute them throughout the administration. Rummy titled the compilation *Rumsfeld's Rules.* But even long after the Ford days, he was still adding to the list.

Part Three: The Tape
September 11, 2001 – June 31, 2005

Rumsfeld Rule: "The absence of evidence is not necessarily evidence of absence."

Chapter 12
September 11, 2001

Rummy was standing at his desk, getting his daily intelligence briefing from Torie Clarke, the assistant secretary of defense for intelligence. Clarke was in her early forties and had short, dirty blonde hair and energetic blue eyes. Rummy found her smart, tough, and endearing. Unlike the generals he interacted with—stars plastered on their shoulders—Clarke wasn't intimidated by Rummy. She could hold her own with anyone at the Pentagon. And she didn't waste his time with politics or worry about hurt feelings. When they spoke, she got to the point. I watched Rummy interact with dozens of his underlings, and Clarke was his favorite. Jenkins was a close second.

There was a muted television on a stand a few feet from them. It was tuned to CNN because an airplane had struck one of the World Trade Center buildings in Manhattan. Rummy had been to the World Trade Center several times on business. He and Clarke both thought it was a terrible accident and Rummy had immediately told Jenkins to work with the chiefs and assess how the military could help. "Clinton's amateurs are still running the FAA," Rummy told her, shaking his head.

"In Zimbabwe, Mr. Secretary, we have evidence that terrorists with links to the ruling government are planning to attack our embassy," Clarke said. She was standing close to him, resting her notepad on the edge of his desk. Rummy nodded a few times but kept looking over at the television. "They tried to attack the embassy before, several times. We recommend targeted strikes at several of their known installations in Zimbabwe combined with the clear message through established communication channels that if we see any further indication of a planned strike on US assets—"

Rummy's eyes widened as he looked at the television in horror. He leaned forward and raised his hand toward Clarke. She turned from Rummy to the television. CNN showed the second World Trade Center building exploding as another plane flew into it. Rummy's heart started pounding against his ribcage. He turned from the television to Clarke and stared deep into her eyes. His Adam's apple bobbed up and down several times and he swallowed some air. "We are under attack," he said. His hand shaking, he picked up the phone and called Cheney. He and Clarke watched the television as dark smoke billowed from both towers.

Ring …

Ring …

Ring …

There was no answer.

"Meeting adjourned," Rummy said to Clarke.

"Understood, Mr. Secretary." She turned around and started walking toward the door.

"No, wait, stay here," Rummy said, taking a few steps toward her and placing his hand on her shoulder. Clarke could see intense fear and vulnerability in his eyes.

"Of course."

Then the door to his office opened violently. Jenkins rushed in and slammed the door behind him. He stared wild-eyed at Rummy and Clarke. No one spoke. The three of them just looked at each other. Rummy's hands were in his pockets. He didn't know what to do. He kept looking at his phone, wanting Cheney to call him back. Dick always seemed to get smarter as things got harder. He'd know what to do.

"What should we do?" Jenkins finally asked.

"I'm trying to get ahold of the Vice President," Rummy said. He looked at Jenkins for a few seconds and then blurted out, "Get the chiefs in here right away."

"Will do," Jenkins said, and walked out of the office.

Rummy turned back to the television set and watched the towers burn. He could feel his bottom lip quivering, but he couldn't stop it. His poker face had crumbled, and he knew it. "What's next?" he asked Clarke. "Is this the iceberg's tip or its core?"

Clarke shook her head. She'd never seen this look of distress on Rummy's face before. "I don't know."

On my watch, he thought. *A major attack on our soil, that could get bigger and bigger and bigger, all on my watch as secretary of defense.* His heartbeat was getting faster and faster. He wiped away several small beads of sweat from his brow. He started to feel disoriented, dizzy. He reached over and grabbed his glass and took a sip of water. *Should I call the president directly?* he asked himself. Bush was traveling. *Was it Texas? Maybe Oklahoma?* He couldn't remember. No, he would wait for Dick to call him back. He looked at the phone again. It sat silently on his desk. Then he looked at the television. The towers blazed.

Several of the chiefs entered the room with Jenkins. They weren't talking, just standing near Rummy's desk, watching the muted television. It was quiet. No one seemed to know what to say or do. Rummy looked at the phone again.

"Okay," Rummy began, realizing he should speak. "Obviously we need to lock down the airspace surrounding the Pentagon. That's step one. Lock it down."

"Understood Mr. Secretary," someone said.

"Then we have two overarching objectives. The first is to figure out what the heck happened in Manhattan and whether anything similar is happening anywhere else. The second is to come up with responsive options for the president. On the first—"

Suddenly the room started shaking and they could all hear and feel a deep, rolling, thundering explosion. The room shook for four or five seconds straight. Rummy put his hand over his chest as his eyes danced around the shaking room. He knew that if the Pentagon—one of the largest buildings on the planet—was shaking then something big had just happened. Earthquake? No, that was wishful thinking. They were under attack. He couldn't tell how close it had been, though. He walked to the large window behind his desk and opened the drapes and looked outside but from this vantage he couldn't see anything unusual, just the Pentagon parking lot and a bunch of trees. It looked like any other autumn day. A sharp pain was building in his lower abdomen. He looked at the chiefs, who were just standing there. Then he looked at Clarke and said, "Wait here for Dick to call back." He paused a moment, then said, "But evacuate if you need to." Then he strode across and out of his office. He turned left and started running down the Pentagon's wide hallway, toward where he thought he heard and felt the explosion. He didn't really know why he was running but staying in his office doing nothing simply wouldn't work. He needed to act, to move, to do something.

So he ran.

"Don't go there Mr. Secretary," Jenkins said, trailing after him, jogging awkwardly and reaching out toward Rummy with his hand. "It's not safe." Rummy ignored him and kept running. His tie was flung over his left shoulder as he sprinted down the hall.

After several minutes of running, and then jogging, Rummy started to walk. He was panting heavily and ran a hand through his sweaty hair. He played squash several times a week and was in good shape for someone in their late sixties. But even a sprint fueled by powerful doses of adrenaline and fear could only last so long. After a few minutes of walking, he could see smoke up ahead down the long hallway. Then he could smell it. With each step, the smoke grew darker, thicker, more ominous. He started coughing as the smoke entered his throat. Eventually his right hand was extended in front of him, attempting to shield him from the fumes as he walked closer and closer toward where it was coming from. Then he saw an exit door on his left and burst through it to the outside. The sun was bright, scolding his eyes. The air was filled with the rank stench of thick smoke. After a few steps away from the building he could see the destruction. The Pentagon had been hit. *By a bomb*, he thought at first. Then he saw massive shreds of burnt metal scattered around the area. And then he realized: *No, by another plane.* His head shot upward and he spun around frantically, trying to see if another plane was accelerating toward the building. He saw nothing but open sky.

Then he looked back down and started moving toward the fire. Dense billows of rising smoke moved violently and erratically upward toward the sky. The dark, swirling clouds were a harrowing contrast to the bright flames from which they emanated. He kept walking straight toward the wreckage. He could feel the heat gripping his face and penetrating through his suit and into his skin. His throat clenched. He coughed some more. He was terrified by what he saw but the fear of doing nothing, of turning away from the smoldering building, was even more powerful.

A young army officer came up from behind him and grabbed his arm, which Rummy jerked away. The officer said, "Mr. Secretary, it's not safe! We're handling this, you should evacuate." Rummy ignored him and headed toward the fire. He smelled the dense, hot, nauseating smoke and felt it seep deep into his body and press against the lining of his lungs.

On my watch, he kept saying to himself. *On my watch. The United States of America is under attack on my watch.*

As he got closer, he saw the devastation in increasing detail. Victims were being carried to ambulances. Blood was dripping from stretchers onto the ground. Sirens were blaring. People were screaming. He kept going straight to the fire and smoke. Closer and closer. He was not reasoning any of this in his mind; he just had an instinct, an urge—a primordial need—to be in the middle of everything, to do something. He didn't know what action to take militarily or strategically—he needed to talk to Cheney—so he chose physical action to fill the void.

As he got closer to the rubble and flames he saw two people carrying a stretcher who looked wobbly and uneven. They nearly dropped the person they were carrying, but Rummy was able to leap forward and grab the side of it, stabilizing them and helping them move ahead. Together they carried the victim, whose leg had been injured, into an ambulance. The ambulance's up-close flashing lights and hair-raising sirens made Rummy even more disoriented. Then he turned around and looked at the building and the fire and the smoke and wondered: *What else has been hit? Where else has the US been attacked? Who did this? What more is to come?*

All on my watch.

After helping another stretcher make its way to another ambulance Rummy stopped and surveyed the scene. He was still panting. Sweat was running down his face. His hands were on his hips. He had grasped the scope of what happened to the Pentagon. A large plane had crashed into the building. He shook himself. His job wasn't to pull people out of the wreckage, it was to make sure there was no wreckage in the first place. He needed to go back to his office and do his job. As he turned and started walking, he saw a piece of silver metal on the ground, about two feet long. It looked like a piece of airplane debris. He picked it up. It was hot. Just barely able to hold it in his bare hand, he took it with him. *If I survive this attack*, he thought, *this can go in a museum—a piece of the plane that hit the Pentagon and was recovered by the secretary of defense.*

When he got back to his office, Clarke was still there, a few feet from the standing desk. Rummy's heartbeat steadied seeing her. She seemed calm, in control. "Has Dick called back yet?" he asked.

"No."

"Any other attacks?"

Clarke looked back to the TV, now playing footage of the Twin Towers rescue effort.

"Not yet."

"Get Cheney on the phone ASAP."

"Okay. I'll work on that while you call Joyce," Clarke responded.

Rummy's heart sank. "Good idea." He'd been so rattled he hadn't thought of calling her.

He picked up the phone and called her at their home in Chevy Chase, Maryland.

"Don... Don is that you?" She answered after half a ring.

"Yes," he said, still breathing heavily. The sound of her frantic voice made his eyes get wet. "It's me."

She started to cry. "Oh, thank God! Honey, how are you? Is everything okay?"

"I'm fine sweetheart, just fine. We have everything under control. Are you okay?"

"I'm fine, everything is normal here, like any other day. But God, I saw what happened in New York, and now they're saying the Pentagon was hit too! Are you sure you're okay?"

"Yes, yes, I'm okay. The plane hit the other side of the building and now we have the whole surrounding airspace locked down and safe. So you don't need to worry about me. How are the kids?"

"They're fine. I've spoken to each of them in the last 30 minutes and they're all fine. We're all just worried about you. What on earth is happening?"

Rummy was trying hard to project a calm and steady voice to Joyce, to give her the impression that he wasn't deeply shaken. He didn't think it was working. She knew him too well. "Okay, stay home and tell the kids to stay home too. I will send additional Secret Service details to each of you, if I can. I need to get to work. I will call you within a few hours."

"But Don, what's happening? What is all this?"

"We're still sorting it out."

"Folks on the news are saying it's terrorists from the Middle East. Is that right?"

"There will be time to figure out who it was later. For now, try to stay calm," Rummy said. "You don't need to worry. The best thing to do right now is try to relax and go about your day around the house. I know that's hard but listening to reporters and trying to guess what happened will only make things worse."

"Can you come home? Or at least leave the Pentagon? What if another plane hits—"

"I can't leave. But I will come home tonight. We can talk about all this when I get home. But for now, I need to stay focused."

"Okay ... okay. I understand."

"I love you," Rummy said.

"I love you too."

He hung up and looked back at Clarke. "Cheney?"

"Working on it, Mr. Secretary."

Rummy stood behind his desk watching CNN. Smoke was pouring out of both towers. Several minutes later, the phone finally rang.

"Dick, is that you?" Rummy asked as he picked up the phone.

"Yes, I'm here. It's me," Cheney said.

"You okay?"

"Yes, I'm fine. You?" Cheney said. His voice was deep, steady, unfazed. He sounded exactly like he always did.

"Hanging in there. The plane hit the other side of the Pentagon, so I'm fine but the damage is hard to fathom." Rummy was trying, and failing, to sound as under control as Cheney.

"Glad you're okay," Cheney said. "The scene in New York is mind boggling."

"It is."

"Both towers."

Rummy said nothing.

"We are at war," Cheney said.

"Yes, we are. On our own soil."

"That's right."

"What are you hearing from the intelligence community?" Rummy asked.

"Not much. Too early. Fog of war still."

"Me too. What should we do?"

"Well, it's hard to have a concrete plan at this point, but one thing is clear: we need to eliminate possible threats wherever we see them," Cheney said. "Anything that might cause more harm. It's our only option. Every plane in the air is a potential weapon. As we get more information we can refine and narrow our orders. But for now, tell the generals to shoot down any planes that veer off route and stop communicating with air traffic control."

"Will do."

"We should cancel all flights in and out of the country that haven't taken off yet."

"Yes, good idea. I can handle that." Rummy looked over at the television and saw the towers still burning. He inhaled deeply.

"And I'd get out of the Pentagon if I were you," Cheney said. "Or at least well below ground, like me. We don't know exactly who the enemy is, let alone the full extent of their capabilities."

Rummy nodded. He looked over at Clarke, who was standing with Jenkins several feet away, and covered the phone with his hand. "Make arrangements for us to move to a new, safe location underground. Make sure it's fully connected to all communication channels."

She nodded and turned and walked out of the room. Jenkins continued to stand still and look at Rummy.

There were a few seconds of silence. Rummy could hear Cheney breathing into the phone. Then Rummy asked, "Where's POTUS?"

"I've been told he's on his way back to Washington."

"Has he weighed in on any of this?"

"Not yet. It's just me and Condi running the show for the West Wing. She's not helping much."

"Big surprise. Al-Qaeda, right? Bin Laden? That's our best guess?"

"I think so. Not substantiated yet but yes that's the best guess. There were 19 Saudis on the first plane, apparently. So Al-Qaeda likely played a role here. Are you hearing anything about that?"

"Not much. Folks here are stunned from the plane hitting and waiting on clarity and guidance from POTUS."

"Yeah, let me see what I can do there. But it's on us until he wakes up and gets involved. Could be awhile."

"Understood and agreed."

There was another pause for several seconds.

"Rummy," Cheney said.

"Yes?"

"We need to eliminate all threats as soon as we see them. Every single one. No sitting around thinking about pros and cons. No worrying about diplomacy or legalities. No asking ourselves if something is proportional or allowed under this convention or that treaty. If we see something we don't like, we destroy it immediately. Period."

"I was just about to say the same thing."

"We have no idea how bad this will get, but it will only get worse if we sit on our hands."

"Yes, agreed."

"Okay, call me if anything material comes up. Calls to my desk are now being forwarded to this location."

"Sounds good. Let's check in either way in an hour or two," Rummy said.

"Talk to you then."

Rummy hung up the phone. He felt a little better now, having talked to Cheney. Then he turned back to the television. Jenkins saw a look of sheer terror spread across Rummy's face. He turned to the television. One of the towers was collapsing into the ground.

Rummy got home that night at 12:45 a.m. His security detail had doubled to eight Secret Service agents, and he didn't object. He had someone double check his secure phone line was working in case anyone needed to reach him. Joyce was at the door when he arrived. He closed the door behind him as he entered and they embraced. He cried as she just held him. They didn't speak. He put his head on her shoulder and sobbed. His shoulders bobbed up and down as tears fell from his cheeks onto her nightgown.

When his head hit the pillow about an hour later, after Joyce had fallen asleep, his mind was racing a million miles an hour. He thought about the known knowns: *Terrorists hijacked planes and attacked The World Trade Center and the Pentagon. They tried and failed with another plane, which was brought down by the passengers who fought back.* Then he thought about the known unknowns: *Who was behind this? Have there been other attacks that I don't know about yet? Has anything happened since I got home? What else is the enemy planning that could happen tomorrow or the day after or the day after that?* Then he asked himself the key question: *What are the unknown unknowns that I'm not contemplating at all? What is the surprise that nobody is thinking about on top of this huge surprise we've already received?* He thought and thought and thought as the back of his head mashed into his pillow. He twisted and turned. His stomach was aching in a sharp knot of winding, twisting, tightening stress, fear, and anger.

On my watch, he thought, staring at the ceiling in the dark with wide-open eyes. His pupils were dilated. His nostrils flared. His teeth grinded loudly as he squeezed the sheets hard with both hands. *On my watch.*

Chapter 13
November 19, 2001

A little over two months later, Rummy strode into the Pentagon press room. The wide brown podium went up nearly to the center of his chest. An American flag stood to his right, and a large, oval-shaped logo of the Pentagon hung behind him. He looked serious and focused. He'd been smiling a lot less recently.

Next to him was General Richard Meyers, the new Chairman of the Joint Chiefs of Staff. Meyers was tall with boyish features. He spoke with a slight lisp, which reminded Rummy of his old friend, now treasury secretary, Paul O'Neill. Meyers' height bugged Rummy, especially since the two men now regularly stood next to each other at press conferences watched by millions of people around the world. Now in his late sixties, Rummy's short height still pissed him off. "If I was 6'3, I would've been president instead of H.W. Bush," he once said—only half-jokingly—to Cheney. "And I would've won reelection!"

But Rummy generally liked Meyers. Unlike Shinseki and most of the other generals, Meyers was duly respectful and deferential to his boss. Though Rummy's respect for Meyers' intellect only went so far.

The topic of this day's briefing: the nascent Afghanistan military campaign. The main target was Osama Bin Laden, chief of the Al-Qaeda terrorist network and the architect of the September 11th attacks. Bin Laden and Al-Qaeda were being given refuge in Afghanistan by the ruling Taliban regime. The campaign was going well and Rummy's confidence—in the military, the country, and himself—was sky high. He'd quickly become a global celebrity, a fact he loved while pretending to ignore. Journalists from all around the world now hung on his every word.

Rummy's disdain for the press was legendary. As he told me numerous times, he thought reporters were a bunch of ankle-biters whose mission was to take whatever tiny little scraps of information they could find or (sometimes) manufacture—virtually never representative of the whole picture—and spin dramatic narratives to sell papers. When I would push back and note that the press was an important check on power in a democratic society, Rummy would scoff: "Well, that may be true. But surely they can be a check on power without being so dishonest." I always found it ironic that someone so hostile to reporters was also so infatuated with seeing his name in the paper.

The object of his most visceral disdain: unidentified sources. To Rummy, one had to know *who* was talking to understand *what* was being said. A "senior official" could be a deputy assistant at the Labor Department—who was privy to nothing important—or the secretary of state (who didn't even always have the facts or right perspective). Anonymous gossipers could hardly be trusted to convey accurate information, yet they fueled the booming industry of American news.

Joyce would often remind him that reporters "have their job to do and you have yours." She was right, he knew, but he still considered them a nuisance.

Rummy was a little nervous standing there behind the podium—one wrong word would reverberate around the world—but he looked confident and in command.

A heavy-set reporter with a beard, from Newsday, lobbed up the first question. "Mr. Secretary, have any special operations troops gone into caves and tunnels hunting the Al-Qaeda and Taliban leadership? And have you fairly sharply defined the area where you think bin Laden is?"

"It'd be foolhardy for me to try to speculate about any of that," Rummy replied. "The Al-Qaeda and Taliban leadership can be any number of places, and they move frequently, so to try and think that we have them contained in some sort of a small area would be a misunderstanding of the difficulty of the task."

Question number two, from a bearded *New York Times* reporter in a suit and tie: "Secretary Rumsfeld, despite the success that you've enjoyed in this military campaign, I'm sure you won't be surprised to know that there are still critics of the administration. If we are to believe *The Washington Post*, some of these critics are right here in this building. Apparently one anonymous four-star general accused you of micromanaging the war. What's your response?"

Rummy rolled his eyes and exhaled into the microphone before answering. "When General Carias was here, he responded to that very question. He explained how he was not being micromanaged but rather being given the right amount of room from the civilian leadership to run the war. I thought it was an accurate and persuasive answer."

"What about the four-star general?" the reporter asked.

"The *anonymous* four-star general?"

"Yes. Any response?"

"I just responded."

A reporter in a red blouse from *The San Francisco Chronicle* raised her hand and Rummy nodded in her direction. "Respectfully, Mr. Secretary, do you have a more responsive answer to the accusation that you're micromanaging the generals?"

"Again, I just gave one. Let me try this again. Think about what takes place. The president says, 'Go after terrorists.' I sit down with the defense establishment, and a plan is developed, and General Carias is in charge of that. And he then presents that plan to me, and we talk about it with the advice of the chiefs. And then, at some point, we present it to the National Security Council and the president. If it's approved, General Carias then goes off and implements that plan. He goes out and makes a series of very tough calls—he and the people under him. And I delegate to him the authority to strike targets. He goes and uses that delegation of authority, makes his judgments, and he has to balance successfully striking our targets against trying to avoid collateral damage and civilian casualties. So he makes a series of judgments. And to me—"

"Mr. Secretary," she persisted, "I think we all understand the general procedure with which our strategy is decided. The question is if you are interjecting yourself too much over the advice of our generals. Do you have anything to say on that subject?"

Rummy's mouth formed a frustrated smile and he shook his head. "Well, you're going to have a bunch of people who aren't involved, and they're going to look at it, and they're going to say, 'Well, gee, if I'd been doing it, I would have done this. I would have done more of that or a little less of this or I would have done it faster or slower.' And the fact that there are one or two anonymous people who seem to have observed something that they might have done differently, well, that isn't surprising at all."

The reporter kept trying. "But again, Mr. Secretary, is your—"

Rummy cut her off: "Next question."

Chapter 14
February 5, 2002

"This makes no sense," Rummy fumed. "None. Zero." He scowled. "How can you definitively conclude that Iraq does not have weapons of mass destruction? It's a huge country. It's 169,000 square miles. With forty-plus million people. They've had them and used them before. Again, the absence of evidence is not evidence of absence."

"Sure Mr. Secretary, but we've looked long and hard. So have other countries. So has the UN. No one has found anything."

"General Shinseki, I don't want to have to say this again, but just because you have not found something does not mean it doesn't exist." Rummy's dark brown eyes shone through his glasses. The row of four-star generals on the other side of the table in Rummy's office made faces that ranged from nervous, to perplexed, to infuriated.

"But why would we conclude it *does* exist?" General Shinseki said, his face red and his fingers shaking as he held his yellow notepad in his hands.

"I'm saying we shouldn't conclude it doesn't. This is especially true given the deceitful nature of the Iraqi regime. It doesn't take a whole lot of imagination to picture Saddam hiding his weapons from inspectors, now does it?"

"What's the point then? We can only draw a conclusion if we find them?"

"Excuse me?"

"By your logic, we'll never rule it out, Mr. Secretary, so you're saying we either find them or say we don't know."

Rummy shifted in his seat. "The world's complicated, General. It's messy. It's hard. You have the information you have, not the information you might want. That's not my fault.

But we can't take shortcuts with how we think about these things, the stakes are too high." The generals just stared back at him from across the table. "Meeting adjourned," Rummy said.

He looked to Jenkins to his left and said, "James, stay here."

Everyone else rose from the table and left the room. Rummy walked over to his standing desk. Jenkins followed.

"What are we going to do with these clowns?" Rummy said.

"I think you're handling it the right way. This is just more pushback like we've been getting since the beginning. If they don't like it, well, too damn bad."

"Shinseki really doesn't like me, does he?"

"Again, too damn bad."

Rummy smiled before changing the subject. "The intelligence community is in shambles," he said. "Tenet is doing some good work, but it takes time to repurpose and redirect a large ship with lots of momentum in the wrong direction. They still can barely put one foot in front of the other."

Jenkins nodded.

"Eight years of Clinton's indifference took a toll."

Jenkins nodded again.

"Iraq has weapons of mass destruction," Rummy said. "They must. We know they have the intent and the capability and a history of using them."

"No doubt about it," Jenkins said.

"And we can't trust a word Saddam says now. That's about the easiest conclusion one could possibly reach. He's a pathological liar."

"Every other sentence he utters is a lie."

"I met Saddam about twenty years ago. There's no limit to his ruthlessness. He's a brutal, sadistic tyrant."

"Yes indeed," Jenkins said.

Rummy's voice got lower. He pushed his glasses up his nose. "So ... listen ... keep this off the books, nothing in writing anywhere, understood?"

Jenkins wasn't sure what Rummy was getting at, but replied, "Understood."

"Nothing in writing."

"Understood, Mr. Secretary."

"Let's get some of our best and brightest DOD intelligence folks on the ground in Iraq. And give them one goal: find evidence of WMDs. That's it. All day. All night. Eat, sleep, breathe one thing and one thing only. *Find evidence showing Saddam has WMDs.* This clown show at the CIA that keeps swinging and missing is hurting the country."

"I can make that happen."

"Report back on progress in one week."

Jenkins nodded firmly.

"And ... again ... James ... don't write anything down or let anyone say anything about this. Just get it done."

"Understood."

"Report back in one week."

"Will do."

Rummy nodded and Jenkins walked out of the office. Then he began dictating a snowflake.

> *From: Secretary Rumsfeld*
>
> *To: National Security Council Principals: Vice President Cheney, Secretary of State Powell, Treasury Secretary O'Neill, National Security Council Advisor Rice.*
>
> *Copy: Karl Rove*
>
> *Date: February 5, 2002*
>
> *Subject: Weakness is Provocative*
>
> *History has proven time and again that weakness in international affairs is provocative. We sat on the sidelines in World War Two and then came Pearl Harbor. It wasn't until America got*

involved that the tide turned toward the Allies. We tried to be nice to the Soviet Union through détente, and they only grew stronger. I know firsthand from watching Kissinger manipulate Nixon and Ford. It wasn't till Reagan and Schultz confronted the Russians with strength that America won the Cold War. In recent years, we allowed terrorists and dictators to consistently harm us with impunity. For example:

- *The terrorist bombing of PanAm flight number 103 in 1988*
- *The attempted assassination of former President George HW Bush in 1993*
- *The first World Trade Center bombing in 1993*
- *Our shameful military retreat in Mogadishu in 1993*
- *The Kosar Towers bombing in 1996*
- *The East Africa embassy bombing in 1998*
- *The USS Cole bombing in 2000*

The Clinton administration was feckless with terrorists and we paid a heavy price. One can draw a straight line from Clinton's weakness to the events of September 11th.

Never again!!

Our campaign in Afghanistan has been a show of strength, no doubt. But it's not enough. We must do more. We must lean forward. Iraq is a breeding ground for more terrorists and therefore, if we do nothing, more terror. We must redouble and broaden our efforts to show strength and the focus must be Iraq. The world must know that choosing to be an enemy of the United States is a very bad decision, a decision that has consequences.

I look forward to discussing this at Thursday's NSC principals meeting.

When Rummy's head hit the pillow that night, he thought about the same thing he now thought about every night: September 11th. The same pain he felt in his stomach when the Pentagon started shaking would come back every night. He saw images of the people being carried on stretchers to ambulances. Their screams echoed in his head. He smelled the dense smoke oozing from the smoldering wreckage. He felt his throat clench as he tried to breathe. In retrospect, everyone *now* knew the scope of the attacks that day. But at the time the planes were hitting the buildings no one knew how vast the destruction would be. No one knew what would happen next. It was horrifying. And next time could be so much worse, he worried. The potential for destruction was so vast. Americans' way of life depended on 300 million people waking up every day and having the freedom and confidence to participate fully in society. This is what allowed schools to open; markets to function; businesses to create products, services, and jobs; artists and athletes to entertain; researchers to discover new truths; the public square to flourish. People needed to get out of bed each day without fear in order for America to work. The violent dysfunction in the Middle East jeopardized all that. And the asymmetric threats—where just a few people could do so much damage—made the challenge immense. It was his job, as secretary of defense, to defend his country.

"Never again," he said softly. Already asleep, Joyce moved just a little. "Not on my watch. Never. Again."

To Rummy there was one way—and one way only—to prevent another attack: action. If it was to avoid another day like September 11th, the United States had to act aggressively on the world stage to root out and destroy its enemies. This approach would not only incapacitate America's adversaries, it would send a strong message to would-be adversaries that trying to harm Americans had big consequences. Cheney felt the same way—and the two men powerfully reinforced each other's views.

In my experience with both men—which was substantial—Cheney and Rumsfeld didn't think identically. Cheney was more conservative, more paranoid, and less concerned with the human toll of war. Rummy was more pragmatic, more detail-oriented, and less of a big-picture guy than his one-time protégé. That said, the overlap between them was significant. They were both nationalistic foreign policy hawks. They were both obsessed with preventing another terrorist attack.

"Never again," Rummy whispered as he stared at the ceiling with open eyes.

Chapter 15
June 9, 2002

"That's exactly right, Mr. President," Rummy said. "Precisely. Doing nothing in this instance is just as much of a decision as doing something."

Bush nodded at Rummy from his chair in the White House Situation Room. He sat at the head of a rectangular table that took up most of the small room. The air smelt like stale coffee. Cheney was to Bush's right; National Security Advisor Condoleezza Rice to his left. Rummy sat to Rice's left, directly across from Secretary of State Colin Powell.

"Colin what do you think?" Bush asked, fidgeting in his seat.

"The truth is that we don't know whether Iraq has WMDs or not. We just don't," Powell said in his baritone voice. "And if—"

"But why does that matter?" Rummy interjected, looking Powell in the eyes. "If Saddam doesn't have them now, which is unlikely, he can easily get them."

Powell leaned forward. "The American people won't go for it, Don. They care about *actual* WMDs—not just speculation about intent and capacity—and we need their support."

"Yes, we need their support, but we also need to lead and not follow. We need to make the right decision and then persuade the American people to follow us. That's what leadership is all about."

"And if we can't?" Powell asked.

"If we can't persuade them?" Rummy said.

"Yes, if we can't convince the American people to support regime change in Iraq?"

Rummy exhaled audibly before responding. "We must try. We can't fail to do the right thing because the whims of public opinion happen to be against us or because of concern that we won't cross some arbitrary threshold of public support. Iraq is a threat to the United States, to the whole world, irrespective of whether at this exact moment they have operational WMDs or not. It's the capability and intent that matter."

Cheney quietly jotted down a note.

"Condi what do you think?" Bush asked.

"Mr. President, I agree with Colin. I don't think we can persuade the American people to invade a sovereign nation that has not attacked us if that nation doesn't have weapons that can harm us, doesn't have WMDs. And I think we would need to prove that they do, not just make the assertion. And without the weapons, I don't think 'the right thing to do' is as simple as Don seems to think."

Rice turned to Rummy after she spoke, half surprised he hadn't cut her off. While she and Rummy started off getting along well, friction between them arose after September 11th. Rummy found her process for getting information to Bush haphazard and dysfunctional—thoughts he shared with her in an open, even confrontational, manner. Rice found Rummy condescending and gratuitously aggressive during meetings. It was a tension that only grew with time.

"We must have the public's support," Powell said, looking Bush in the eyes, "that's the key lesson from Vietnam. And, Mr. President, we won't have public support for invading Iraq without *clear evidence* that they have WMDs. If we don't have that—"

"Mr. President, if I may," Rummy said. Bush turned from Powell to Rummy. "This debate seems to be premised on the notion that because we haven't found them yet, that means Iraq doesn't have WMDs, and we have to affirmatively prove the contrary in order to take action. By golly I think that's the wrong premise. They very likely *do* have WMDs. That should be our assumption." Rummy turned from Bush to Powell. "The burden should be on those who think Iraq doesn't have them. They should have to prove Saddam doesn't have the weapons. Showing weakness and leaning toward inaction under Clinton for eight years was a colossal error in judgment; it led directly to September 11th. We simply can't repeat that mistake."

Then Rummy turned back to Bush. He noticed that the president's nostrils seemed to remain in a constant flare throughout the conversation.

"But even if Saddam doesn't have WMDs," Rummy continued, "I still think regime change is the right policy. He's invaded two of his neighbors. He's brutalized his own people. He tried to kill your father." Bush squinted and gave Rummy a perplexed look but didn't say anything. "All I'm saying is that even if the very unlikely scenario were true that Iraq didn't have WMDs, we would still need to do the right thing and force regime change."

"If I may Mr. President," Powell said, raising his hand up off the table. "It's so easy for a civilian to simply say 'force regime change,' but the reality of this idea is incredibly complicated. Secretary Rumsfeld is pointing out one lesson he's learned from history, to be proactive. Another lesson we've learned from history is the paramount importance of having public support for major military initiatives. Vietnam was—"

"I know a thing or two about Vietnam," Rummy said, cutting him off again. "I was secretary of defense when we withdrew." Powell's face reddened. Rummy continued: "We lost public support in Vietnam because the military was cautious and tentative, refusing to use the force necessary to achieve the objective. The reason—"

"That's far too simplistic," Powell said loudly. Some spit came out of the right side of his mouth. "Those of us on the ground understood that the key—"

"Okay, okay," Bush said, placing both of his palms on the table. "Look. We can all agree we haven't found WMDs in Iraq. We just haven't. Not yet. Don, if we ever do, we'll revisit this question. For now, let's keep the focus on Afghanistan."

Condi nodded in agreement, clearly relieved. Though she knew Cheney and Rummy were relentless and this debate was far from over. Time and again she'd seen them seemingly lose a debate, only for Bush to change his mind later. Often the change was unannounced, and members of the administration would find out randomly that presidential decisions had been reversed. Cheney's weekly lunch with Bush was a particularly vulnerable hour of Bush's time.

"Will do, Mr. President," Rummy said straight-faced. The status quo in Iraq made him very nervous. He didn't like the idea of simply waiting and watching Saddam. And he didn't think Bush really understood the threat. But Bush was the president, and Rummy respected the chain of command. He would stand down, for now.

Powell smiled softly and briefly. He liked this result. But he was fuming that Rummy interrupted him to lecture everyone on the true nature of Vietnam. As if Rummy understood better from books what Powell learned firsthand on the ground.

Cheney leaned back in his chair and jotted down another note on his yellow pad.

When Rummy got back to his desk he dictated a snowflake:

> *From: Secretary Rumsfeld*
> *To: Chief of Staff Jenkins*
> *Date: June 9, 2002*
> *Subject: Foreign Leaders' Statements About September 11th*
>
> *Before every meeting I have with a foreign leader, I want to see what they said—verbatim—about the United States after September 11th. Where they stood in the immediate aftermath of that day will*

be important to their country's standing with the United States going forward.

Chapter 16
June 17, 2002

"Dick, what the fuck are you guys doing with Iraq?" Treasury Secretary Paul O'Neill said, eyes intense and lisp strong. His white hair shone brightly under the lights in Cheney's office.

"Excuse me?" Cheney responded from behind his cluttered desk. A large picture of colonial America wrapped in a thick, expensive frame hung on the wall behind him. He didn't like the question. Or more specifically, its tone.

O'Neill was sitting upright on the edge of a chair in front of Cheney. He'd just taken his seat. "You and Rummy are pushing hard on Iraq. I see the mobilization happening across numerous areas."

"And?"

"Do you really think we're anywhere near ready to invade? Do you really think we have any clue what will happen in Iraq and the Middle East if we bomb this helpless country to smithereens? It's good to be proactive but we should be prudent too."

"Now, Paul, I appreciate the questions, but we have this under control. You can stay focused on the sanctions regime."

"Stay in my lane?"

Cheney nodded. "Yes, stay in your lane."

"That's it?"

"Yes, that's it."

"Fine," O'Neill said. He looked Cheney in the eyes for a few seconds and then got up and left.

Cheney made a mental note to talk to Rummy about O'Neill's increasingly erratic behavior. He was vehemently opposed to the major tax cut Cheney maneuvered through Congress. And now he seemed to be against regime change in Iraq. The last thing they needed was a treasury secretary as smart as O'Neill trying to thwart their key initiatives.

Chapter 17
June 31, 2002

"We've got him on our side now, today," Cheney said from behind his desk. "*Right now* he thinks Iraq has WMDs. But Colin and Condi could easily change his mind again. They could convince him at any moment that there's no WMDs. That's what he thought just a few days ago."

"Like a leaf in the wind," Rummy said, shaking his head. "Our dear POTUS."

"Reminds me of Herbert Walker. A little more testosterone, a little less brains."

Rummy's face brightened into a smile. "Yeah, but we should celebrate the pluses, too. You've accomplished a lot already Mr. Vice President. That tax cut was no joke."

"Indeed," Cheney said, smiling, crossing his legs. "And more to come. Anyway, I haven't said this to anybody other than Lynne, but between us, he seems a little off lately. He was sharper during the campaign and our first year in office. More on point. More focused. I can't put my finger on it, but something seems off."

Rummy squinted at Cheney and tilted his head to the left, concerned to hear this. He remembered the empty wine bottle in the hotel bathroom when Bush interviewed him about becoming secretary of defense. He thought to himself perhaps there was a connection. "Any idea what might be going on?"

"No, can't really put my finger on anything specific."

"Hm."

"In any event, we need to stay focused on Iraq," Cheney said. "Bottom line: everything with POTUS is WMDs. If we want regime change, we need to convince him that Iraq actually has WMDs—and we need it to stick. He's not concerned with capabilities. He doesn't care about past usage. Or intent. Or the fact that Saddam is a pathological liar and brutal tyrant."

"My goodness. Did he learn anything from September 11th? So if Saddam doesn't have WMDs today but could have them in a month that doesn't even matter?"

"Bingo."

"It has to be right now ... he has the weapons right now?" Rummy asked.

"Yep."

"He probably does have them."

"Yes indeed."

"So what do we do?"

"We stay on top of him ... get him to understand the situation ... don't leave him alone in the same room with Colin or Condi," Cheney said, smirking.

"Understood."

Then Cheney lowered both his voice and his chin. "How's Jenkins' intelligence shop doing in Iraq?"

"Hard at work. Still trying to pin down where the WMDs are."

"Nothing?"

"Nothing that I've seen," Rummy said. Then he smiled. "Yet."

Cheney smiled back. "*Yet.*"

Chapter 18
July 4, 2002

Rummy worked an 18-hour day at the Pentagon on the Fourth of July. As usual, he had a driver take him both ways so he could work in the car. Joyce had become so used to him working all the time that she hadn't even asked if he'd be home for the holiday. He dictated 21 snowflakes before lunch, including this one:

> *From: Secretary Rumsfeld*
> *To: National Security Council Principals: Vice President Cheney, Secretary of State Powell, Treasury Secretary O'Neill, National Security Council Advisor Rice*
> *Copy: Karl Rove*
> *Date: July 4, 2002*
> *Subject: Saddam Hussein*
>
> *A reminder of what Saddam Hussein said about America on September 11th, 2001:*
> *"America is reaping the thorns planted by its rulers in the world."*
> *And a few other reminders about what we conclusively know—what's beyond debate—about this murderous dictator, Saddam Hussein:*
>
> - *Shelters terrorist organizations within Iraq, including Al-Qaeda*
> - *Employs nuclear scientists and technicians*
> - *Attempted to assassinate the Emir of Kuwait and George H.W. Bush in 1993*
> - *Admitted in 1995 that Iraq had a nuclear weapons program prior to the Gulf War, which caused the program to cease operations*

- *Tried to buy high-strength aluminum tubes used to enrich uranium*
- *Likely maintains stockpiles of VX, mustard gas and other chemical agents*
- *Attacked Iranian and Kurdish populations with mustard gas and nerve agents*
- *Produced tens of thousands of liters of anthrax*
- *Repeatedly kicked out UN weapons inspectors from Iraq*

I look forward to discussing this at the NSC principals meeting this week.

Chapter 19
August 18, 2002

Colin Powell's face reddened as he stared at the small stack of paper before him. He was sitting at his desk at the State Department, reading a draft of the speech Cheney planned to give in Tennessee the following week. He got the draft from Cheney's office that morning. Powell circled and underlined a sentence from the speech, his pen pressed so hard against the paper that the ink was jagged and runny: *There is no doubt that Saddam Hussein now has weapons of mass destruction.*

He wrote in the margin: *Absolutely not!! Cannot say this. Not true. No way!*

Powell pressed a blue button on his phone and said, "Get me Deputy Armitage right away."

A few minutes later Richard Armitage waddled into Powell's office. Armitage was short, 30 pounds overweight, and bald. He had arthritis in both knees and walked slowly and gingerly, cringing with each step. In his early 60s, he'd been friends with Powell for decades. They came up together in the military. He was known for being pragmatic, logical, tough as nails, and for having a particular disdain for Rummy, who interviewed him to be deputy secretary of defense in early 2001. He joked to Powell that the H in Donald H. Rumsfeld stood for hubris.

"What's up?" Armitage said, pulling up his pant legs a few inches before slowly sitting down in one of the two chairs facing Powell's desk. There was a thin layer of sweat on his bald head, which glistened in the light.

"Dick ... Fucking ... Cheney is about to give a speech in a few days and say unequivocally to the whole world that Iraq *does* have WMDs. No hedges. No qualifications. Look at this." He leaned forward and turned the papers around and put the speech in front of Armitage.

Armitage leaned forward and looked at the text Powell underlined. He read it out loud:

There is no doubt that Saddam Hussein now has weapons of mass destruction.

His head lurched backward and he looked up at Powell. "Wait … what?"

"It's right there," Powell said, tapping the text sharply with his pen.

"But it's a lie," Armitage said. "Is he serious?"

"This is the current draft."

"These lunatics. This is FUBAR." Armitage was famous for using this acronym, commonly uttered in military circles. It stands for Fucked Up Beyond All Reason.

Powell nodded. His eyes were glowing with rage.

"What can we do?" asked Armitage.

"I need to get to the president. The whole world will be watching the speech. The administration. Congress. Our allies. Saddam. We can't walk out on this plank. We can't lie. We need to be accurate about what we know. We can't base a war on a lie. These bastards who've been in suits their whole lives … who've never worn the uniform in combat … they just don't understand war."

Armitage's head bobbed up and down twice in an affirming nod. "Do you know if POTUS has seen the speech yet?"

"I don't. Will call Condi now."

Chapter 20
August 20, 2002

From: Secretary Rumsfeld
To: National Security Council Principals: Vice President Cheney, Secretary of State Powell, Treasury Secretary O'Neill, National Security Council Advisor Rice
Copy: Karl Rove
Date: August 20, 2002
Subject: Regime Change in Iraq

It's hardly new or unique to want regime change in Iraq. The idea that this is a novel or extreme position is utter hogwash. This is what President Clinton (of all people!) said on December 19, 1998:

"We began with this basic proposition: Saddam Hussein must not be allowed to develop nuclear arms, poison gas, biological weapons, or the means to deliver them. He has used such weapons before against soldiers and civilians, including his own people. We have no doubt that if left unchecked he would do so again ... So long as Saddam remains in power he will remain a threat to his people, his region and the world. With our allies, we must pursue a strategy to contain him and to constrain his weapons of mass destruction program, while working toward the day Iraq has a government willing to live at peace with its people and with its neighbors."

As the critics and skeptics of our administration's foreign policy get louder and louder—an inevitability—it's important that we remind the American people about Saddam's long history of using WMDs, invading Iraq's neighbors, and shooting at US aircraft, among other disturbing misbehaviors.

I met Saddam. I looked him in the eyes. He's a madman. And there has long been a broad consensus in this country—and among *our allies—that regime change in Iraq is the right policy. September 11th only reinforced this and strengthened the justification.*

Chapter 21
August 24, 2002

Two days before Cheney's speech, the National Security Council and their deputies convened in the Situation Room at the White House. Tensions ran high.

"Mr. President, Vice President Cheney simply can't say this," Powell said to Bush. "He can't say there's no doubt Iraq has weapons of mass destruction. It's not true. There is doubt."

Powell had known Cheney for decades. They collaborated successfully during the first Gulf War. And Powell respected Cheney, even if he found him cold and hard to connect with on a personal level. He didn't enjoy this direct confrontation with the Vice President, but the stakes were too high to stay silent.

Bush turned to Cheney and raised his eyebrows.

"Yes, I can say it, Mr. President," Cheney said. "And I should. The odds Iraq doesn't have WMDs given their past behavior and known intent are negligible. There's a—"

"Why don't we say that then?" Powell interjected. He was sitting on the edge of his seat, motioning dramatically with his arms. Rummy found it unprofessional and thoroughly unbecoming of the sitting secretary of state. "I'm fine with that articulation," Powell continued. "The odds they don't have WMDs are negligible. That's fine. Say that. The world will be watching this speech. The international community will hold us to what we say."

"Rummy, what do you think?" Bush asked. All eyes shifted across the table to Rummy.

"We should say it Mr. President." Rummy consciously sat back in his chair and didn't gesture with his hands, trying to draw a calm contrast to Powell's animated presentation. "Having 100 percent certainty of anything in foreign affairs is rare. That shouldn't be the litmus test for making a straightforward assertion."

Bush looked at Condi.

"I agree with Colin," she said. "This is too important to go beyond what we know. The international community is hanging on our every word with Iraq. And the truth is we don't know whether or not Saddam has WMDs. We just don't."

Rummy responded: "I don't understand why some of us are more concerned with the *international community* and what they—whoever exactly they are—think about our speeches than we are with doing the right thing, with saying what needs to be said."

"That's not fair," Condi responded. "I'm talking about key allies, nations that we depend on in Afghanistan and elsewhere. The UK, Australia, Israel among them. They rightfully expect us to be truthful and accurate with our public assertions, especially in matters of war and peace. They will remember what we say, and if we say Iraq has WMDs and it turns out they don't, well, it will be a big problem."

Rummy shook his head the entire time Condi spoke.

"For what it's worth, Mr. President, I agree with Colin and Condi," O'Neill chimed in from the far end of the table. The treasury secretary tended not to get in the middle of national-security debates in front of the president unless there was an explicit economic component. He was making an exception. Everyone turned to him. "We can't go to war based on exaggerations."

Rummy forgot that he was trying to appear calm and slammed his hand down on the table. "It's not an exaggeration! It's a common sense and fair conclusion based on what we know."

O'Neill tried to respond: "I just don't think that's—"

Rummy wouldn't let him: "Any other approach is giving Saddam the benefit of the doubt, which is absurd. He's a brutal tyrant. He threatens the region and the world."

"We aren't giving Saddam anything of the sort," Condi responded. She sat near the edge of her seat and shifted her gaze from Rummy to Cheney and then back to Rummy. "We're respecting empirical reality. We're respecting the facts. We don't know if the statement Vice President Cheney wants to make is actually true. I'm frankly surprised there's such little concern about accuracy here."

Rummy sneered. "There *is* concern for accuracy—"

"Okay, okay. Thank you everyone," Bush said, taking over the conversation. "Good debate." He took a deep breath, leaned back in his chair, and looked up at the ceiling for several seconds. Then he looked at Cheney. "Dick, don't say it. You can say we *think* he has WMDs, or our intelligence *suggests* he has stockpiles, or whatever. But you need to hedge. Don't say we know for sure he has them."

"But Mr. President," Cheney said. "I think it is—"

"No Dick," Bush interrupted. "We don't actually know. So don't say it."

Cheney nodded.

Powell smiled.

Condi turned to her agenda to see what the next topic of discussion would be.

O'Neill jotted down a note on his yellow pad.

Rummy exhaled loudly.

Chapter 22
August 26, 2002

Two days later, Dick Cheney strode onto the stage in Nashville, Tennessee for his speech at the Veterans of Foreign Wars national convention. His pace was brisk, a speed he could only sustain for a few seconds, which, thankfully, was all that was required to get from his chair to the podium. Heavy set with thin white hair and a huge forehead, he was wearing a black suit and red tie. He was a little nervous, but overall calm and steady.

The boisterous crowd was chanting, "USA! USA!"

Cheney smiled and waited fifteen seconds for the crowd to calm down. He didn't love the politics side of his job; his passion was actually governing. But he did appreciate the dopamine bath provided by an adoring crowd. This long pause allowed his panting to subside. With some sweat on his brow, he began the speech. Several minutes in, he turned his focus to protecting the United States from another terrorist attack:

"The danger to America requires action on many fronts all at once. We are reorganizing the federal government to protect the nation against further attack. The new Department of Homeland Security will gather under one roof the capability to identify threats, to check them against our vulnerabilities, and to move swiftly to protect the nation. At the same time, we realize that wars are never won on the defensive. We must take the battle to the enemy."

Paul O'Neill was a thousand miles away at the Treasury Department watching the speech on CSPAN with his deputy Kenneth Dam. "These guys don't know what they're getting us into," he said. "He's all but declared war and we're not ready for it."

Cheney continued. "Much has happened since the attacks of 9-11. But as Secretary Rumsfeld has put it, we are still closer to the beginning of this war than we are to its end. The United States has entered a struggle of years—a new kind of war against a new kind of enemy. The terrorists who struck America are ruthless, they are resourceful, and they hide in many countries. They came into our country to murder thousands of innocent men, women, and children. There is no doubt they wish to strike again, and that they are working to acquire the deadliest of all weapons. Against such enemies, America and the civilized world have only one option: wherever terrorists operate, we must find them where they dwell, stop them in their planning, and one by one bring them to justice."

O'Neill was shaking his head so swiftly that Dam was concerned he might sprain his neck. "Put another way," O'Neill said, "let me translate this: we can do whatever we want, wherever we want, whenever we want, to whoever we want. That's the license we have given ourselves. There's no limiting principle here."

Then Cheney pivoted to Iraq. "The case of Saddam Hussein, a sworn enemy of our country, requires a candid appraisal of the facts. After his defeat in the Gulf War in 1991, Saddam agreed under U.N. Security Council Resolution 687 to cease all development of weapons of mass destruction. He agreed to end his nuclear weapons program. He agreed to destroy his chemical and his biological weapons. He further agreed to admit U.N. inspection teams into his country to ensure that he was in fact complying with these terms. In the past decade, Saddam has systematically broken each of these agreements."

Colin Powell was in his office at the State Department watching the speech with Armitage. "He's really pushing the envelope," Powell said. "Do you think he's going to say it?"

"No way," said Armitage. "He's not going to say Iraq has WMDs. The president told him to hedge, so that's what he's gonna do."

Powell looked concerned. He shifted his gaze from Armitage back to the television. "Cheney and Rummy had 24 hours to get the president to change his mind. I'm not so sure we have the full picture."

Cheney turned the page of his printed speech and continued. "Intelligence is an uncertain business even in the best of circumstances. This is especially the case when you are dealing with a totalitarian regime that has made a science out of deceiving the international community. Let me give you just one example of what I mean. Prior to the Gulf War, America's top intelligence analysts would come to my office in the Defense Department and tell me that Saddam Hussein was at least five or perhaps even 10 years away from having a nuclear weapon. After the war we learned that he had been much closer than that, perhaps within a year of acquiring such a weapon."

O'Neill's eyes narrowed as he stared at the television screen. "The word *perhaps* is carrying a lot of weight in that sentence. This is all fiction. We're marching to war on assumptions." Dam just nodded at his boss silently.

Cheney marched ahead. "Saddam also devised an elaborate program to conceal his active efforts to build chemical and biological weapons. And one must keep in mind the history of U.N. inspection teams in Iraq. Even as they were conducting the most intrusive system of arms control in history, the inspectors missed a great deal. Before being barred from the country, the inspectors found and destroyed thousands of chemical weapons, and hundreds of tons of mustard gas and other nerve agents."

"I think he's going to say it," Powell said to Armitage.

"He's not going to say it. He wouldn't do that. It's too important. He's not going to stand up in front of the whole world and lie through his teeth about the central basis justifying military action against Iraq."

Powell grit his teeth. He wasn't so sure.

Cheney continued. "To the dismay of the inspectors, they in time discovered that Saddam had kept them largely in the dark about the extent of his program to mass produce VX, one of the deadliest chemicals known to man. And far from having shut down Iraq's prohibited missile programs, the inspectors found that Saddam had continued to test such missiles, almost literally under the noses of the UN inspectors."

Powell and Armitage were glued to the television, understanding this was where in Cheney's draft speech he'd claimed unequivocally that Saddam had WMDs. Powell's heartbeat was racing. His arms were crossed against his chest. Armitage kept standing up from his chair, adjusting his pant legs, and sitting back down. Both men squinted at the television.

"Simply stated," Cheney continued, *"there is no doubt that Saddam Hussein now has weapons of mass destruction."*

"Mother ... Fucker!" Powell screamed. He threw his pen across the room. It slammed against the wall before bouncing on the floor a few times. Armitage stood up violently, sending his chair tumbling behind him, and stomped his right foot into the floor twice. "FUBAR," he said. "Fucking FUBAR!"

Then Cheney doubled down. "There is no doubt he is amassing them to use against our friends, against our allies, and against us. And there is no doubt that his aggressive regional ambitions will lead him into future confrontations with his neighbors—confrontations that will involve both the weapons he has today, and the ones he will continue to develop with his oil wealth."

Paul O'Neil shook his head. "No doubt? No fucking doubt Dick? My friend Richard B. Cheney, who I've known for thirty years, is a liar. He's looking the whole world square in the eyes and lying through his teeth."

Cheney carried on. "We are dealing with a dictator who shoots at American and British pilots in the no-fly zone, on a regular basis, the same dictator who dispatched a team of assassins to murder former President Bush as he traveled abroad, the same dictator who invaded Iran and Kuwait, and has fired ballistic missiles at Iran, Saudi Arabia, and Israel, the same dictator who has been on the State Department's list of state sponsors of terrorism for the better part of two decades. As former Secretary of State Henry Kissinger recently stated: 'The imminence of proliferation of weapons of mass destruction, the huge dangers it involves, the rejection of a viable inspection system, and the demonstrated hostility of Saddam Hussein combine to produce an imperative for preemptive action.' If the United States could have preempted 9-11, we would have, no question. Should we be able to prevent another, much more devastating attack, we will, no question."

Powell and Armitage just stared at the television, blank-faced. Defeated.

O'Neill's head was still shaking. "There are millions of variables all interacting dynamically once you go into Iraq. The outcome can't be predicted."

Rummy, watching the speech at his standing desk at the Pentagon, alone, simply smiled. *Well done, Dick*, he thought. *Well done.*

Chapter 23
August 29, 2002

Paul O'Neill walked into Cheney's office without a scheduled meeting. Cheney had his foot propped up on his desk and was reading *The Washington Post*.

"Sorry to interrupt, Dick, but I need a few minutes of your time."

Cheney nodded, removed his foot from the desk, and placed the newspaper in front of him. He and Rummy had been growing more and more disappointed with their old friend from the Ford days. O'Neill's unwavering rationality just didn't jive with their post-September 11th fervor.

O'Neil focused on keeping his voice calm and respectful, but he got right to the point: "Look, I haven't heard one word suggesting we have a good handle on what will happen if we invade Iraq." Cheney took a deep breath through his nose and stared back at him. He was frowning and his blue eyes rested in puffy pink pockets. "I know, I know, I'm treasury secretary, not defense secretary. But I know a thing or two about getting things done and what works and what doesn't work in the world."

"You do," Cheney conceded, giving a single head nod.

"And we don't have a handle at all on whether this is going to work. Sure, we can level Baghdad and smash the country beyond recognition. But then what? We are rushing into a hornet's nest teeming with millions of people, many of whom are unhinged and desperate. We have no clue what shape this will take, what the consequences will be. We just don't know."

"I appreciate your concerns Paul but—"

"Wait, wait, before you tell me not to worry about it, to stay in my lane, let me say this: I know doing nothing is a terrible option. I know. I get it. But with the status quo at least we have some basis for what to expect, some sense of what Iraq and the region will look like. But with an invasion? Everything could get worse and stay worse for a long time. It could take decades to find a new equilibrium and the new equilibrium could very well be worse. A stable democracy is not the natural state of human organization, especially in the disorienting aftermath of brutal dictatorship. We don't have a solid basis for assuming Iraq will improve if we take out Saddam, Dick. It could easily get worse."

Cheney stared at O'Neill without saying anything.

O'Neill stared back. Then he continued: "And I know ... I know ... weakness is provocative. Rummy's line. But that's just a slogan. Making a big mistake and blundering on the world stage has negative consequences, too. And *that's* weakness, making a big dumb mistake is weakness, not strength."

Cheney crossed his arms. "Anything else?"

O'Neill stared at him for several seconds and then got up and walked out.

Cheney looked up at the ceiling. He tapped his finger on his desk twice. He asked himself if the smartest guy he knew was really so wrong about Iraq? Was O'Neill really this off base? Yes, he was wrong, Cheney concluded. O'Neill simply didn't have all the facts. He and Rummy did. Saddam's threats far outweighed the potential negative outcomes of an invasion. It didn't matter how smart you were if you didn't have all the facts.

Then he placed his foot back on the desk and resumed reading the paper.

Chapter 24
August 30, 2002

Jenkins entered Rummy's office and closed the door. He walked up to Rummy, who was standing at his desk. "Mr. Secretary," he said. He had a serious look on his face. His bloodshot eyes sat inside dark and puffy pockets.

"Yes, what is it?"

"The team on the ground in Iraq has obtained audio of Ambassador Aziz talking to Qusay, Saddam's son. The conversation was yesterday."

"Interesting," Rummy said. He didn't like the look on Jenkins's face.

"It's from the bug we planted a few weeks ago in a shed outside Saddam's palace in Tikrit."

"Okay ... continue."

"Both men explicitly say that there are no WMDs, that Iraq doesn't have WMDs. Here's a translation," Jenkins said, placing a small stack of paper on Rummy's desk.

Rummy picked up the papers and started to read. He had an angry, skeptical look on his face. His nostrils were flaring. He looked up at Jenkins and then back down at the papers. Heaps of adrenaline started coursing through his body.

Hussein: These bastard Americans keep saying we have WMDs. Did you see that monster Cheney's speech last week?

Aziz: Yes, I did. Total bullshit. Lies. Lies. Lies. Why do you think they do that?

Hussein: To justify their war.

Aziz: Can't we just tell them we haven't had WMDs in years?

Hussein: They won't listen, they will say we are lying, they will say we are misleading the international community, that we are tricking the UN inspectors. No matter what we say we cannot get them to accept it.

Aziz: So we'd have to prove we don't have them for the Americans to back off?

Hussein: Yes.

Aziz: But that's impossible.

Hussein: Exactly.

Aziz: How do you prove a negative?

Hussein: I know.

Aziz: Should we recommend to Saddam that we restart our programs, then? If they're going to say we have them we might as well have them, right?

Hussein: I'm not so sure.

Aziz: How long would it take to restart everything? How long until we actually had usable weapons being produced?

Hussein: A few months. Most of the infrastructure is still in place.

Aziz: It might make sense to do so.

Hussein: But Saddam doesn't want them. He still thinks they're more trouble than they're worth.

Aziz: True.

Hussein: Perhaps he's right. Right now, war is fifty-fifty. If we get caught with WMDs it goes immediately to one hundred.

Aziz: I agree.

Hussein: Okay ... okay. The status quo is best. No WMDs.

Aziz: I agree.

"Okay," Rummy said, squeezing the paper tight between his fingers. He paused for several seconds, thinking. "Have we verified the authenticity of this thing?"

"Yes, in every which way," Jenkins said. "It's real."

Rummy looked down at the papers, then back up at Jenkins. He cleared his throat before speaking. "This is interesting, but it's just noise from the Iraqi leadership. How do we know that they weren't aware of the bug, that this isn't calculated misinformation?"

Jenkins adjusted his tie. "We don't, but we don't know anything isn't calculated misinformation. What we do know is that it's relevant and it's meaningful. Obviously."

Rummy looked down at the transcript and read it again quietly, intensely. He looked up at Jenkins, his eyes sharp and intense. "The point of this operation was to *find* evidence of WMDs, not disprove the existence of WMDs."

Jenkins nodded slowly. "But I still think we need to tell—"

"No, no. Don't tell anyone about this."

"But—"

"No," Rummy said. "Do not tell anyone anything about this."

Jenkins looked Rummy in the eyes a few seconds before answering. "Understood," he replied.

"No one."

"Understood."

"Burn it."

Jenkins looked down at the floor and then back up at Rummy. "Will do."

Chapter 25
February 5, 2003

George Tenet smiled and put both of his large, hairy hands on Colin Powell's shoulders, looking him in the eyes. "You've got this," the director of the CIA told the secretary of state, squeezing his shoulders hard.

Powell smiled and nodded. He turned to his right and looked at John Negroponte, the director of national intelligence, who gave him a knowing stare and a firm head nod. "Yes, you do," Negroponte said.

Powell nodded again. His heart was racing. He was about to do what the president of the United States had asked him to do: declare war. It was a huge risk, and he knew his legacy hung in the balance. But over Armitage's vehement objections, he committed himself to laying the foundation for the United States to invade Iraq. Unlike Rummy and Cheney, he felt a deep ambivalence about whether invading Iraq was the right thing to do. He didn't know if it was justified. And he didn't know if it would work. But saying no to the president was a violation of the chain of command—the code he had lived by for four decades. Above all, he was a loyal soldier.

"Time to get moving," Powell said.

The three men walked down the long, narrow hall towards the floor of Assembly Hall at the United Nations. Their shoes clanked on the tile. Powell held a binder containing his speech in his right hand, clenching it hard.

"Thank you, Mr. President," Powell said a few minutes later, sitting at the large circular table, joined by representatives of the countries in the UN Security Council. His eyes had dark pockets under them. He had been at the CIA all week with Tenet—night and day—reviewing the intelligence, building the case. He cleared his throat and began: "Mr. President, Mr. Secretary General, distinguished colleagues, I would like to begin by expressing my thanks for the special effort that each of you made to be here today."

A thousand miles away in Cheney's office, Rummy and Cheney were watching the speech on C-SPAN. Cheney's foot was perched on his desk. Rummy was sitting in a chair, his legs crossed, his fingers squeezing the arms of the chair hard. He was nervous. A lot rode on how Powell's speech was received, both at home and abroad. Rummy was more and more convinced with time that regime change wasn't simply a good idea but was absolutely essential to America's security. Every day Saddam was in power the threat only got bigger.

A few blocks from Cheney's office, Paul O'Neill was watching alone in his office in his luxurious Washington D.C. apartment. The room was hazy with smoke from his cigar. A tall glass of gin rested in his right hand. Bush had fired O'Neill just a few months earlier, on Cheney's prodding. As Cheney said to Rummy after he was canned, O'Neill's brain power only helped if he was on board, if their interests were aligned. "We don't want our adversaries to be smart and energetic. We want them dumb and lazy."

Powell's voice was deep and strong as he continued. "This is an important day for us all as we review the situation with respect to Iraq and its disarmament obligations under UN security council resolution 1441. Last November 8, this council passed resolution 1441 by a unanimous vote. The purpose of that resolution was to disarm Iraq of its weapons of mass destruction. Iraq had already been found guilty of material breach of its obligations, stretching back over 16 previous resolutions and 12 years."

O'Neill was staring at the television through a plume of smoke. He muttered to himself, "How on earth did Rummy and

Cheney get Powell to do their dirty work? He was on the right side of this just a few months ago."

"Resolution 1441 was not dealing with an innocent party," Powell said, "but a regime this council has repeatedly convicted over the years. Resolution 1441 gave Iraq one last chance, one last chance to come into compliance or to face serious consequences. The material I will present to you comes from a variety of sources. Some are US sources. And some are those of other countries. I cannot tell you everything that we know. But what I can share with you, when combined with what all of us have learned over the years, is deeply troubling."

O'Neill shook his head. "Of course you can't share everything we know," he said out loud. "You're only going to share what incriminates Iraq. You're not going to share the exculpatory material, nor all the ambiguity and inconclusiveness that pervades the whole body of evidence."

Powell moved his glasses up his nose. His fingers were interlocked and a microphone was a few inches from his mouth. "What you will see is an accumulation of facts and disturbing patterns of behavior. Unfortunately, Iraq's behavior demonstrates that Saddam Hussein and his regime have made no effort—none at all—to disarm as required by the international community. Indeed, the facts show that Saddam Hussein and his regime are concealing their efforts to produce more weapons of mass destruction."

Rummy nodded as Powell spoke. He thought it was going well and his hands now merely rested on the arms of the chair. He had reviewed the speech two days earlier. As he expected, Powell had rejected most of his suggested edits. *That's okay*, Rummy thought. *The overall thrust of the speech is right where it needs to be.*

Powell continued. "This effort to hide things from the inspectors is not one or two isolated events, quite the contrary. This is part and parcel of a policy of evasion and deception that goes back 12 years, a policy set at the highest levels of the Iraqi regime. We know that Saddam Hussein has what is called 'a higher committee for monitoring the inspections teams,'" Powell said. "Think about that. Iraq has a high-level committee to monitor the inspectors who were sent in to monitor Iraq's disarmament. Not to cooperate with them, not to assist them, but to spy on them and keep them from doing their jobs."

"Yes, they are devious," O'Neill said loudly, scowling at the screen. "Yes, they are liars. Yes, they did not cooperate with inspectors! But that *does not mean* they have weapons of mass destruction. You aren't meeting your burden of proof Mr. Secretary."

"You okay, hun?" his wife asked, peering her head into his office.

"Yes, I'm fine, don't mind me," he responded without looking up from the television set.

"You sure?" she asked.

He looked up at her. "Sorry, yes, yes, I'm okay."

"Okay," she said with a shrug, "whatever you say," before walking away.

And the loyal soldier charged ahead at the UN. "Everything we have seen and heard indicates that, instead of cooperating actively with the inspectors to ensure the success of their mission, Saddam Hussein and his regime are busy doing all they possibly can to ensure that inspectors succeed in finding absolutely nothing. My colleagues, every statement I make today is backed up by solid human sources. These are not assertions. What we're giving you are facts and conclusions based on solid intelligence."

"A human said it so therefore it's true?" O'Neill said, a little softer so his wife wouldn't hear him. He took a puff of his cigar. "*This* is the best we have? None of this establishes what we say it establishes. Maybe Saddam has WMDs, maybe he doesn't. We're going to destroy a country on a hunch."

Powell concluded his speech with a plea to the international community. "Today, Iraq still poses a threat, and Iraq still remains in material breach. Indeed, by its failure to seize on its one last opportunity to come clean and disarm, Iraq has finally worn out the grace of the international community. My colleagues, we have an obligation to our citizens. We have an obligation to this body to see that our resolutions are complied with. We wrote 1441 not in order to go to war. We wrote 1441 to try to preserve peace. We wrote 1441 to give Iraq one last chance. We must not shrink from whatever is ahead of us. We must not fail in our duty and our responsibility to the citizens of the countries that are represented by this body."

By the time Powell's speech ended the nervous pit in Rummy's stomach had disappeared. He looked at Cheney and said, "that'll work," with a smile.

"Yes, it sure will," Cheney said.

Chapter 26
March 17, 2003

General Shinseki sat down at his desk at the Pentagon. He looked at the inbox tray sitting in front of him and cringed. He could tell what had been placed atop the pile: a snowflake from Rummy. After staring at it for about fifteen seconds, he reached over and picked it up.

> *From:* Secretary Rumsfeld
> *To:* General Shinseki
> *Date:* March 17, 2003
> *Subject:* New Reporting Structure
>
> General Schoomaker will henceforth report directly to me on all matters relating to Iraq. Please cease inserting yourself in between us in the chain of command.

Shinseki crumpled up the paper into a ball and shook his head. He clenched his jaw hard and squinted. "That bastard," he said softly, before throwing the ball of paper in the trash.

Chapter 27
March 19, 2003

President Bush sat at his desk in the Oval Office and spoke to the nation:

"My fellow citizens, at this hour, American and coalition forces are in the early stages of military operations to disarm Iraq, to free its people and to defend the world from grave danger. On my orders, coalition forces have begun striking selected targets of military importance to undermine Saddam Hussein's ability to wage war. These are the opening stages of what will be a broad and concerted campaign. More than 35 countries are giving crucial support—from the use of naval and air bases, to help with intelligence and logistics, to the deployment of combat units.

"To all the men and women of the United States Armed Forces now in the Middle East, the peace of a troubled world and the hopes of an oppressed people now depend on you. That trust is well placed. The enemies you confront will come to know your skill and bravery. The people you liberate will witness the honorable and decent spirit of the American military. In this conflict, America faces an enemy who has no regard for conventions of war or rules of morality. Saddam Hussein has placed Iraqi troops and equipment in civilian areas, attempting to use innocent men, women and children as shields for his own military—a final atrocity against his people.

"Our nation enters this conflict reluctantly—yet, our purpose is sure. The people of the United States and our friends and allies will not live at the mercy of an outlaw regime that threatens the peace with weapons of mass murder. We will meet that threat now, with our Army, Air Force, Navy, Coast Guard and Marines, so that we do not have to meet it later with armies of firefighters and police and doctors on the streets of our cities. Now that conflict has come, the only way to limit its duration is to apply decisive force. And I assure you, this will not be a campaign of half measures, and we will accept no outcome but victory."

At the Pentagon, Cheney and Rummy watched the speech together, silent and satisfied.

At the State Department, Powell and Armitage watched together, nervous and tormented.

At his apartment, O'Neil watched alone, angry and distraught.

In Baghdad, huge American bombs rained down from the sky. Men, women, and children who had nothing to do with Saddam or Bush or Cheney or Rummy—who just wanted to get by each day—had their lives ended in an instant. The air was filled with screams, the land with smoldering rubble, the streets with blood.

At a grocery store in the Karkh neighborhood of Baghdad, the owner was stocking the shelves with food when a bomb landed in the produce section nearby. The roof of the store caved in. His right leg was severed from his body and his skull crushed flat against the concrete floor.

At a small house on the corner of Yarmouk Street and 618 Avenue, a mother was putting her son to bed. A multi-ton bomb landed on their roof. Both of their bodies were instantaneously eviscerated in the explosion.

Just outside a military installation in nearby Radwaniyah, five teenage Iraqi soldiers were hiding in a dark brown tent surrounded by trees. None of them had ever heard of Dick Cheney or Donald Rumsfeld. The shrapnel from a bomb that destroyed the installation hit the tent like a snowstorm. Only two of the teenagers survived. One who survived lost both his legs. The other suffered brain damage and never spoke again.

In an underground bunker in Tikrit, Saddam Hussein was hiding with his sons and Tariq Aziz. They had five million dollars in cash with them.

All around the world people watched the images of US bombs destroying Iraq, the lights of the exploding bombs flashing wildly in the night's sky.

Chapter 28
May 6, 2004

There it was. Sitting atop his standing desk. A fresh copy of Rummy's favorite publication, *The Economist*. It was one of the few things Rummy respected that wasn't American made.

"The least partisan and most substantive analysis out there," he once said to Cheney about the British magazine. "The US media just makes everybody some caricature and it's all a salacious cartoon—a fairy tale—of rivalry and personality. Even the so-called top publications. Once in a blue moon they get something right. Usually by accident. *The Economist* actually analyzes the issues and lets the facts lead to the conclusion. They don't have an agenda. Or at least not much of one."

Resign, Rumsfeld, was the title of this edition, just above a picture of an Iraqi prisoner at US-controlled Abu Ghraib prison in Iraq, dressed by the guards as some sort of freaky scarecrow. The scandal at Abu Ghraib had broken a few days before. Pervasive and sadistic abuse of captured Iraqis at the hands of US military personnel. The images of the abuse—now seen all round the world—profoundly undermined America's role as a global moral leader.

Rummy was furious when he learned about Abu Ghraib a few months before it became public. He'd ordered a full investigation and wanted the stiffest punishments possible. It was on his watch, he knew. Yet he didn't find himself culpable.

"If you mobilize hundreds of thousands of people and ask them to leave their families behind and go into harm's way, well, by golly, some small number will inevitably break the rules," he said to Cheney on the phone the day before. "It's disappointing, but not surprising."

"No doubt," Cheney said.

"There will always be a small percentage of bad actors. Any city of several hundred thousand will always have a jailhouse. And those who break the law should be punished."

Cheney nodded. "And don't forget the Clinton effect."

"Yes!" Rummy said, seizing Cheney's point. "The leadership in the region is still dysfunctional from Clinton's neglect."

"And that's a mess that doesn't get cleaned up quickly."

"The real problem here … the real problem is public relations. Those images are awful. They really are. So … Dick … I'm going to offer POTUS my resignation. It's the right thing to do. Perhaps if I leave the administration can move past this."

"No, no, no Rummy. You don't need to. You shouldn't."

"I should. I'm a distraction."

"POTUS might not accept it."

"Well, I'm going to offer it and give him the option. He deserves the offer."

"This isn't your fault though Rummy."

"I know … I know."

But here was *The Economist* blaming Rummy. They weren't the Washington press. They weren't partisan hacks. They weren't always right, of course, but they had reasons, sound logical reasons, for their conclusions. Rummy's stomach fluttered with nervous excitement seeing his name on the cover of one of the world's most respected and highly read publications. He knew the story wouldn't be friendly, but he still liked seeing his name there. He picked it up and felt the thick magazine in his hands. He ran his fingers over his name. Then he opened it up and went to the article.

The secretary of defence, Donald Rumsfeld, should resign. And if he won't resign, Mr. Bush should fire him.

Rummy read the first few paragraphs. They were blaming him, just like the American press was. Then he stopped reading and looked out the window, squinting. He tried to open his mind to the possibility that they were right, that the abuse at Abu

Ghraib really was his fault. He once heard that Charles Darwin always gave extra attention to disconfirming evidence, the facts and data that went contrary to his conclusions. Then he would adjust his conclusions accordingly. Rummy liked this process and often advised people to follow it.

He flipped back to the cover. *Resign, Rumsfeld.* He looked back out the window. Then back down at the cover. He tried hard to open his mind to the notion that they were correct. Was *The Economist* right? Was it really his fault? Should he be held responsible for what happened at Abu Ghraib? He gave the notion the fairest opportunity he could muster to settle into his mind and change his thinking ...

... But he couldn't do it. They didn't know what they were talking about. There were millions of US military personnel all around the world. Many of them were in highly stressful environments. The best conceivable central management from the Pentagon wasn't going to eliminate bad actors everywhere. His job was to have good leaders on the ground and make sure the right rules were in place and the right punishments meted out when they were broken. And he was doing precisely that.

He tossed the magazine into the garbage bin beside his desk and went back to work.

Chapter 29
May 8, 2004

"I will check with Ambassador Bremer, Mr. President," Rummy said, fidgeting in his seat in the Situation Room. The room was filled with NSC principals and their deputies.

"You don't know current troop levels in Baghdad?" Bush asked, squinting. The president's nostrils widened and contracted as he spoke.

"Not sure on all the specifics Mr. President, since Ambassador Bremer took responsibility for Iraq right after the initial invasion, after DOD toppled Saddam's regime."

Like everyone else in the room other than Cheney, I was floored that the secretary of defense didn't know the basic facts about troop levels. The truth was, I think, that he did—he just wanted to distance himself from the whole thing.

"Colin, do you know?" Bush asked.

"Yes Mr. President. There are currently 244,500 troops in Iraq. I was briefed on it last night."

"Where we at with oil?" Bush asked. He looked at Rummy first. Then turned to Powell. Cheney squirmed in his seat.

Powell answered. "We've come a long way in a short time. We've secured most of the fields and refineries, but there's more work to do. And of course these are favorite targets of the insurgents, so the situation is not linear."

"And how is security in the Green Zone? Any improvement?" Bush asked Powell. Powell raised his eyebrows and turned to Rummy. Bush looked back at Rummy and said: "You'll need to check with Ambassador Bremer, who's been in charge since shortly after the invasion, right?"

"I'll report back just as soon as I connect with him, Mr. President."

Chapter 30
May 11, 2004

Paul O'Neill was sitting on the wide leather couch in the living room at his Washington D.C. apartment. He was with Ron Suskind, a Pulitzer-prize winning author and *Wall Street Journal* reporter. O'Neill was wearing a thick pink sweater and his gold Rolex glistened under the chandelier hanging from the room's tall ceiling. Suskind was a few feet to O'Neill's left, also on the couch. He was short, with wavy brown hair and a plump face that resembled a happy leprechaun. Unlike O'Neill, his demeanor was cheerful and energetic.

O'Neill handed Suskind a CD containing all his papers as treasury secretary. The whole file. "Here it is, everything. Write your book. I just want to see a draft every now and then."

"Thank you, Mr. Secretary."

"Shine some light on this mess."

Suskind smiled at the overflowing pot of gold he had received. He was looking at it intently and holding it with both hands, like a premature firstborn. He nodded. "Will do." His eyes bounced from the CD to O'Neill a few times. And then the interview began. "It seems you were right. Iraq is not going well."

"Yes indeed," O'Neill said.

"The insurgency is big and getting bigger."

O'Neill nodded.

"Cheney and Rumsfeld don't seem to think so, though."

"They sure don't."

"Are they seeing something we aren't?"

"No, no, they aren't seeing anything different. We are all looking at the same sheet of music, they're just singing a different song."

Suskind laughed. "Are they delusional?"

"No, I don't think they're delusional."

"Are they lying?"

"No, I don't think they're lying."

Suskind's head tilted to the right. "Well … are they stupid?"

"No, they're definitely not stupid."

"So if they're not delusional and they're not lying and they're not stupid, what are they then?"

"They're overconfident," O'Neill said. "Which is a pernicious bias. They're not biased towards any particular ideology or political persuasion in foreign policy. Not really. They're biased towards themselves, toward their own previous judgments, their own previous statements. They're interpreting everything that comes in, all the new facts, as being consistent with their preexisting beliefs."

"They seem smart and rational. They've accomplished a lot over the years. Both of them."

"The smartest people in the world rarely escape the affliction of being biased towards themselves. Confirmation bias is very hard to disentangle from, you have to beat it our of yourself. And then you have to build a huge wall—and a moat—to make sure it doesn't come seeping back in. And you have to nurture that moat, adding to it consistently, protecting your psyche from the bias. They don't do that."

Suskind was writing all this down on a yellow notepad. He leaned in. "Why not?"

"Ego."

Suskind raised an eyebrow motioned with his hand, urging O'Neill to continue.

"Not the normal kind of ego, that needs people to agree with it. They don't care if journalists disagree with them. Not really. Rather ego in the sense that they need their judgments to be correct, they need to be the wise, prescient thinkers. Their self-worth would collapse if they were wrong and their critics—their inferiors—were right."

"Interesting."

O'Neill crossed his legs and leaned back into the couch. "The thing that complicates all this is that the critics usually *are wrong*. And it's important to think for yourself in leadership positions; you don't want to just follow the whims of public opinion. And they do have a lot more information than the press. But if you *never* listen to the critics, well, that becomes a license to do whatever you want. And that's when, eventually, big mistakes will happen."

Suskind was entranced, hanging on O'Neill's every word. "So what do you do then? If you can't listen to the critics but you also can't ignore them?

"Good question," O'Neill said. He paused several seconds before answering. "You do the best you can. You don't just dismiss the whole thing. Take Rumsfeld … Rummy … I've known him for decades. Since the Ford days. A brilliant guy but he has a cognitive flaw. He loves the poem *If* by Kipling; I've heard him talk about it multiple times. There's a line in that poem—and it's a great poem—the line says: *If you can trust yourself when all men doubt you, But make allowance for their doubting too.* That's his problem right there: he trusts himself when all men doubt him—big time—but he doesn't also make allowance for their doubting too. He just swats all the doubting away."

"He trusts his own judgment too much?"

"That's right, he's too self-confident. He's very smart but he doesn't understand, doesn't accept, the limits of his own knowledge."

"Isn't that kind of ironic, that the guy famous for articulating the three tiers of knowledge—known knowns and all that—doesn't grasp what he knows and what he doesn't?"

A smile broke through on O'Neill's face but then just as quickly disappeared. "I hadn't thought about it that way before, but yes, I think that's a fair point."

Suskind smiled as he wrote all this down on his notepad. "What happens from here? Do you think we go after Iran? I've been hearing rumors that might be on their agenda."

"We might, as long as Cheney and Rumsfeld are in charge."

"In charge? But Bush is president."

O'Neill gave Suskind an impatient look.

"Okay, okay," Suskind responded, holding up both hands, palms out.

O'Neill continued: "Inaction makes them nervous. That's another character trait of Cheney and Rumsfeld that the country, the world, is subject to right now. The status quo makes them shiver. They have to do something … they have to act … they have to move. It's paranoia rooted in their own egos. They think the world left alone will fall apart and it needs their hands to shape it. So it's a staggering proposition but I would not rule out that we go into Iran even though Iraq is a complete mess."

Suskind shook his head and smiled. "If their egos are so big … well … why don't they try to avoid big mistakes and preserve their legacies?"

"Again, part of why their egos are so big is that they think they don't care about their legacies, they think that they are above public opinion. And going against public opinion actually makes them more comfortable in their own superiority. It reinforces it." Suskind was listening intently as O'Neill continued. "It's admirable not to focus too much on public opinion. But if you ignore it too much that's bad too. There's a happy medium. Even though it's a mirage it has substance. The paradox of public opinion is that it's often false yet by its very existence it can become true. It can be a self-fulfilling prophecy. If too many people hate a good thing it can turn bad. Perceptions matter, especially in a democracy. And ... well ... that's why I just gave you that CD."

Suskind looked down at the CD on his lap and smiled. He looked up and saw on O'Neill's face that he wanted to wrap things up. "Just a few more?" he asked.

"Okay," O'Neill said, looking at his watch.

"Can Cheney and Rumsfeld be persuaded, can they change?"

"I doubt it. They're in their sixties and are rich and have been wildly successful at everything they've done—hardly the elements in people open to self-reflection. They always have an answer for the criticism. Stuff happens. You go to war with what you have, not with what you might want. And so on."

"Sounds like they've set everything up so nothing can get in the way of them doing exactly what they want."

"Correct."

Though O'Neill had only said a single word, Suskind's pen was carving into his notepad, spinning more furiously than at any other point during their conversation.

Suskind's book, *The Price of Loyalty*, is an important work. It does a great job of capturing how misguided Cheney and Rummy really were. Other than some mistakes with how he characterizes me, it's mostly accurate from start to finish.

Chapter 31
September 2, 2004

"FLIP, FLOP! FLIP, FLOP!"

The crowd was going wild.

"FLIP, FLOP! FLIP, FLOP!" The chant highlighting Democratic presidential nominee John Kerry's tendency to change his political positions was thunderous. The walls at Madison Square Garden shook.

"FLIP, FLOP! FLIP, FLOP!"

And Dick Cheney, standing behind the podium, underneath a huge American flag, lights pouring down on him—at the center of everything—was sporting the biggest smile of his life.

"FLIP, FLOP! FLIP, FLOP!"

Cheney was wearing a dark blue suit and red tie. He had been keeping his concerns about the insurgency in Iraq to himself, his wife Lynne, and Rummy. Here at the Republican National Convention, everything was as it should be. He looked calm, confident, focused. He was beaming as he soaked in the crowd's energy.

"FLIP, FLOP! FLIP, FLOP!"

Rummy was watching from home, admiring Dick's contrasting personality traits. He was quiet and kept his views to himself in large meetings. He was introverted and cerebral. Yet he could turn it on and be charismatic and charming in public. He was both a substantive leader and a talented politician. Cheney preferred the nuts and bolts of government, but he could go all-in on the sport of politics, too. He pulled no punches excoriating Kerry. He howled into the microphone that Kerry's "habit of indecision" could not be tolerated for a nation fighting the war on terror. "On the question of America's role in the world, the differences between Senator Kerry and President Bush are the sharpest, and the stakes for the country are the highest."

The crowd got louder.

"History has shown that a strong and purposeful America is vital to preserving freedom and keeping us safe. Yet time and again, Senator Kerry has made the wrong call on national security." Cheney then contrasted Bush's "clear message" with Kerry's "message of confusion" and disturbing pattern of changing his mind and flip flopping on key issues.

"Senator Kerry says he sees two Americas," Cheney said. "It makes the whole thing mutual—America sees two John Kerrys." The crowd went berserk. Cheney stood at the podium, soaking it in.

"FLIP, FLOP! FLIP, FLOP!"

Chapter 32
February 18, 2005

Bush was a few minutes late to the Iraq briefing in the Situation Room. He flopped into his chair awkwardly. The chair rolled away from the table, and he had to pull himself back with both hands. His eyes were puffy. His tie wasn't centered well, and his shirt was too tight around his neck. He missed a few spots shaving that morning. Looking down at the table he said, "let's get started," in a voice that was a little too loud for the occasion.

General Tommy Carias's face was on the big flatscreen mounted to the wall, to Bush's left. He was at Central Command in Tampa. "Mr. President, I am leading the briefing today," he began. "I won't sugar coat things. We have problems."

Bush looked up, first to his right. Then he found the screen to his left. Squinting, he seemed to have trouble seeing Carias. "Go on," Bush eventually said.

Rummy and Cheney looked at each other.

"We are experiencing what I would call catastrophic success," Carias said. "That is, our initial military campaign was so successful that Iraq's military and civilian institutions essentially disappeared."

"And now why is that catastrophic Tommy?" Bush asked, getting his footing.

"Well, because it has created a void. There are no functioning government institutions. There's no civil order. And it's becoming more and more clear that the void is being filled by insurgents."

"If I may interject to make one discrete point Mr. President," Rummy said. Everyone turned to Rummy. "The intelligence community never, not once, warned that this insurgency was possible, let alone likely. We were confident that the initial military operation would be a success. And it was a historic success. But we weren't on notice of a potential insurgency."

Bush nodded once at Rummy without saying anything and then turned back up to Carias. "Go on Tommy."

"The insurgency appears to be a mix of former Baathist regime members, local criminal elements, and foreign terrorists that have come into Iraq from Iran and Syria."

"That's right, Mr. President" Rummy interjected. "You may know that Saddam let out over one hundred thousand prisoners from Iraqi jails in the weeks leading up to our invasion. The intelligence community also failed to predict this."

Bush looked at CIA Director Tenet. Then back at Rummy. "Now, Don, you've been critical of the intelligence community for many years, am I right?"

"Yes indeed."

"I remember talking about it with you way back when … before assuming office."

"Me too."

"So then shouldn't we have expected intelligence failures? Shouldn't we have assumed they would occur before we invaded?"

Rummy fidgeted in his seat before answering. "Perhaps we should have Mr. President. But I don't—"

"Maybe we wouldn't know exactly what they'd be, the intelligence failures, but seems we shoulda built this right into our expectations—that we wouldn't be able to predict everything with precision—while we were advocating for the invasion to begin with."

Rummy nodded. "But Mr. President if I may, that doesn't quite—"

"Not much point in harping on it now," Bush interrupted. Then he turned back to Carias. "Go on Tommy."

Rummy sat stone-faced. Carias waited a few seconds and then continued. His bright face beamed down from high on the wall.

"So the insurgency has a mix of elements, but they appear to be coalescing around a common purpose: to wreak havoc. And it's working. They are—"

"If I may, Mr. President," Rummy said, leaning forward in his chair. "We anticipated that the insurgents—"

"No, Don, I want to hear from Tommy," Bush said, holding his palm up at Rummy but continuing to look up at Carias. "Please continue."

Rummy slouched back into his chair. After a brief pause Carias continued. "They … they are a hard enemy to fight, Mr. President. They are dispersed broadly throughout the country. They don't wear uniforms and have ample weaponry. The country is flooded with weapons that Saddam used to control. And, most of all, they are fearless fighters with nothing to lose."

Bush turned from Carias and stared at Rummy for several seconds. Then he turned back to Carias, exhaled loudly, and lifted his hands up off the table before thumping them back down. "Well … fuck," he said.

Chapter 33
February 27, 2005

"Barbara is in the Oval Office a lot more these days," Cheney told Rummy from behind his desk. "Goes in there a few times a day."

"Gee whiz," Rummy replied. While his relationship with Bush had deteriorated in recent months, Rummy still cared for Bush on a personal level. He was genuinely saddened by what he was hearing. His primary concern, however, was for the country.

"In there sometimes for almost an hour at a time, just her and the president," Cheney said.

"An hour?" Rummy asked.

"Yeah ... not good."

"Not good at all. Can we help him?"

"I don't think there's anything we can do to help him directly at this point. It's a personal thing he needs to sort out with himself and his family. Our focus should be on how this impacts the government, the country."

"Well, what do you think we should do?"

Cheney sighed. "Keep paying attention, for now. We'll have to do something if he doesn't get better soon."

Rummy nodded. "Indeed we will."

Chapter 34
March 2, 2005

The Situation Room was quiet. Various cabinet officials were seated at the table. Their deputies were in the chairs behind them.

Cheney was sitting next to an empty chair at the head of the table. Bush was nowhere to be found.

It was 10:16 a.m. and the meeting was supposed to have started at 10 a.m. Long famous for his punctuality, Bush had been late to meetings with increasing frequency. The only sound in the room was of papers shuffling and people, most well past middle age, breathing unevenly and loudly. Rummy heard a faint snoring sound but wasn't sure from who. The faces of several generals were on the screens on the wall.

Condi, now secretary of state after Powell resigned, exchanged perplexed looks with her deputy Robert Zoellick.

Cheney finally said, "Let's just get started. I'll fill the president in later." He looked at Chairman of the Joint Chiefs, Richard Meyers, who was down the table to Cheney's right. "Richard, how about an update on Iraq."

"The insurgency is still gaining strength Mr. Vice President. Ambassador Bremer's decision to disband the Iraqi army was a mistake. The Iraqi military was a deeply flawed institution, but it had at least some cohesion, some stability. What we are seeing now is anarchy. There's just nothing to grab onto."

"That's right," Rummy said. "The military objective was successfully achieved, but the diplomatic efforts to achieve a stable government are falling flat." He turned to Condi. "Respectfully Ms. Secretary, I think we can and should do better on the diplomatic side. After all, Ambassador Bremer has worked for the State Department for many years. All the elements for success are there; we just need our diplomats, like Ambassador Bremer to have a clear and effective message on the ground."

"No doubt about it," Cheney said. Looking at Condi, he said, "What can we do to fix the diplomatic situation?"

"Well ... Mr. Vice President ... I don't think that's a fair way to characterize things at all," Condi said. "President Bush sure doesn't see it that way. He thinks—"

Rummy cut her off: "All the generals agree Condi. The military campaign was a huge success, so big they call it a 'catastrophic success.'" He held up his hands and made air quotes with his fingers. "It's diplomacy ... or a lack thereof ... that's causing the problems we're facing now."

She shook her head. "The military, supported by our allies, succeeded in wiping out the country. A huge hammer came down on a small nail. But it failed to maintain order in the aftermath. That's not a lack of diplomacy; that's merely phase two of any military campaign. You need to maintain order through force, not just blow things up and leave the rest to people in suits."

Rummy knew that Condi had always been closer to Bush than he was, and that with Iraq not going well Bush had been moving more and more toward her and further away from him and Cheney. It was a dynamic he didn't like at all. With Bush not in the room, he vented his frustration: "Oh that's just utter hogwash ... respectfully. The military's job was to remove Saddam. It succeeded. The State Department and Ambassador Bremer are supposed to bring order and stability. They have brought anything *but* that. The decision to disband the Iraqi military was a disaster."

Taken aback at Rummy's direct confrontation, Condi looked around the room. It was awkward for everyone. "I don't think it's productive to litigate this now, without the president in the room. I will just say that you've transparently gerrymandered the lines of responsibility to make DOD look good and State look bad. I firmly disagree."

Chapter 35
March 5, 2005

While most cabinet meetings were consumed with discussions about Iraq, behind the scenes Rummy and Cheney were also focusing on a new target: Iran. While they knew it would be hard to convince Bush to take action, regime change in Iran was the final move in their grand strategy to transform the Middle East. While Saddam was the more visible and belligerent threat, it was Iran whose tentacles in the region had the most reach. Their proxy terrorist organizations had wreaked havoc for decades. Rummy and Cheney thought that whatever challenges America's military was having in Iraq paled in importance compared to the Iranian threat. They were convinced it was only a matter of time before this terror was felt within America's borders.

Rummy dictated a snowflake:

From: Secretary Rumsfeld
To: Chief of Staff Jenkins
Date: March 5, 2005
Subject: Iran Campaign

Please connect with Undersecretary Bolton on Iran immediately. Do not inform anyone else of this effort for now. Just Bolton. The status quo is not working. We need details. We need operational specifics. We need a rock-solid plan in case things continue to get worse with Iran. Report back in one week on this effort. The status quo isn't working.

Chapter 36
March 16, 2005

Cheney was sitting at the table in the West Wing, waiting for Bush to join him at their weekly lunch. He checked his watch: 12:19 p.m. He stared at his salad and had two thoughts. First, the salad was gross. All wilted lettuce and underripe tomatoes. Second, the country couldn't have its president falling off the wagon. There was too much at stake. And it was going to go public, eventually, and probably soon. He and Rummy talked about it again that morning. They agreed that the time to act was drawing near.

He looked at his watch again. It was 12:26. Without touching the salad, he got up and left.

Chapter 37
May 20, 2005

Rummy stepped into Cheney's office and closed the door behind him. He walked up and sat down in one of the chairs facing his desk. Without speaking he just looked at Cheney, who folded *The Washington Post* and placed it on his desk.

"It's bad," Cheney said, shaking his head.

Rummy took a slow, deep breath in, trying to calm his nerves. He spoke softly: "It's a disease, a real one. I've seen this before. Doesn't matter if you're a janitor or the president of the United States. It gets you the same way."

"Yeah, it got me years ago, as you know. Almost lost Lynne a few times cause I couldn't keep it under control. Still something I have to contend with."

"Indeed."

"Barbara confirmed to me that he fired the Secret Service agent who tried to stop the whisky deliveries. She said he's never been this bad. She's really shook up."

Rummy draped his left leg over his right. "I'm sure she is. Must be an absolute nightmare. Even more so for her than him, in a way. Do you think the press has a sense?"

"*The Post* noted he's not in public as much lately. They blamed it on Iraq, the insurgency, saying he's trying to avoid questions from the press. I don't think they have a sense yet of what's really going on, though. But they will. And soon. It's inevitable."

"We have to do something."

"Agreed," Cheney said.

"What would our enemies think?"

"I know."

"Our allies?"

"I know."

"What do you think we should do?" Rummy asked. "Can you give him an ultimatum at your next lunch?"

Cheney gave Rummy a skeptical look. "If he shows up."

"Or the next time you see him?"

"I'll ... yes."

"Worthless to try?" Rummy asked.

"Not worthless, but low likelihood of success. Very low. Look where he is now ... already this far gone. What more could be at stake than there already is? If it's gotten to this point, I'm not sure what even a strong ultimatum would do."

Rummy nodded. "We can try though. Stop drinking completely and at once or we'll invoke the 25th Amendment?"

Cheney nodded. "Sounds about right."

"What else can we do?"

"I'll have Addington put something together on the 25th Amendment, to make sure our ducks are in a row."

"Better than impeachment and removal."

"If he doesn't quit, those will be the two options—impeachment or 25th Amendment."

Rummy stood up and straightened out his pant legs. "We need to move fast. The status quo is not acceptable." He took a few steps toward the door and then stopped and looked back at Cheney, who stared back at him. They were both thinking the same thing, though neither dared say it: Dick might be president soon.

Chapter 38
June 17, 2005

Paul O'Neill was sitting at the desk in his home office with CNN on the television mounted to the wall. In front of him: a prodigious stack of thoroughly read newspapers and a tall glass of gin. It was 5:30 p.m. He'd been anxiously awaiting Cheney's speech. The White House announced that morning that Cheney would be speaking live to the American people later in the day, a fact that made O'Neill nervous. Why, he wondered, would the White House, and not the Vice President's office, announce the speech? Someone on CNN—a balding pundit with a scratchy voice—asked the same question.

Then Cheney appeared on the screen. The camera zoomed in closely on his face. His skin was light pink; his right eye opened wider than his left. O'Neill thought he was in the White House Press Room but wasn't sure. "My fellow Americans," Cheney began, "I have the following statement from President Bush to read to you."

O'Neill's pulse accelerated. Cheney's expression was serious, his tone somber, his voice deep. His double chin jiggled as he looked up and down from his prepared remarks. "Dearest Americans, it is with a heavy heart I have made the decision to resign from the presidency. The world is far too dangerous and complicated for the greatest country on earth to have its leader not at full strength. I will be back in public life in due time, and will continue to dedicate myself to promoting America's interests and freedom for all people. But for a short time, I need to pause and focus on myself and my family. As so many of you know, addiction is a vicious disease that chooses its victims indiscriminately. It has chosen me."

O'Neill's heart sank. He had sensed something wasn't right with Bush but never had a good handle on what was really going on. He was more concerned for the country than he was for

Bush, though. He knew what this meant. "Iran," he said out loud, softly.

Cheney continued reading: "When I selected Vice President Cheney five years ago to be my running mate, the principal reason was in case a moment like this arose. A seasoned leader with decades of government experience will now take the helm. You are in the most capable of hands. Serving my country as president has been the greatest honor of my life. I'm proud of all that my administration accomplished, at home and abroad, over the course of four-plus years. Thank you for the honor of serving this great country."

Cheney looked up. His face still filled the whole screen. O'Neill slowly shook his head back and forth, his eyes fixed on the television. He remembered the times he'd come to Cheney to warn him that the administration wasn't prepared to invade Iraq, that he and Rummy needed to slow down and be more realistic about the endeavor. Cheney had rebuffed him. Gotten him fired. And yet here things stood: Iraq was in shambles, just as O'Neill predicted. He took a swig of his gin, letting the liquid swirl around in his mouth before swallowing. He wondered what had happened to Cheney, the bright and rational leader he knew in the Ford days, the remarkably solid and effective secretary of defense under Bush Senior. Why had he changed so much? It was September 11th, O'Neill concluded. That day dramatically changed both Cheney and Rumsfeld. Scared them. Traumatized them. Rewired them. They'd lost their sense of proportion in the fervor of trying to prevent another attack. O'Neill thought they were playing into the terrorists' hands: one of the goals of terrorism is to disorient the enemy, to make it lash out and overreact. He thought that was what the US was doing in Iraq … and would soon do in Iran.

"As the president indicated," Cheney continued, "he has resigned from office and in a ceremony a few minutes ago, Chief Justice Rehnquist swore me in as president of the United States. I take this oath very seriously. I will not relent in serving America's interests. I will not relent in protecting our nation."

Then Cheney paused and the camera started to pan out. Slowly. O'Neill saw that someone was standing behind Cheney, to his left. He could see a black suit emerging ... but couldn't tell who it was at first. The screen slowly captured more of the room. O'Neill squinted: Who was next to Cheney?

Then he saw it was Rummy, who had a serious look on his face, almost a frown. O'Neill smiled. "Of course," he said softly.

Cheney continued: "Secretary Rumsfeld will assume the office of vice president of the United States. His nomination will be before the Senate later today and we expect his swift confirmation at this essential moment in our nation's history. We should all be grateful that a man of his experience, skill, and character will assume this important office."

Rummy stood still, staring into the camera. Neither his face nor his body seemed to move at all.

"Further changes to the cabinet are underway and we'll be making additional announcements in the coming days," Cheney said.

O'Neill wondered what the other changes would be. He knew one thing for sure: Condi was gone. The hawks were now in charge.

Chapter 39
June 31, 2005

Two weeks later Rummy stood at his desk in the Vice President's office. While he didn't like the smaller office, he was enjoying the new role. In one fell swoop his purview had grown from national security to just about everything. Cheney had him involved in all the administration's most important matters, including efforts to eliminate the Department of Education and pass another gigantic tax cut.

Intellectually, Rummy couldn't have been happier, voraciously tackling one big challenge for the country after another. But there was one psychological discomfort nagging at him: virtually all of his power derived from Cheney. While the vice president was a constitutional officer, its formal powers etched into law were slim. He'd always gotten along with Cheney and expected that to continue. But he also knew that if things soured between them, he'd be marginalized quickly. *There's only one seat at the top of the food chain*, he thought. *Dick has it. I don't.* The difference between being president and being vice president might seem small from certain angles, but in actuality it was vast across the board. He was as powerful as Dick decided he would be; it was that simple. He tried, and mostly succeeded, not to let this fact impact his work.

As Rummy worked through his papers, he dictated a snowflake:

> *From:* Vice President Rumsfeld
> *To:* Secretary of State John Bolton; Secretary of Defense Paul Wolfowitz; Vice Presidential Chief of Staff James Jenkins
> *Date:* June 31, 2005
> *Subject:* Regime Change in Iran

Please update me this week on Iran. We need a detailed war plan on President Cheney's desk in the next month. He is asking about this consistently. Iran is harming US interests in the region every single day. Doing nothing is just as big of a decision as doing something. Every day—every minute—of inaction compounds the problem.

Part Four: Iran
(July 20, 2005 – October 24, 2005)

Rumsfeld Rule: "Certainty without power can be interesting, even amusing. Certainty with power can be dangerous."

Chapter 40
July 20, 2005

Rummy stood at the podium in the White House Press room and pulled the microphone down an inch or two. Joyce was to his left. His face was focused, his eyes fixed on the camera, his heartbeat murderously fast.

"My fellow Americans," he began. "Tragedy has struck our nation. The president has died. While the medical analysis is still underway, it appears to have been a heart attack. I knew president Cheney for more than three decades. While his time in the Oval Office was limited, history will remember him as a strong leader, a great president, and a good man." Rummy paused and pushed his glasses up his nose. "I have two messages tonight. First, to the American people: Your government is strong. Secretary of State Bolton will assume the office of vice president. His nomination is with the Senate. We will continue to fulfill the vision of strength and purpose laid out by President Cheney at home and abroad. The last several months have been filled with turmoil and change. But my promise to you is this: stability is now here. My administration places the United States in calm and steady hands. My second message tonight is to America's enemies: Do not misunderstand this transition to be a sign of weakness. America has never been stronger. We will continue to defend our national interests at home and abroad. And we will do so proactively, erring, as we must, on the side of action over inaction. This is the philosophy on which this nation was founded, on which it has grown into the world's sole superpower, and on which it will continue to prosper."

After his speech, Rummy and Joyce walked to the Oval Office. They slowly, even tentatively, entered the hallowed room and looked around quietly. "Can I have a few minutes, honey?" he whispered. "I will meet you in the residence."

"Of course," she said with a smile. She kissed him on the cheek and left the room. As she walked back to the residence in the quiet night Joyce felt a powerful mix of emotions. She was profoundly sad about Dick, whom she had been friends with for decades. Her heart ached for Dick's wife Lynne, who she'd become closer to in recent years. She knew the Cheneys not as the famous political power couple so often swirling in public controversy, but rather as nice, likable friends who were fun to spend time with. And she was nervous for Rummy. She knew her husband well enough to know that he wasn't going to be timid from the Oval Office. Decades of pent-up ambition were about to be unleashed. He didn't need an electoral victory and corresponding mandate to be a fiercely aggressive president. She sighed as she walked and made a mental note to confirm the Secret Service would increase the security detail for their family.

Meanwhile, Rummy was soaking it in. There he was: alone in the Oval Office, as president, for the first time. He stood in the middle of the room, arms hanging by his sides as he breathed in deeply. Freshly cleaned, the smell of pine sol blended with the aroma of flowers from several pots. He had been the guest of various presidents in this room hundreds of times since the 1960s. He thought of his meetings here with Nixon in the heat of the Watergate scandal. He thought of his endless sessions with Ford hashing out the broad sweep of his policies both at home and abroad. He thought about Carter and Clinton, dangerously mismanaging the country for twelve years from this room.

He always loved being in the Oval Office, where history was made. If he ever caught himself getting used to it, he would scold himself for the lack of perspective. Being in the Oval Office was not something to be taken for granted. Ever. And now, in his early seventies, it was his. A middle-class kid from the Chicago suburbs. *His* room. *His* office. *His* stage for making history.

Finally.

A wave of adrenaline cascaded through his body.

He sat down at the Resolute desk, which was empty. Rummy already ordered the staff to clear out Cheney's things. He rested his hands on the broad, rock-hard surface of the desk. Freshly polished, it glowed under the moonlight entering the room through the windows.

He looked around. He thought of Dick and was struck by sadness.

Dick was a good man, Rummy thought. *The most caricatured politician in history. He was courageous enough to do what was right even if the whole world thought he was wrong. Just as good leaders are supposed to do.*

Rummy remembered the first time he met Dick, when the young graduate student from Wyoming came into his office at the Office of Economic Opportunity for a job interview. Rummy thought Dick was bright and focused, but nothing too special. A little too dull, a little too dry. He never thought the two of them would collaborate for thirty-plus years or that one day he'd succeed Dick as president of the United States.

He wiped his eyes and walked out the door and asked his assistant for a notepad. She handed him one, along with a black ballpoint pen. As he walked back to the desk he wrote: *Call Lynne*. He hadn't yet.

Then he sat at the desk and absorbed the quiet of the room. The importance of the room. The power of the room. He closed his eyes and exhaled and let the power of the room enter his pores and seep into his body. Then he opened his eyes and looked around at the furniture and the walls and then out the window. It was late. The bulbs mounted to the outside of the building were beaming light down onto the bright green lawn.

I'm president of the United States, he thought. *Me. Donald Howard Rumsfeld. It happened.* He smiled. It was a big smile.

Then he picked the notepad back up, grabbed the pen, and composed a snowflake:

From: The President
To: Chief of Staff Jenkins
Date: July 20, 2005
Subject: Iran Campaign and Joint Session of Congress

One: Accelerate planning on Iran and have a report to me and Vice President Bolton in one week. The plan should include specific steps to initiate the campaign.

Two: Make arrangements for a speech before a joint session of Congress within six weeks. I need to speak directly to the American people in that setting.

He put the pad and pen down on the desk and leaned back in his chair. He had calls with a dozen heads of state the next day. *Keep them short*, he thought, *other than China and Israel. Don't tip our hand but take folks' temperature on Iran.*

Then he looked at the painting on the wall of Cheney's great grandfather Samuel Fletcher Cheney, a Civil War general. *Hm*, he thought, *whose portrait will I put up there? Teddy ... yes Teddy.* He was thinking of Teddy Roosevelt, one of his favorite former presidents. "A true rebel," Rummy often called him.

He looked around the room again, leaning back in his chair. He was nervous, excited, terrified, and joyful—all at the same time. He thought about the history books that would be written in five, ten, fifty years. He didn't know what they'd say exactly. But he knew this: He would no longer be a footnote, merely another minion of other men, of other presidents. He would be the focus of historians. They would write the type of books about him that he read about other presidents. His picture would be on the walls of schools, with the other presidents, all around the country. The 45th president of the United States. His name would be uttered endlessly all around the world. President Rumsfeld. President Donald Rumsfeld.

It was his show now: his office, his government, his country, his world.

He took a deep breath and smiled. *It happened*, he thought. *It really did.*

He was the president of the United States.

Chapter 41
August 2, 2005

Rummy was sitting at the Resolute desk in the Oval Office. His standing desk was to his left, but he'd found himself sitting down more now that the Oval Office was his. It made him feel more presidential. And there was too much adrenaline coursing through him now to ever feel sluggish sitting down. To his right was Vice President John Bolton and Secretary of State Torie Clarke. To his left Defense Secretary Paul Wolfowitz. Straight ahead was Chief of Staff James Jenkins.

"Iraq is tough, no doubt, but this is comfortably in line with what we expected," Rummy said. Then he recited a *Rumsfeld Rule*: "No plan survives first contact with the enemy." Everyone nodded.

He'd been president for about two weeks. He loved the new view of the Oval Office from behind the Resolute desk. It was psychologically explosive, in a euphoric way, to have his perspective so thoroughly transformed. Instead of jockeying for the president's attention with a bunch of other competing personalities, now all eyes were fixed on him, all the time. The experience of the room was different from this angle, the feeling of being there totally new. It was surreal. He liked push-back from his subordinates and good debate; but he also thoroughly enjoyed the effusive deference now cascading his way.

"Saddam is out of power," he said, "so despite the messiness—diplomatic messiness that resulted from our catastrophic success militarily—the campaign has been a clear net positive." Everyone nodded again. "I suspect within six months we'll see tangible progress on the ground. Especially now that Bremer is out and the focus will be on rebuilding the country and not rehabilitating his image." Bolton chuckled loudly and his bright white teeth emerged beneath his thick silver mustache. Rummy continued: "What we can't let happen ... what we won't let happen ... is for Iraq's instability, however temporary it may be, to embolden Iran. They are the other regional powerhouse and, in some ways, pose an even bigger danger than Iraq did under Saddam."

Everyone knew where he was headed.

"As you all know well, Iran and their proxies have been behind so many of the region's problems. So many terrorist attacks on our allies. So much instability. I mean, their stated goal is to destroy Israel. These are the conditions from which groups like Al-Qaeda emerge, from which events like September 11th happen. Every day they are harming our interests abroad and endangering us at home." He paused and turned to Wolfowitz. "What's the current status of our planning for a campaign?"

"The chiefs are working with their teams around the clock, Mr. President." He cleared his throat. "Their focus is dual: Winning in Iraq, preparing for Iran."

"What's the timeline? When could we be ready to invade?"

"One month if we had to. Two preferred."

"And the diplomatic side?" Rummy asked, turning to Clarke.

"Full court press, Mr. President. We've got cooperation on bases from most key regional players. The UK is on board. Australia too. Israel of course. Several countries in Eastern Europe."

"Still no support from Old Europe?" Rummy asked with a smirk. When he referred to Old Europe publicly in 2003, the international press went bananas. Little did they know that he said it all the time privately. I once asked him what the dividing line was between Old and New Europe and he said, "Not sure on the precise line—the key is that France is Old." I used to joke that the two things Rummy disliked most were the American press and the French government.

Clarke gave Rummy a wry smile. "None, Mr. President. Old Europe doesn't want anything to do with Iran. They know we will clean up their messes and protect them even if they do nothing."

"So they do nothing," Bolton said.

"Exactly," Clarke said. "France has all but closed the door in our faces."

Rummy shook his head. "We need to change the incentives. Right now they know that they can sit on their hands and we will bail them out. So—surprise, surprise—they sit on their hands."

"I would have thought the whole World War Two thing, you know, where we came in and saved them, would have led to a little more appreciation," Bolton said. "They'd be Germany if it wasn't for us."

Rummy chuckled.

"Nope," Clarke said, "no appreciation ... all that is long forgotten."

"We've been carrying their defense burden for them for far too long," Rummy said. "They think Clinton is still president. Well, he's not." He began tapping his fingers against the desk, relishing that it was his. "Let's discuss NATO at the next NSC meeting. We're still dealing with some of the same problems in Brussels we had when I was NATO Ambassador for Nixon. We need higher contributions from Old Europe or things will change."

"Our bases in Iraq will be useful Mr. President," Wolfowitz said. "We can repurpose capabilities toward Iran."

"Synergies," Rummy said enthusiastically, slapping his right hand on the Resolute desk. The word reminded him of the Searle days.

"Exactly," Wolfowitz said.

"Good," Rummy said, turning back to Clarke. "And we'll take what we can get from our actual allies, but obviously whatever coalition we muster will have no say whatsoever in what we do. None. We need to display leadership."

"Understood Mr. President. We lead; they follow."

Rummy smiled. "Exactly." Then he scanned the group and pounded the desk. "We're a decade late on Iran. Maybe two. Inaction won't be tolerated in this administration. It's time to act."

Chapter 42
August 10, 2005

Arizona Senator John McCain opened *The Wall Street Journal* at his office desk at the US Capitol. It was early morning, and the 72-year-old military veteran was alone. He was wearing a dark brown suit and gray tie. His hair was white, his eyes brown, his coffee black.

The lead headline on the top right corner jumped out at him: *President Rumsfeld Says Iran a Threat to US Security*. He squinted, fidgeted in his seat, and felt a flash of anger run through his chest. He squeezed the paper and held it up close to his eyes and read the headline again. "What on earth?" he said out loud. He read on:

> *In a speech Wednesday to the Chicago Economic Club, President Rumsfeld focused not on Iraq, where over two hundred thousand American troops are deployed, but rather its neighbor, Iran. "The Iranian regime continues to threaten not just its neighbors but the entire international system of nations. The reach of their influence, and therefore the magnitude of their threat, only gets bigger with time. This must not be allowed to continue."*

What is this lunatic doing? McCain thought, shaking his head. *Iraq's spiraling out of control and now he's laying the groundwork to invade Iran?* He pressed the buzzer on his desk and a few seconds later his assistant came in.

"Yes, Senator?"

"Please arrange a call with Vice President Bolton. Soon as possible." McCain and Bolton had been friends for decades.

"Will do."

Chapter 43
August 18, 2005

"My fellow Americans," Rummy said from behind the Resolute desk, staring into the camera. His hair was combed sharply from left to right—not a hair out of place. "On my orders, the United States military has initiated targeted airstrikes against the Iranian government in Tehran. The regime's threat to the United States has become intolerable and leaving them unchecked cannot continue. We did not invite this confrontation, but we cannot shirk from it either."

Without looking down, but pausing briefly and awkwardly, he turned over the first page of his printed remarks. The font size was huge so he could read it easily. Clarke told him several times during his practice sessions to be more fluid when he turned the pages and he'd thought he finally had it down. But he couldn't pull it off now, with the camera rolling.

"Doing nothing is no longer an option. Time combined with inaction will only make things worse, leaving the challenge of addressing this pernicious threat to future generations under far worse circumstances. Indeed, the situation in Iran has been getting worse—the threat increasing—for many years. The reason America has constantly struggled with the Middle East is because of our own indecision and inaction. The status quo is a downward spiral. It will not continue. Not on my watch."

Chapter 44
August 26, 2005

"Mr. Speaker," the Sergeant-at-Arms of the House of Representatives proclaimed in a booming voice, "the president of the United States."

Rummy slowly and triumphantly walked into the House Chamber at the United States Capitol. He shook hands as he strode down the center aisle. His suit was dark blue, his tie red, his smile huge. He was soaking it all in. The experience was even better than he'd imagined all those years. Truly exhilarating. After several minutes he arrived at the podium, which had been lowered to just the right height. He'd sent four separate snowflakes that week making sure the podium was not set too high. He didn't want to look short.

He placed the print-out of his speech on the podium and peered out at the sea of faces, smiling proudly. He was one of them before—many times—just another congressman from just another district, blending in with the crowd. But not anymore. Now he was president, and they were all there to see him. The new perspective made his cheeks get hot. It felt like a dream.

Behind him were Vice President Bolton and, to Bolton's left, Speaker of the House Nancy Pelosi.

He squeezed both sides of the podium hard and then began: "My fellow Americans, after two successive unexpected presidential transitions within a matter of months, the executive branch is now stable and strong. My administration is brimming with experience, competence, and patriotism. As always, our most important focus is America's national security. And we are more secure as a nation now than we have been in decades."

Bolton leaped from his chair and clapped feverishly. Watching the tape later that night, Rummy thought he looked awkward and eager and, next time, needed to relax. Rummy liked Bolton's hardline approach to foreign policy, but was uncomfortable with his limited domestic political talent. He worried voters would find Bolton awkward when it came time to run for reelection.

Pelosi squinted and shook her head. About half the Republicans in the crowd stood and clapped. Everyone else remained seated. *Only half of my people standing?* Rummy thought. He squeezed his printed speech hard in his hands.

"With Iraq, the critics are focused on what is going wrong," Rummy said, glaring at the Democrats to his right. "Big surprise. But what is going right is momentous. Saddam Hussein was a threat to the entire world. And now he's gone. His regime was toppled quickly in one of the most successful military campaigns in history. Iraq held free and fair elections. I repeat: *Iraq held free and fair elections.* Contrary to much of the reporting in the press, this is a historic achievement and not something to take for granted. Iraq's elections are an important step in moving the Middle East toward democracy and away from extremism. Moreover, the insurgency in Iraq is in its last throes. The strength of American and allied forces is simply too much for this ragtag band of terrorists, cast-offs, and has-beens. Complete victory is on the horizon. Iraq is on the path to democracy."

Rummy paused. Again, about half the Republicans stood and clapped. Everyone else remained seated. Rummy made a mental note to have Jenkins create a list of all Republicans who weren't standing during the ovations. There would be consequences. The Republicans needed to be unified behind their president or they would get walloped at the polls. He knew there was disagreement within the party about going into Iran, but these disagreements were for behind closed doors. He focused on not letting his face show his displeasure.

"We are likewise on the path to victory in Iran. Our troops and our allies are defending freedom in Iran, and their heroic efforts are paying dividends every day. While the enemy is fighting back and achieving some limited success on the battlefield, our forces will prevail. The fight in Iran was not of our choosing, but we will not relent until we achieve total and complete victory."

Pelosi shook her head and mouthed "nonsense" several times, though Rummy couldn't see her.

Rummy cleared his throat and continued. "In both Iraq and Iran, it is essential for the United States to show strength and be proactive on the world stage. Inaction is just as consequential as action. Indeed, inaction for decades, in Iraq and Iran and elsewhere in the Middle East, is why we as a nation found ourselves vulnerable on the morning of September 11th, 2001. My administration will not let that happen again. Ever. We will never cease being proactive in defense of this nation."

A little more than half the Republicans stood and clapped. Everyone else on both sides of the aisle stayed seated.

McCain sat stone-faced in his chair.

Chapter 45
August 27, 2005

The next day McCain walked briskly to the podium in the Senate Chamber. He was pissed. The room was packed with senators from both sides of the aisle. He got right to the point:

"President Rumsfeld's brazen war with Iran must stop. It is a radical and misguided diversion from Iraq, an active conflict that requires the United States' full attention and effort. Far from being in their 'last throes,' as President Rumsfeld put it, the insurgents in Iraq are gaining momentum every day, and our military must focus there with increased resources and renewed purpose. I will be introducing legislation this week to stop the Iran campaign—a revised version of the War Powers Act—and to reaffirm Congress's constitutional role as the sole branch of government empowered to declare war. Article 1 of the Constitution could not be more explicit about this. It says: 'Congress shall have the power to declare war.' And Congress has declared war eleven times in our history, beginning with a declaration of war against England in 1812. I am confident this legislation will pass by an overwhelming and veto-proof margin—and that both sanity and our constitutional order will be restored."

McCain was scowling. His eyes were glossy and intense, his voice angry. He continued: "President Rumsfeld was not elected by the American people, as either president or vice president. He assumed the Oval Office through chance and tragedy. His mandate has always been limited. And yet he has taken it upon himself to expand the powers of the presidency beyond recognition and to plunge our military into a needless and damaging conflict with a nation that did not and does not pose a substantial threat to US interests. We must focus on Iraq and this disastrous diversion in Iran will only get worse if we do not end the campaign right away. I will not stop until this is accomplished."

There was a standing ovation on both sides of the aisle. Only a handful of Republicans stayed seated.

Chapter 46
September 29, 2005

"Will we win in court?" Rummy asked William Barr, his attorney general, from behind the Resolute desk. Barr was heavy-set with a short and simple brown hair cut. Cheney worked with him in Bush Senior's administration, when he was a young attorney general. Shortly after assuming the presidency, Cheney had convinced him to come on board as attorney general again. Rummy thought he was tough and smart—a strong advocate for expansive presidential powers—and kept him on.

"Could go either way at the Supreme Court, which is where this is headed, Mr. President. Congress has the better technical argument on the law. The Constitution does expressly say Congress, not the president, has the power to declare war. So the courts have a valid basis for upholding McCain's legislation. But the practicalities of taking this power away from the president are enormous. There's a reason why the president, the commander in chief, has assumed this power in practice over the years. A nation can't fight wars by committee. Ginsburg, Breyer, Stevens, and Souter will vote against us. Scalia, Thomas, and Alito are locks for us, though. So it'll come down to Roberts and Kennedy, both of whom should be receptive to our arguments. But you never know. I'd give us a 60 percent chance of winning."

"Mr. President," Rummy's assistant said, opening the door with a slight knock.

"Yes."

"Secretary Wolfowitz is here. He says it's an emergency."

"Send him in."

Wolfowitz walked in. Barr started to get up. "You can stay," Rummy said.

Wolfowitz sat down in the open chair next to Barr. He was shaken. He looked Rummy in the eyes. "This morning, Mr. President ... this morning Iranian-backed terrorists breached the

US Embassy in Baghdad and took hostage several dozen of our people there, including ... um .... including ... Secretary Clarke."

Rummy stared at him stone faced. He had sent Clarke to Baghdad just a few days earlier. His heartbeat thumped against his chest. "What?"

"It all happened quickly," Wolfowitz continued. "The Iranians have control ... they have control of the top floor of the building. Our security forces appear to have the rest of the building secured. It's only a matter of time before this hits the press."

"Is Torie okay?" Rummy asked.

"We don't know."

"But is she ... is she ..."

"We don't know Mr. President."

"Do we have a military response in motion?"

"General Carias has already ordered several thousand additional troops to the area. We're still working on a specific plan. Obviously, we don't ... we don't want to do anything that would get our people killed."

"So ... is Torie ... she's on the top floor?"

"That's our understanding."

"Can we establish a line of communication with Tehran, to start negotiating?"

"We have ... yes ... we have reached out to Tehran."

Rummy was picturing Clarke's face as he listened to Wolfowitz. Her smile always made him feel good and he'd missed her recently. Having people around him like Clarke who could confidently withstand his interrogations reduced his anxiety about delegating important tasks. He thought perhaps he made a mistake sending her to State, that chief of staff would have been better. When he was secretary of defense he saw her nearly every day. As president it was much less.

He didn't know what to do now, so his reflex—use overwhelming force—kicked in: "Tell Carias to prepare the biggest series of strikes he can imagine. Shock and awe squared. If the Iranians don't release Torie and the other hostages immediately, we unleash the full might of the American military. This whole thing will get a lot worse for them if they don't comply. We've used restraint so far. If they don't release the hostages, that will stop."

Wolfowitz looked down at the floor. Then back up at Rummy. "Will do."

"Get Torie back home safely."

Wolfowitz nodded.

"I want a report on Carias's plans hourly. Every hour I want an update. Understood?"

"Understood, Mr. President."

Two hours later John McCain was in his office on the phone with a campaign donor from Tucson. His Chief of Staff Mark Salter walked in with a look on his face that McCain knew was serious.

"I'm sorry Bob, I need to call you back," McCain said, lowering the phone from his ear but still holding it in his hand. "Yes, Mark, what's up?"

Without speaking, Salter grabbed the remote control on McCain's desk and turned on the television. CNN came on and showed footage from outside the US Embassy in Baghdad. There was a mob of people in the streets. The ticker blazed across the screen: "Secretary of State Torie Clark and staff held hostage by Iranian terrorists on top floor of US Embassy in Baghdad. The Iranian regime is refusing to negotiate their release."

McCain's eyes widened and mouth opened. He slammed the phone down into the socket. "This is insane!" he screamed. "Ronald Fucking Dumsfeld is ruining this country. What a disaster!" Then he picked the phone up again and slammed it back down.

Later that day Rummy sat at the head of the table in the Situation Room. General Carias' face filled a screen on the wall. Bolton sat to Rummy's right, Wolfowitz to his left. "Begin," Rummy said, looking up to Carias.

There was a pause. "Me, Mr. President?" Carias said.

"Yes, you."

"Okay, Mr. President, thank you. We are seeing a large and growing insurgency of Islamic extremists in Iran, much like we have seen in Iraq. The Iranian military itself is not causing significant problems—its capabilities are as limited as we assumed—but the extremists who have come in from other countries in the region, including Iraq, well, they are proving to be a difficult foe."

Looking at his new director of national intelligence, Larry Di Rita, Rummy asked: "Where was the intelligence community on this Larry? They totally missed the insurgent element in Iraq and you're telling me they've dropped the ball—again!—in Iran."

Di Rita resisted the urge to remind Rummy that the intelligence community did, in fact, warn him about a potential insurgency in Iran. Repeatedly. "That's right," Di Rita said, "Tenet dropped the ball again. Our new approach is gaining better insights, more signal, but we're still sorting out the mess."

"I don't want to hear about Tenet … about the prior regime anymore Larry. You own this now. Fix it."

Di Rita nodded. "Will do."

"What about Torie?" Rummy asked Wolfowitz. "Any change?"

"Nothing new, Mr. President." Wolfowitz said.

Rummy clenched his teeth and shook his head. "Nothing?"

"I'm sorry Mr. President."

"Okay, tell me right away once we have her back safe."

"You'll be the first to know."

"Get her back safe."

"That's our number one priority right now."

Rummy looked up to Carias. "Now, how can we increase the pressure on the insurgents in Iraq and Iran? I want a huge surge in both countries."

"We are working on plans now," Carias said.

Rummy turned back to Wolfowitz. "Are we confident the terrorist attacks at home are behind us? We can't allow these extremists to weaken the American people's confidence that our nation is safe and secure."

"We are working with state and local officials and making significant progress safeguarding our cities ... but we can't rule out further attacks. We've disrupted numerous Iranian terrorist groups domestically, but several are still operational."

"No more Nashvilles," Rummy said. It had only been a few days since Iranian-backed terrorists detonated a bomb on a commuter bus in Nashville. "Do whatever it takes. No more attacks at home."

Wolfowitz took a sip of water and nodded. "Understood, Mr. President."

Rummy turned to Barr. "When will the martial law orders be ready?"

"This week Mr. President. OLC head Yoo is reviewing a draft now."

"I'd hate to use them but I'm glad we'll have them ready. Our enemy's whole goal is to terrorize our people, to use fear to destroy our freedoms. It won't happen ... not on my watch."

Barr nodded.

"And are we ready for tomorrow's argument?"

"Yes indeed. General Clement is fully prepared, as he always is. He's going to tell the court—"

"We need to send a very strong message to Iran," Bolton interjected, looking at Wolfowitz. "We need to show our strength."

"Yes, Iran and Iraq need to understand there's a new regime in town," Rummy said, looking around the table and up at the screen. He slammed his right fist against the table. "We need to ramp this up in every possible way. Across the board. Pull every lever at our disposal. Mobilize and deploy every tool of American power. I will handle the domestic squabbles with Congress and the courts. We need to focus on the Middle East, on showing Iran and Iraq and the insurgents in both countries and the terrorists here that if they attack us, we will attack them much harder. Every time. Cause and effect must be explicitly clear. No exceptions. Their only option is full surrender."

Everyone nodded.

"I want an update on Torie in one hour," Rummy said, looking at Wolfowitz.

"Yes, Mr. President," Wolfowitz said.

Chapter 47
September 30, 2005

The next morning Solicitor General Paul Clement rose and walked confidently to the podium at the United States Supreme Court. His second home. He wore a dark blue suit and turquoise tie. The gallery was jam-packed with spectators. Barr was sitting in the front row.

The clerk initiated the proceedings as he always did: "Oyez, oyez, oyez."

Chief Justice John Roberts sat in the middle of the grand courtroom, four justices on each side of him—all draped in black robes. "General Clement, you may begin."

"Mr. Chief Justice and may it please the court. Article 2 of the United States Constitution vests the executive power in the president of the United States. The president is the commander in chief of the military. Inherent in this role is the sole power not only to wage war but to declare war in the first place. Those two powers are not just inherently intertwined; they are one and the same. Any other reading of the Constitution makes no sense and thus, under traditional canons of construction, is void. The framers of the Constitution would not have reposed the war power in the shifting, ephemeral majorities of Congress—a large, unwieldy, hyper-political group of representatives, none of whom sit in the chain of command or have access to key diplomatic channels. This is the president's domain—full stop. Accordingly, Congress's renewal and revision of the War Powers Act must be struck down. There are—"

"Excuse me, General Clement," Justice Ruth Bader Ginsburg interrupted. "What are we supposed to do with Article 1? Your argument runs headlong into Article 1's language that 'Congress shall have the power to declare war.' It couldn't be more clear. Setting aside the practicalities you reference, how do we reconcile your argument with this express language?"

"The Constitution also says that the president is the commander in chief, Justice Ginsburg. The president can't fulfill this role if a 535-person super committee tells him when he can and can't defend the nation's interests abroad. That wouldn't make sense."

"Whether it 'makes sense' or not, it's plainly written in the Constitution," Justice Antonin Scalia said. "Justice Ginsburg is right about this aspect: there's really no ambiguity there."

"Well, Justice Scalia, even if that's true, you should nonetheless do what the whole of the US government has done for decades: interpret it to allow for the practical necessity that the president must have free reign to be the commander in chief."

"So you want us to rewrite it?" Ginsburg asked.

"No, Justice Ginsburg. Not rewrite it; interpret it consistent with our constitutional design and core national traditions. Moreover, if the court isn't sure about this, about what the answer should be, it need not go there. It need not strip the president of this key power in the middle of two wars and in the aftermath of the largest terrorist attack on US soil in our history. The court can instead simply rule that this is a political question best left to the political branches, and leave it there."

Barr was sitting in the front row of the gallery, nodding his head. He thought it was going well.

Chapter 48
September 31, 2005

"Those bastards," Rummy said from behind the Resolute desk the next day. "Are you sure?"

"Yes, one hundred percent," Jenkins replied.

"And at the Pentagon no less?"

"Yes, yesterday afternoon. At the Pentagon. I saw the tape from the security team. McCain and General Shinseki walking into Shinseki's office together."

Rummy placed two closed fists on the desk. "Wow, wow, wow." Few things in life gave him more anxiety than disloyalty from his subordinates. He was steaming.

I know," Jenkins said. "Hard to believe."

"Shinseki is going outside the chain of command."

"Yep."

"Plotting against his own president at a time of war."

"That appears to be the case."

"We cannot have this. We're already facing fierce opposition from Democrats, the press, even some Republicans. We can't add our own generals to the list. If they want to disagree, that's fine. Do it behind closed doors. But fraternizing with the enemy simply can't be allowed."

"I'll have him reprimanded"

"No. I want him gone. Today. Have Barr work up a list of options, of how to get rid of him—immediately."

"Respectfully, are you sure that's wise, sir? Now might not be the best time to fire a general."

Rummy stared at Jenkins for several seconds. "I want him gone."

Jenkins nodded slowly without speaking and then left the room.

Chapter 49
October 1, 2005

Rummy's old friend Ned Janetta was sitting at his favorite seat at his favorite bar in Chicago, *The Lodge*. It was happy hour, and he was drinking his second *Old Style* beer. With each gulp a thin layer of white foam latched onto his thick mustache for a few seconds before disappearing. CNN was on the television behind the bar and the talking heads were—as usual—focused on Rummy. It smelled like beer, peanuts, and stale cigarette smoke.

"The president of the United States has gone rogue," the guest, some attorney, said. "Right in the middle of the disaster in Iraq he decides to invade Iran. Now both houses of Congress have passed veto-proof legislation saying he can't do that. Yet he isn't budging."

"What's next?" the host asked.

"We are smack dab in the middle of a constitutional crisis. The courts have always been the last word on the law; presidents have always respected their rulings. Always. It's not clear that's still true. Not as long as Donald Rumsfeld is president. As far as I can tell, the ruling is up in the air. Both sides were asked hard questions. There didn't appear to be a clear consensus among the justices. The government raised some good points about the practicality of giving Congress the power to declare war, but the court has to be worried about the implications of unchecked presidential power in this area. And also what would happen if President Rumsfeld simply ignores a ruling against him."

"You think it's possible Rumsfeld simply ignores the Supreme Court's ruling?"

"That's right."

"That would be a pretty bold approach for someone who wasn't even on the presidential ticket during the last election."

"Well, the president is a pretty bold person. We've all seen that."

The bartender, Nicholas, turned from the television to Janetta. "Ned, you know President Rumsfeld personally, don't you?"

Janetta smiled. "Yup ... since we were kids," he said with unmistakable pride in his voice. He took a gulp of his *Old Style*. The foam sank into his mustache. "We grew up together, went to Princeton together."

"Weren't you ... weren't you his—"

"I was his campaign manager when he first ran for Congress. We won. He was 29."

"So you must know him well, then."

"Very well, yes."

"How's this all going to end up?"

"No idea," Janetta said.

"No idea?"

"Rummy isn't gonna budge. I know that much."

"Really, even if the Supreme Court rules for Congress?"

"Oh yeah. That would mean little to him."

"Really?"

Janetta leaned back in his chair. "A million geniuses could all tell him he's wrong and he'd still never give an inch."

"What do you mean?"

"He trusts his own judgment far more than everybody else's combined. He just won't listen to critics and opponents, even when it's a judge ruling on something."

"Interesting," Nicholas said, refilling Janetta's beer.

"And he's still a wrestler, like he was in high school and college. He needs to fight, to push, to make other things bend to his will. It's just his nature."

Nicholas tilted his head to the left. "I don't think being president is much like a wrestling match, though. That's too simplistic a comparison."

"I just mean he likes the fight to change things. Needs it, even. But he forgets that the status quo is okay sometimes too. Sometimes doing nothing is actually the best alternative."

Nicholas got a beer for another patron and then came back to Janetta. "But Ned, President Rumsfeld seems like a smart guy. I mean ... would he really ignore a court decision?"

"You're right, he's brilliant. But he has a blind spot. It's the same blind spot most geniuses have: he thinks he's even smarter than he is. He's overconfident. His confidence is effective in a way. It allows him to do great things. He ran for Congress in his twenties ... and won! He was the youngest secretary of defense in our whole history. He made millions from a standing start in just a few years as CEO." Janetta took another gulp from his *Old Style* before continuing. "But it also leads to mistakes. Causes him to misjudge certain things—like we've seen with Iraq and his idea that he can transform it into a model of democracy. So the very same confidence leads him to overestimate what he can do. It's a great strength and a great weakness at the same time."

"So nothing will stop him now? He's just gonna ignore everybody and plow ahead in Iran like he has been?"

Janetta's voice lowered. "There's only one thing in the world that can get him to change his mind. We shouldn't expect it to happen, but it could."

"What's the thing? What would get him to cave?"

Janetta didn't respond.

"What's the thing, Ned? What gets the president to cave? Ned?"

Janetta still didn't respond. He just shook his head and took another gulp of his beer.

Chapter 50
October 9, 2005

Attorney General Barr walked gingerly into the Oval Office. Rummy looked up from behind the Resolute desk. Just from the way Barr held his shoulders, tight and tense, Rummy could tell that it was not good news.

"I've just received word that the court is going to rule against us, Mr. President," Barr said, "A clerk in Justice Thomas's chambers let Clement know. They're going to rule for Congress … they're going to say that Congress has the power to declare war, not the president."

"Are you serious?"

"Yes … I'm serious," Barr said, taking his seat. "The order should issue later today. They are upholding McCain's legislation. It was a 5-4 decision, so it was close. But Justice Kennedy sided with Congress. We lost."

Rummy stared stone-faced at Barr. He was disappointed but not shocked. He knew he was pushing the envelope legally. "What are our options?"

"We really only have two. We can accept the order and withdraw from Iran in a manner consistent with the legislation. This would—"

"And option two?"

"Well, the alternative is to openly disagree with the court and say that they don't get to decide this, that we have Article 2 prerogatives and we do not accept the legitimacy of their decision. We would be interpreting the commander-in-chief powers to be beyond both legislative and judicial oversight. No checks. No balances. The executive has all the power. This would be … momentous, to say the least. Ever since the 1804 case *Marbury v. Madison* every president has accepted the Supreme Courts's orders … whether they liked them or not. Truman. Nixon. Reagan. Every president. Even at times of war."

Rummy stared at Barr. He was grinding his teeth, soaking in what he was hearing. "But it's really up to me, right? Judges have gavels. Presidents have troops. There's nothing they can actually do to force my hand, right?"

Looking Rummy in the eyes, Barr moved his glasses up his nose and nodded. "In an empirical sense, yes, that's right. It all comes down to force ... that is ... well ... force is always the last step in the political analysis. As long as the military accepts your orders, then, yes, it's up to you."

"And what would this say to our enemies, if some court overruled my judgment to initiate hostilities? What would that tell the world about American power? What would that tell the world about American weakness? Can you think of a more effective way to embolden our enemies than to allow five lawyers to overrule the commander in chief at a time of war?"

Barr nodded. "I understand your point, Mr. President. But I must add that if you decide not to follow the court's order Congress will go absolutely apeshit. Both sides. You will be impeached. McCain will push hard to get enough senators to remove you from office. The press will go bananas too. Even *The Journal* and most conservative outlets. It will be a legitimate constitutional crisis. I'm not saying it's not worth it. But I'm telling you what will happen. We will need to be prepared, have contingencies in place."

Rummy squinted at Barr and tightened his fists. "So option one is we capitulate and abandon our mission and the critics just go on and find something else to go nuts about. And option two is we do the right thing and continue with the mission in Iran, and our critics stay nuts about it. Either way the critics go nuts."

Barr didn't respond.

"Am I missing anything?" Rummy pressed.

"That's one way to look at it, Mr. President."

"Thank you, Mr. Attorney General. I have what I need."

Rummy looked back down at his papers and Barr got up and walked out of the room.

Two hours later McCain held a press conference at the Capitol. Two dozen senators—evenly distributed across the political aisle—stood behind him. His pale, almost translucent skin shone under the bright lights. Spit flew out of both sides of his mouth as he waved his arms wildly and hollered into the microphone:

"The Supreme Court of the United States has issued its ruling. We won! The power to declare war resides in Congress and not the president, as expressly set forth in the United States Constitution. Ignoring this order would be a treasonous high crime under the Constitution's Impeachment Clause. We expect the president of the United States to withdraw all United States forces from Iran as outlined in the legislation. If he does not do so we will seek—and we will obtain—his impeachment and his removal from office."

Meanwhile, Rummy was sitting at the Resolute desk being briefed by General Carias and Wolfowitz. "More bad news, Mr. President," Wolfowitz said. "The situation at the embassy hasn't improved. The hostages are still captive, though we think they're being fed something and given water. The Iranians still refuse to communicate directly and it's unclear what their plans and intentions are. Intelligence reports suggest at least two Americans have been killed."

Rummy's mouth cracked open, but he didn't speak for several seconds. "Was … was …"

"We don't know if Secretary Clarke was one of them." Carias said.

"We don't know one way or the other?" Rummy asked. His voice cracked and both Wolfowitz and Carias were taken aback at the palpable fear in his eyes.

"Thats right, Mr. President. We just don't know," Carias said. Rummy leaned back into his chair. "Okay ... go on."

"On the battlefield in Iran, the losses are mounting," Wolfowitz said. "The insurgency is, frankly, out of control. We need to either quadruple our forces—no easy task—or get them out of there right away. Though it's important to note that even if we do quadruple them there's no guarantee we will prevail."

"Quadruple them. Can you imagine what would happen if we withdrew, if we left, what Iran would think, what message that would send to our enemies ... to the world?"

Wolfowitz looked worried. His Adam's apple bobbed up and down before he spoke. "Mr. President ... um ... how ... um ... how are we factoring the Supreme Court's decision today into our thinking?"

"Excuse me?"

"The court's decision today ... upholding McCain's legislation. How are we thinking about this?"

"We're not. Five partisan Democrat lawyers in robes aren't stripping me of core presidential powers." He looked at Carias. "Quadruple the forces in Iran."

"Okay, Mr. President. Will do."

That night Rummy flew to Iraq. He would visit troops there and in Iran and be back home within 48 hours. While hesitant to leave Washington with everything going on, he felt compelled to look American soldiers in the eyes and thank them for their service.

He often worked nearly straight through overnight flights. This flight was no different. His pile of papers to review was nearly a foot tall. While he didn't take much time to sleep, he did write a letter to Joyce.

My dearest Joyce,

I write to you from somewhere high above the Atlantic Ocean, on my way to visit the troops in Iraq and Iran. It's the middle of the night and there's nothing but darkness outside the plane's windows. It makes me miss you, the light of my life.

It's been an incredibly busy and hectic time lately—being president is even more demanding than I expected—and I'm sorry that I have been distant. As always, you deserve better than me. And, as always, I deserve less, much less, than you.

As I sail through the air on this quiet night, I've found more clarity of thought than I've had in months. I see your beautiful smile so vividly, and I can't wait to be back in Taos with you after my presidency concludes. The moment my time of service ends, our time together—you and me—will begin once again.

For now, I must focus on the security of our nation and our people. We've done the right thing in both Iraq and Iran. I'm getting a lot of heat right now, and that must be hard on you and the family. But rest assured, as I know you do, that America under my leadership will be on the right side of history. Knowing that you are by my side, that you support and believe in me, gives me the strength to do the right thing in the face of so much criticism. Deep down I know that no matter what the world throws at me, everything will be okay because I have you.

I would rather have you with me and the whole world against me than vice versa. It's not a close call.

I thank you. I love you.

Don

Chapter 51
October 12, 2005

Three days later General Carias and Wolfowitz were back in the Oval Office with Rummy. Carias went first. "Mr. President, we have a problem."

"What?"

"Several key generals, including Thalblum and Julian, are concerned about the Supreme Court's ruling and the implications for the country if we refuse to obey the court."

"You've got to be kidding me," Rummy said.

"I wish I was."

Rummy's face flashed with anger. Seeing the nervousness on their faces made him miss Clarke—her confidence, her charm. He leaned in and squeezed his fists. "Can they be persuaded? Should I speak with them?"

"Perhaps they can be. But I'm not so sure," Carias said.

"So these folks—these storied military generals—they'd rather follow a bare majority of the Supreme Court than the commander in chief?"

"They're worried about the country, about American democracy, if court orders aren't followed," Wolfowitz said. "American civics is deep in the DNA of our military leaders and they're uncomfortable with the current situation. Uncomfortable may be putting it lightly."

Rummy squeezed his fists. "Okay ... well ... fire them. Get patriots in there who respect the chain of command. I will worry about the court and the Congress and American democracy. Our generals should stay focused on winning these wars."

Carias and Wolfowitz sat silently.

"Okay?" Rummy asked.

Wolfowitz looked at Carias and then back at Rummy. "We also have concerns Mr. President. Giving the court the last word on constitutional issues has served the country well for two hundred years. We're concerned about the long-term implications of ignoring them. You have sound judgment, we know that. But the next president may not."

"You sound like a Democrat," Rummy said. They didn't respond. They just stared at him. "But, Paul, what about the long-term implications of letting Iran run roughshod over the Middle East, of filling the void left by Saddam? Civics won't matter if we don't have a country and we won't have a country if we don't proactively defend ourselves."

"Those are valid concerns, Mr. President," Wolfowitz said. "I understand where you're coming from. I do. Which is why I suggest we withdraw for now and try to gain a broader consensus for the war in Congress, and in our military. Include others more in the planning, in the strategy, so they have more of a stake in it. One element of this is their egos ... they want to be included and to feel like they have some amount of influence in what we're doing. Right now they feel disrespected and ignored. We can work with Congress and our generals and then go back into Iran if it makes sense at the time."

Rummy smiled and shook his head. "Meeting adjourned," he said tersely. "Get out."

The two men stood and walked out of the room.

Chapter 52
October 19, 2005

After firing Wolfowitz and Carias and four other generals, Rummy installed General Peter Pace to lead the wars in Iraq and Iran. He instructed Vice President Bolton to assume the responsibilities of secretary of defense while he looked for a replacement for Wolfowitz with any shot of getting confirmed in the Senate. Anyone who supported the war in Iran wouldn't get past McCain and his allies.

"The House introduced Articles of Impeachment this morning," Bolton said, pushing his glasses up his nose and looking at Rummy from a chair in front of the Resolute desk.

"What took them so long?" Rummy said dryly.

"Yeah, not a surprise."

"What are the articles?"

"Violation of the constitutional requirement that only Congress can declare war. Ignoring a court order. Disregarding duly enacted legislation. Asserts they are all High Crimes under the Impeachment Clause."

"Impeach me all day long. I don't care," Rummy said. "We need to say focused on doing what's right."

"Absolutely," Bolton replied.

"We'll lose in the House, but I doubt they can get two thirds of the Senate to remove me. There are still some true Republicans in the Senate. History will be on my side. We got into this mess through inaction and I'm not going to just sit around and let courts and hacks in Congress dictate American foreign policy."

"I agree completely. Regime change in Iran is the defining issue of your presidency, one that will echo positively throughout the world for years to come. We can't sit idly by while the Middle

East gets more and more dangerous every day. Do not back down, Mr. President."

Rummy nodded, appreciating Bolton's consistent hawkishness. "Never," he said.

Chapter 53
October 22, 2005

Rummy was standing at his desk in the Oval Office, getting things done. A thick stack of papers sat on his desk, just next to his tape recorder. He was happy, fully entranced by his work. Despite everything going on around him, the psychic splendor of the presidency—his lifelong dream fulfilled—was as thick and powerful as the moment he heard Cheney had had a heart attack.

The door opened without a knock. He wasn't expecting any visitors. Not appreciating the interruption, some adrenaline picked up in his bloodstream and his nostrils flared. He was about to tell whoever was entering they needed to leave.

Then he saw it was Joyce. She was wearing a dark green dress and blue sweater. She looked distraught. Rummy put down his pen. "You okay honey?" he asked. Typically, she would tell him she was coming before entering the Oval Office. She walked straight toward him, slowly. She didn't respond.

His concern grew. "Everything okay honey?" he asked again.

She exhaled. "No ... Don ... it's not." She walked up to one of the chairs in front of the desk and stood behind it. She put both her hands on the back of the chair and stared at him. Her expression was blank. Her green eyes alert and glistening. "Everything is not okay."

He looked at her with deep concern. "What's going on? Tell me what's going on."

"I've never questioned anything you've done professionally in fifty years."

"Yes," he said. "That's true."

"I've always supported you fully."

"Yes ... yes, I know. You have."

"This has to stop."

He instantly knew what she was talking about, but he asked anyway: "What do you mean?"

"This, this battle with Iran, this battle with your own country. It has to stop."

He paused a few seconds, looking her directly in the eyes. "Joyce ... my love ... you don't ... you just don't understand. You don't have all the facts." He was still standing at his desk.

She shook her head. She was calm and confident. "I have *enough* of them. You can't just dismiss my opinion because you have facts I don't, or alternatives are worse, or there are unknown unknowns."

"Hun, you just—"

"No, listen to me."

"Okay, okay."

"Sometimes Don you're just wrong and even if you can poke holes in what the critics say you're still wrong. Even if you have more facts than they do, you're still wrong. Even if the alternatives are difficult ... you ... are ... still ... wrong. You just are."

Rummy stared at her as she spoke.

Her eyes started to water. "They have Torie, Don. *They have Torie.*"

He nodded. "Yes, they do."

"I love you with all my heart, and that will never—ever—change. But you're wrong about all this. You just are. It's right in front of your face but you can't see it. You have to get us out of Iran. You tried. It didn't work. Time to move forward. Do other things. Big things. Be a great president. You've always wanted to be president and now you are. Make the country better in the ways you've wanted to for decades. But first just get out of there."

Rummy's arms hung limply at his sides as he stared into her eyes. Joyce walked around to his side of the desk, and he turned toward her. She stood right in front of him.

"Just leave Iran, Don."

"But ... Joyce ... weakness is prov—"

Joyce put her finger on his lips and stopped him mid-sentence. "It's provocative. Weakness is provocative. I know, I know. We *all* know. But here's the thing: doubling down on a big mistake is the embodiment of weakness." She lifted her arms to hug him. They embraced. She leaned back, her hands still touching him, just above his hips. "You need to get out of there."

He looked at her, squinting. He nodded very slightly. She kissed him softly on the lips.

Then she turned around and slowly walked out of the room. Rummy watched her exit, standing, rooted in place like a tree, his arms still hanging by his sides.

Chapter 54
October 24, 2005

"My fellow Americans," Rummy said two days later from behind the Resolute desk. A television camera was several feet in front of him. Big bulbs were pouring light down onto him. He felt the warmth on his face. "I have ordered our military to do a full withdrawal from Iran. United States forces have achieved their limited mission in Iran of inflicting substantial damage to Iran's military and civilian institutions. The mission has been a success." He looked down at his papers and then back up. "As part of this withdrawal process, we have reached an agreement with the Iranian government. All the American hostages being held at the US Embassy in Iraq will be released, including Secretary Clarke." He paused and stared into the camera for several seconds before continuing. "To be clear, we are not doing this because of domestic pressure coming from certain quarters. The president, as commander in chief, has the unqualified, uninhibited authority to wage war on behalf of the United States. Any alternative to this endangers the country. Rather, we are withdrawing because it is the right thing to do on the ground. Our objectives in Iran were limited. And we achieved them. I want to thank our troops and their families for their skill in the mission and their sacrifice for our country."

Part Five: Taos
January 8, 2010 – September 19, 2018

Rumsfeld Rule: "Big (and bad) things can start from small beginnings."

Chapter 55
January 8, 2010

I never visited Rummy at his home in Taos after his presidency. Others from the administration did, though, including Bush and Bolton. Jenkins was there on a regular basis. From what I heard, he and Joyce had a nice life there. I sometimes feel guilty about what I did and how it resulted in Rummy getting ripped away from his quiet home in the dead of night in handcuffs. We had a rivalry, heated at times, but I may have taken it too far.

Oh well. What's done is done. There's nothing I can do about it now.

On this morning, years before his arrest, Rummy woke up and poured himself a piping-hot cup of coffee and sat down at his kitchen table. The walls of the kitchen were almost all windows, and the room was illuminated by a bright mix of light from a sparkling chandelier and the emerging morning sunlight. Outside the sun was rising, casting a light pink and yellow hue over the mountainous landscape. Bright, fresh flowers of various colors lined the countertops.

Joyce was still sleeping. It was quiet.

Rummy removed the thin yellow rubber band encircling *The Washington Post* and placed the paper on the table. It was thick today, which Rummy—still a news junkie at 75—loved as much as ever. He was enjoying the strong scent of the coffee as the steam rose up to his face and disappeared into his nostrils. As always, he scanned each page first, before diving in, to see if there were any stories about—*who else*—Donald H. Rumsfeld.

There was nothing about him on page one. Even though most of the press he got these days was negative, he was still slightly disappointed. The visceral excitement of seeing his name in the paper hadn't faded in 50-plus years. It still made his midsection flutter to see his name in a headline.

The lead story was instead about Barack Obama: *President Obama meets with former President Bill Clinton at the White House. The last article I want to read*, Rummy thought. *No thank you. Obama signals American weakness to the whole world every day and I had to spend years restoring confidence in the White House after Clinton's shameful escapades.*

He re-reviewed the rest of the front page. Exxon Mobil had record profits and peace talks in Palestine had stalled. Nothing too exciting. He took a sip of his coffee. He felt the hot fluid hit his tongue with a mild sting and then dance down his throat into his stomach. He turned the page. He heard the peeling and turning of the paper in the quiet room. He scanned both pages two and three for his name. Nothing. Instead: *Netflix subscribers increased by 25% year-over-year and Chuck Schumer was in some spat with John Boehner about the debt ceiling.*

Total snoozers.

He turned the page again. The room was getting increasingly brighter thanks to the rising sun. He heard the faint sound of the toilet flushing down the hall. *Joyce must be awake*, he thought. He turned the page and started to do the Rumsfeld Scan again.

And there it was. The headline: *Rumsfeld and Bolton charged by international court.*

His eyebrows rose and he sat upright and held the paper up close to his eyes. A mix of nervous excitement and pointed stress coursed through his body. His first thought: *How is this on page five instead of page one?* Then he read the article:

> *Former President Donald H. Rumsfeld and former Vice President John R. Bolton have been charged by the International Criminal Court for their involvement in the United States war with Iraq, which Rumsfeld presided over as US secretary of defense from 2003 to 2005 and US president from 2005 to 2008. In a press*

conference, French prosecutor Patrice Perche accused Rumsfeld and Bolton of violating numerous international laws and committing various crimes against humanity:

"The crimes against humanity perpetrated by Donald Rumsfeld and John Bolton must not go unpunished. Their deceitful war against Iraq resulted in the death of tens of thousands of innocent people and the destruction of that nation's infrastructure, economy, and national identity. We will not stop until justice is served."

The United States has never submitted to the International Criminal Court's jurisdiction and experts think it is very unlikely the Obama administration will change course in this instance. According to former two-time Attorney General William H. Barr, who served as then-president Rumsfeld's attorney general from 2005-2008, "This is a total clown show, a kangaroo court. The US has never and will never submit to the jurisdiction of international tribunals of this nature. Doing so would subject all US officials who operate in the international sphere with potential criminal liability for simply doing their job."

"Ha," Rummy said out loud. "Nice try!" He made a mental note to call his attorney Paul Clement, now in private practice after serving as Rummy's solicitor general. He was sure Clement would confirm Barr's statement that, in fact, the United States has never submitted to the International Criminal Court's jurisdiction and there was nothing for him to worry about. He was confident this was a nonissue. *Being a former president, things like this just happen sometimes*, he thought. *It comes with the territory.*

"Morning hun," Joyce said as she entered the kitchen in her Italian silk, multi-colored robe and headed to the coffee maker.

"Morning," Rummy said, perhaps a little too enthusiastically. "Everything okay? Another hit job in the press?"

"Yes, honey, everything is just fine. You know how it goes."

"Yes I do. Sleep okay?"

"Not too bad. You?"

"Yes, just fine."

Coffee in hand, she kissed him on top of the head and walked back to their bedroom. Rummy looked back down at the headline again: *Rumsfeld and Bolton charged by international court*. He shook his head and took a sip of coffee. "What a joke," he said out loud. And then he turned the page and scanned for his name on page six.

Chapter 56
April 15, 2015

"What's up, Rummy?" Jenkins said. "How was your day?"

"It was great," Rummy said, sitting at the desk in his upstairs home office under a glowing lamp. Jenkins had been helping him with his memoirs for several years, both organizing the files and building the manuscript. He even set up a website with Rummy's papers, including reams of snowflakes: rumsfeld.com. They spoke about the project on the phone almost every evening. Rummy was enjoying the companionship with his old friend almost as much as crafting a story he was sure would bolster his legacy. He'd written a quote from Churchill on a sticky note and taped it to the wall in front of his desk: *History will be kind to me for I intend to write it*. Next to the sticky was Rummy's favorite poem, *If*, by Kipling. Joyce had underlined the words *but make allowance for their doubting too* and drawn a smiley face in the margin. Rummy chuckled when he saw her handiwork.

A printed draft of the manuscript was on his desk and Rummy had Jenkins on speaker phone so he could take notes while they talked. "Chopped a pile of wood so high it almost reaches the shed's ceiling," Rummy continued. "Felt great. That new axe is my best purchase in years." His overalls were dirty from the day's work, and his hands were sticky from the tree sap. He smelled like pine needles.

Jenkins was also at his desk in his home office. He smiled as he held the phone to his ear, picturing 81-year-old Rummy—still vibrant and strong—chopping wood with vengeance. "Ha! Love it."

"And you?" Rummy asked.

"Great day, too. The symposium on the tax bill was a screaming success. Obama has spent his term trying to bankrupt the country. *Spend, spend, spend* and future generations can figure out what to do about it later." Jenkins was now a respected conservative commentator and Senior Fellow at the American Enterprise Institute. He spoke confidently to his old boss, his voice loud and firm. He was more relaxed now, having retired from a long and arduous tenure as Rummy's deputy at Searle and in government. Relieved from the pounding stress of their professional collaborations, a genuine friendship had blossomed. "Shall we get started on the book?"

"Yes, let's," Rummy said, picking up a pen and flipping open the manuscript. "Was thinking about something earlier today. How should we characterize the root cause of the Iraqi insurgency? I don't want to sound self-serving, but we need to explain not just *what* happened but *why* it happened."

"Well, I couldn't agree more. We need to dig into it, really explain it. The historical record needs to be accurate. There are some myths out there that should be corrected. Condi's book was extremely self-serving on this point, among others. She blamed *us* for the insurgency. DoD! Can you believe that?"

"I know, I know. She took absolutely no responsibility for the array of diplomatic failures in Iraq. She was secretary of state yet somehow it was everyone else's fault but hers."

"Yeah, she pretended like she never supported the war in Iraq to begin with."

"Just unreal," Rummy said. "But, you know, O'Neill's book was even worse, the one written by the *Wall Street Journal* reporter. What's his name? Suskind, I think. Paul really didn't have a clue what was happening."

"What a conundrum he was."

"Yep. Smart as could be and a true star in the Ford administration. Jerry used to have him and Greenspan debate the economy in front of us and just listen. Soak it in."

"I remember you telling me about that."

"Then he shows up in the Bush administration and starts acting like a Democrat," Rummy said, shaking his head.

"Yeah, he was a huge disappointment. As for the insurgency, the real answer is pretty simple: Bremer's decision to disband the Iraq military was the decisive factor, the main reason the insurgency got out of hand."

"I tend to agree."

"We won the actual war in weeks."

Rummy nodded. "The biggest and swiftest large-scale military victory ever."

"No doubt. Everything was teed up for success. The glue that was going to hold everything together in phase two was the Iraqi military, with our training and guidance. It still would have been messy, but it would have gone much, much better. Bremer botched it. The insurgency followed."

"A true diplomatic failure," Rummy said. "Bremer was a career State Department official, was in charge of post-war diplomacy. It all should have been a great success. Turned into catastrophic success."

"Successful war. Catastrophic diplomacy."

"Bingo."

"Your management of the generals was essential to that success. Just the right touch. The idea that you micromanaged the generals was such a canard. One of many from the press."

Rummy shook his head. "True, very true."

"It was all total BS. Your leadership was balanced and fair. I found several snowflakes we can quote to establish this, to debunk that narrative."

"Excellent."

"Anyway, it was the subsequent diplomatic mistakes by Condi and Bremer that sowed the seeds of the insurgency. Chiefly disbanding the Iraqi military, but there were other mistakes too."

"Yes," Rummy said, "but let's be careful how we characterize this. We don't want to do what Condi did in her book. We don't want to come off as self-aggrandizing, like we're pointing fingers and deflecting responsibility. We need to state the facts, let them speak for themselves."

"Will need some careful wordsmithing to get it right."

"Exactly. And please look for some contemporary files that show how, in real time, we at DoD knew disbanding the Iraqi military was a big blunder. Let's get those posted on rumsfeld.com."

"Okay, I will take a look," Jenkins said.

Chapter 57
December 5, 2015

"Grampy?" Rummy's twelve-year-old granddaughter Debbie said as she opened the thick metal door into the large shed on his property in Taos. The bright afternoon light rushed into the dimly lit room. Debbie was wearing blue-jean overalls over a long-sleeved white T-shirt. Joyce had just finished braiding her dirty blonde hair into pigtails.

The shed was about twenty yards from the house and had a steel blue roof and log walls. Rummy tried to build it himself a few years earlier but after several frustrating months he capitulated and hired a contractor. The large, single room shed had a high ceiling, a concrete floor, and was filled with hammers, axes, and knives.

Rummy kept busy in the shed fixing things, chopping wood for the fireplace, and working on various projects. In his 80s now, Rummy still couldn't stand being idle. Sitting still just didn't work. In retirement much of his time was filled with various projects in the shed. He was also spending a lot more time with Joyce, which they both loved. He'd noticed in recent years that being away from Joyce had become increasingly stressful. He was just more relaxed in her company.

Rummy was sitting on the swivel stool in the shed in front of his workspace when he saw Debbie come in. He was wearing blue jeans, a thick, long-sleeved button-up shirt with blue-and-white checkers, and a light brown wool vest with lots of pockets. He still shaved every single day—seven days a week—and his chiseled pale cheeks were stubble-free and clean.

"Grampy?" Debbie repeated. "You in here?" Her voice was soft and curious.

"Yes sugar," Rummy replied. Screwdriver in hand, he was in the middle of fixing his lawnmower. "Over here."

She turned to her right and saw him in the corner, behind the eight-foot-tall stack of wood Rummy chopped for the fireplace earlier that week. Looking up from the lawnmower he noticed as she was walking to him that she was holding a newspaper. She looked sad.

"I tried to read this Grampy," she said, approaching him, holding up the paper. "It's about you." His posture straightened and his stomach fluttered. He smiled. "I can't really understand a lot of it," she said, "but I can tell it's not very nice." As she got closer, he realized it was *The Washington Post*. That morning he had read *The Wall Street Journal* and *The New York Times* over his coffee, and was saving *The Post*, along with *The Financial Times* and *USA Today*, for the afternoon.

"Oh really, what does it say?"

She stopped a few feet from him, held the paper up close to her eyes, and started to read it slowly out loud. "Former President and Vice President and Secretary ... of ... Defense and White House ... Chief of Staff Donald Rumsfeld famously art ... articulated ... articulated—"

"Why don't I just read this myself." He reached over and took it from her hands. Standing up and holding the paper with both hands, he saw it was a column in the Opinion Section. The author was some guy he'd never heard of before, Greg Solomano. He read the headline: *Donald Rumsfeld's Contradictions*.

"This should be good," he said sarcastically. "Thank you for bringing this to me. Give me just a few minutes to read it and then we can talk about it, okay?"

"Okay," she said, looking him in the eyes. Then he sat back on the stool and started to read.

Former President (and Vice President and Secretary of Defense and White House Chief of Staff) Donald Rumsfeld famously articulated a three-tiered framework of human knowledge. First, there are "known knowns," he explained. These are the things "we know we know." Second, there are "known unknowns," the things we know that "we do not know." And third, there are "unknown unknowns," the things "we don't know we don't know."

Rumsfeld was right. This is an insightful framework for categorizing human knowledge—which is all too often imperfect and incomplete.

Yet Rumsfeld's most famous endeavors—the Iraq and Iran wars—were profound violations of the principle that people should recognize the limits of their own knowledge. While advocating for war against Iraq, Rumsfeld was far too confident that Iraq had weapons of mass destruction. He thought it was a known known—a certainty—when it was really a known unknown: While we knew that Saddam Hussein had sought weapons of mass destruction, we didn't know, at the time of the invasion, whether or not he actually had them.

We now know he didn't.

Compounding this error in judgment, Rumsfeld was far too confident in thinking that the war in Iraq would be successful. He was convinced that after defeating Saddam's army through sheer force, the United States could turn Iraq into a vibrant democracy.

We now know we couldn't.

Despite Rumsfeld's overconfident assertion that "I don't do quagmires," Iraq is not the vibrant democracy he and others in the Bush, Cheney, and Rumsfeld administrations predicted it would become.

As for Iran, Rumsfeld's brazen initiative to invade that country right in the middle of the fledgling Iraq initiative was thankfully shut down quickly by Congress (which renewed the War Powers Act) and the Supreme Court (which upheld it).

The man known for decades as someone who could get big things done failed as president to win either of these military campaigns.

> But Rumsfeld's contradictions don't stop there. On the one hand, he was a brilliant, dedicated, and farsighted public servant. His work transitioning the military away from a Cold War posture and addressing modern asymmetrical threats involving terrorism and new technologies was necessary and important.
>
> On the other hand, Rumsfeld's overconfidence hampered his ability to build the wide coalitions of allies—domestic and foreign—he needed to accomplish his biggest objectives. And his gratuitous antagonism toward the press was an unforced error in a democratic society where perceptions often matter more than reality.
>
> Rumsfeld's great strengths were thus often marginalized by his profound weaknesses.
>
> Rumsfeld's office announced last week that he is working on his memoirs. The working title, Known and Unknown, is fitting: He is now a known known in American politics—his career in government began in 1962 when he was elected to Congress (at age 29) and ended in 2008 when he lost the presidential election, in a landslide, to Barack Obama. Yet he will be defined by one lasting open question: How could someone so attuned to the limits of human knowledge be so overconfident in his pre-war assessments of Iraq and Iran?
>
> This question—a known unknown—is unlikely to ever be answered definitively. "Freedom," Rumsfeld once said, "is untidy." So, too, will be his legacy.

"Ha!" Rummy said, smiling at the paper. Then he looked up and his eyes met Debbie's. She was standing on her tippy toes, waiting to hear his thoughts. "This was actually not that bad. Most columns about me are hit jobs, saying I'm terrible and a monster. This one just says I was wrong."

"Are they right, were you wrong?"

"No, no, no. They are wrong. I never said Iraq would turn into a vibrant democracy."

"What does it mean to be a vi ... a vibrant democracy?"

"Good question. It just means that a country is like the United States, like us. That it has a good legislature and president and a sound judicial system."

"Ju ... judicial system?"

"Yes, the courts. We have good judges and good lawyers who uphold the law. You know you would make a mighty fine lawyer."

She smiled. "Really?"

"Yes indeed. You're smart and logical, just like the best lawyers."

"So, Grampy, you really didn't think Iraq had those weapons?"

"Well, I wasn't sure, I thought they might have them, and I thought it was important for us to make sure they didn't use them."

"But you always say to know what you know and know what you don't know. That that's the key."

"That's right."

"So what happened Grampy?"

"What do you mean?"

"Were you right about Iraq's weapons? Or were you wrong?"

"It's a good question, my brilliant granddaughter," he said smiling. "I think I did the best I could with what I had."

"But Gram—"

"Now why don't you go back inside the house with your mommy and let Grampy keep working on the lawnmower. This darn thing is finally about to start working again."

"But Grampy," she said, still standing on her tippy toes. "I don't understand how—"

"Now, sugar, you go inside, okay?"

"Okay," she said, her heels returning to the ground. She turned around and walked away slowly, her head down.

Rummy watched her leave. The sharp sunlight rushed into the room again when she opened the door. It just as quickly disappeared when the door slammed shut behind her. Staring at the door, alone and in silence, Rummy thought about Cheney, one of the few people who actually understood the vital importance of removing Saddam and how much worse the world was when Saddam was in power. He missed his old friend. He made a mental note to call Dick's daughter, Liz, who was stirring things up as governor of Wyoming.

Chapter 58
November 5, 2016

Jenkins was staying with Rummy in Taos to work on the memoir. They were in Rummy's office. The manuscript was due to the publishers in a few months.

"Before we get started, one question first," Rummy said. "I need to know. Odds Trump wins on Thursday?"

Jenkins sighed. "Two percent. Maybe three. Pisses me off it's even that high." He was sitting in a chair a few feet from Rummy and a notepad rested on his knee. They'd just had a spaghetti dinner with Joyce and his full, large stomach expanded and contracted mightily with each breath. Rummy was drinking tea; Jenkins was drinking bourbon.

"You really think it's only single digits?" Rummy asked.

"Yes, that low," Jenkins said, taking a pull of bourbon. "I do. We ship him back to Trump Tower on Friday, breathe a sigh of relief for a day or two, and then brace for four years, maybe eight, of Hillary."

"The Clintons just won't go away, will they?"

"Nope, to the chagrin of the country and the world."

Rummy paused before responding. "Maybe she will be better than Bill. I know Robert Gates respects her. He tends to have good judgment about people."

"Don't know if she will be better than Bill, but she will be better than Trump would have been. Guy's a nut job. Can't keep his companies out of bankruptcy and now he wants to run the country?"

"Well, you know I agree that Trump's unfit. Every time I see him, I'm reminded of John Adam's quote about the White House: 'May none but honest and wise men ever rule under this roof.' But I'm still a little—maybe a lot—more concerned than you are that he wins. It's unfathomable to folks like us—that a guy like that could get anywhere near the presidency—but there's a big swath of the American people who've just *had it* with the government. Globalization ravaged their businesses, their towns. And that destruction is what they see, hear, feel, every day. That's what they think about. They're not reading *The Economist*, they're not thinking about lifting strangers in other countries out of poverty through a global economic system. They're thinking about their own lives. They're mad and, frankly, I get it. Snooty elites in government—like us—just keep pushing more and more free trade down their throats. They want to tear the whole thing down."

"I still—"

"And who, and who better than Trump to do that, to tear the whole thing down?"

"You're scaring me Rummy! Trump won't win. He just can't. He better not win. Strong consensus in the press Hillary wins. For once I'm choosing them over you."

"Ha!"

Jenkins smiled. "And no Republican can win the presidency without the endorsement of Donald H. Rumsfeld."

"Don't know about that. Bush refused to endorse Trump too. It's not just me!"

"Okay, okay, book time? Shall we get started?"

"Yes, let's get going," Rummy said. "My first thought: We should delve into President Bush more. I want to be honest, but discreet."

"We could air out a lot of dirty laundry," Jenkins replied. "It'd probably be good for book sales."

"But he's a good man, has a good family," Rummy said. "He had the right intentions for the country. And did a lot of good things. I want to emphasize that, be generous with how he's portrayed."

"Alright, fair enough."

"Maybe we can repair some of his legacy."

Jenkins nodded. "Good idea." He was taking notes while they spoke. "What do you think happened, why do you think he fell off the wagon?"

Rummy uncrossed his legs and pushed his glasses up his nose. "Being president is hard. It's a lonely job. A tough job. You're one person, just like you've always been. Then all of a sudden—boom!—you assume office and in fundamental ways are responsible for the whole world. And sometimes it feels like that whole world is closing in on you. You've got the Congress, the courts, the press, state and local governments, even your own executive-branch bureaucracy—all these important actors you have limited to no control over. They're always thwarting what you want to do, what the country needs. And that's just domestically, with the folks who are supposed to be on your side. It's a shock to the system: you spend decades wanting to be president, trying to be president. Then you get there, and you sometimes feel powerless. I had some dark moments by myself in the Oval Office and in the residency. I can see how someone like President Bush … someone who already had an alcohol problem … how that could rear its head. Having a drink dulls the stress. Having two dulls it some more. When you're feeling that stress you just want it to go away. That's how humans are. You want the pain to go away. He was only a man, and I think he felt like the whole world was closing in on him."

"Well put Rummy. I like that for the book. Helping to explain why President Bush was—"

"No, no, we shouldn't get into it in detail like that. We can mention it briefly for context—we have to—but the more his challenges are in the book the more people will talk about it, remember it, emphasize it. I don't want that to happen."

"Maybe we can include what you just said about being president without tying it to Bush? I think it's important for people to understand that perspective."

"Maybe. Let me think about it."

Jenkins nodded. "Okay, let me ask you this: you said there were some dark moments while you were president. What were they? What were the dark moments?"

Rummy paused for about five seconds. "Well, when the Iranians had Torie, that was very dark. It really shook me. I had actually already been questioning whether I'd given her the right job, as secretary of state. And then I send her off to Baghdad and she gets taken hostage. I really feared for the worst."

"Yeah, that was tough."

"It was. And it was all on me. My decisions led her there." The sound of Jenkins' scribbling filled the room and Rummy raised his hand. "Please no notes right now. We can talk about what happened in the book generally but I'm not writing about this, about my feelings, or anything like that. This is just for me and you."

Jenkins nodded and put his pen down on the desk.

"So that was a dark moment, for sure. She was my friend. Still is. Would have been devastating if something had happened to her. Not just on my watch but directly because of my decisions."

"Any others? Any other dark moments?"

"Yeah, there were others. My first speech to Congress was supposed to be this triumphant moment, something I'd dreamed about for years. Then I get there and half the Republicans refuse to clap when I mention foreign policy, in protest against the Iran campaign. Thanks to McCain. Remember that?"

"I sure do."

"When you're president you really need your party on your side. Your opponents—in Congress, the courts, the press, other nations, even supposed allies—they are all so nasty, so united against you. So many people all around the world are waking up every day focused on—obsessed with—taking you down in one way or another. So you just really do need your party to be with you. Not just politically but emotionally, psychologically. So many people are trying to tear you down and your party is your only real protection. I didn't let it impact my decision making, but it was really tough not having my own folks with me. It was dark."

"Were you ever scared? As president?"

"Was I ever scared?"

"Yes."

"Well … and this … this isn't for the book."

"Understood."

"Or for public consumption at all."

"Yes, understood."

"The answer is yes, every day. I was scared every day I was president. Don't get me wrong: I loved the job. But it was hard and scary. I was terrified that September 11th was actually small, that something much larger could happen. That's part of how terrorism gets its name—you never know what's next."

"We talked about that, I remember."

"Yeah, but I never really shared how it made me feel."

"I guess it was hard to when you're supposed to be the source of stability, the rock for the nation."

Rummy nodded and took a sip of his tea. "The critics of the Iraq and Iran campaigns typically looked at September 11th as some sort of distant, even abstract, historical event. They dehumanized it. They made it academic. But it was very, very real. I felt the heat of the burning Pentagon. I heard victims screaming. I smelt the thick clouds of smoke. I looked into the eyes of the troops we sent to destroy Al-Qaeda in Afghanistan. Now imagine all that much bigger, ten times, a hundred times. I thought about that possibility every day. Yes, I was terrified. And that's why we did what we did."

Jenkins tilted his head to the left. "What do you mean, why we did what we did?"

"That's why we invaded Iraq, why it was absolutely essential to remove Saddam. We simply had to reduce the likelihood of another attack. Same with Iran. We had to act; we had to be proactive." Rummy's voice lowered to nearly a whisper. "It's ironic but the need to show strength with those campaigns was actually rooted in fear, in my own fear."

Jenkins nodded and took a sip of his bourbon.

Rummy smiled. "And if you ever tell anyone I said that I will deny, deny, deny."

"Ha!" Jenkins said.

The two men sat in silence for about a minute. Rummy flipped through the manuscript. Jenkins reviewed his notes.

Then Jenkins changed the subject: "Any regrets from your time in government? Anything you'd do differently?"

They looked each other in the eyes for several seconds. Jenkins could see Rummy turning things over in his mind, but he was confident he knew Rummy's answer.

"None at all," Rummy said, shaking his head slightly, left to right. "We did the best we could with what we had to work with. And we made our decisions for the right reasons. No, no regrets."

"Not one?" Jenkins asked.

"Not one," Rummy said. "You?"

Jenkins fidgeted in his chair and took another sip of his bourbon. "Same with me," he said. "No regrets."

Chapter 59
August 3, 2018

Rummy unlocked his big brown mahogany front door. The lock clanked loudly, interrupting the otherwise quiet morning. He opened the door slowly and reached down to grab *The Washington Post*. His back hurt as he bent and his fingers ached when he squeezed the paper. The other papers hadn't arrived yet. Two tall, bulky Secret Service guards stood watch outside in dark suits, as always. Little red dots were blinking in their ears. Guns were holstered to their hips underneath their suit jackets.

"Good morning!" Rummy said enthusiastically. They both nodded back at him.

The sun was just coming up over the Taos landscape. It was still dark, but a purple hue was slowly emerging in the lower echelons of the sky. Rummy turned back and walked inside, shutting the door softly. Joyce probably wouldn't be up for another hour or two. As he walked toward the kitchen table the lead headline in the top right corner of the front page caught his eye: *Trump fires Bolton.*

Rummy still spoke occasionally with his old Vice President John Bolton, even though tensions between them reached withering levels during their losing 2008 campaign. Bolton had come off as arrogant and unfriendly in his vice-presidential debate with Democrat Joe Biden, and Rummy wasn't happy about it. The campaign team's endless preparation sessions with Bolton emphasizing likability apparently had boomeranged into making Bolton even more unlikable. "From a D-minus to an F," as Rummy put it at the time. He still regretted picking Bolton over Sarah Palin, a then-promising but obscure young politician from Alaska who was now a Tea Party firebrand in the House.

Rummy sat down, his eyes fixed on the paper. His white porcelain coffee mug clanked softly on the table and thick steam emanated upward from his fresh pour. He held the paper up with both hands. He first scanned the article and the rest of the front page for his name. Not finding it, his eyes rose from the bottom of the page back up to the top right corner. He read the lead article:

> *In an early morning tweet yesterday President Donald Trump fired his National Security Advisor John Bolton. Trump tweeted:*
> *"War monger John Bolton has been fired ... I never should have hired him after his failures in Iraq and Iran, two messes I inherited and am in the process of fixing. He needs to learn to keep his mouth shut.. Maybe he will in retirement."*

Shaking his head, Rummy took a slow pull of coffee. He swirled the hot liquid in his mouth before swallowing. He could feel the tingling caffeine doing its work. He kept reading:

> *Bolton, for his part, released the following statement on Twitter several hours later: "I can no longer work for a man with such a little interest in and understanding of the world we live in. Contrary to the president's tweet, I resigned from the Office of National Security Advisor early this morning. It has been a privilege to serve my country."*
>
> *According to people with knowledge of the situation, President Trump and Bolton have had growing tension in significant areas. Bolton, for instance, has long held that the US has unfinished business in Iran after withdrawing from the country in 2005, when Bolton was vice president, not long after invading it in the first place. He was pushing hard and sometimes publicly for further action against Iran, while President Trump has chosen a more isolationist foreign policy. Bolton, moreover, has privately expressed significant concern about the machinations of Trump's private attorney Rudy Guliani, whose foreign initiatives outside standard government and diplomatic channels have consistently rankled Bolton and others.*

Rummy shook his head some more. *Should have taken my advice, Bolton, and never set foot near Trump*, he thought. *I warned you time and again: Trump has no business anywhere near the Oval Office.*

Rummy then took another sip of coffee and turned the page and scanned for his name on pages two and three.

Chapter 60
August 18, 2018

Rummy was chopping wood in his shed when Joyce opened the door. The sunlight rushed into the room. She saw him and said loudly: "Don ... Don ... Paul Clement is on the line."

Hm, Rummy thought, *why is Clement calling?* A bolt of nervousness danced through his body. Clement, still Rummy's personal attorney, was all business. He didn't call just to gossip or see how Rummy's day was going. Clement had recently argued in the federal court of appeals that a class-action lawsuit against both Rummy and Cheney's estate brought by Iraqis injured in the 2003 invasion should be dismissed. US courts, Clement argued, had no business entertaining foreign claims brought by foreign litigants against former US government officials. Clement was worth every penny of his $1,800 an hour, Rummy told friends.

"Coming!" he replied.

Rummy walked through the shed and across the freshly mowed, bright green lawn into the house. Joyce handed him the phone in the kitchen.

"Yes, Paul, how are you?"

"I'm okay Mr. President. How are you?"

"I'm fine, thank you. What's up?" Rummy was staring out the window into the surrounding mountains, listening intently. His right hand held the phone; his left rested on his hip.

"I just received a call from Secretary of State Mike Pompeo."

"Okay. Go on."

"President Trump has issued an executive order stating that the US will no longer oppose extradition for you and John Bolton regarding the International Criminal Court's proceeding."

"What? Really?"

"Yes."

"What does that mean?"

"It doesn't necessarily mean you or Bolton will be extradited to the court, which is at the Hague in the Netherlands. But if the prosecutor sought extradition the US wouldn't oppose it. At least that's what Trump is saying now. This would undoubtedly reverse under a new administration, as it has never happened before. And the implications are ridiculous: if former US government officials can be extradited and charged in international courts, no one serious will ever serve in the government again."

"Is this because of the spat between Trump and Bolton?" Rummy asked.

"Pompeo didn't say. I asked. It must be, but of course he can't say that out loud."

"Can they drop me? I'm just collateral damage. This is about Bolton, not me, right?"

"I asked that too. He said he didn't know … to take that up with the White House."

"I know Trump doesn't like me because I stayed quiet during his campaign, didn't offer support. But this is extreme."

"I agree."

"Maybe … maybe it's just a mistake? Maybe he just meant to do this with Bolton and inadvertently included me?"

Clement could hear the concern in Rummy's voice. "That could very well be true, Mr. President. The prosecutor included both you and Bolton in the same set of charges, so it could have just been a mistake. But the executive order allowing extradition does affirmatively name both of you."

"Hm … okay. I will call Vice President Pence, who I've known for years—a good man—and see what he says."

"Good idea."

"Paul …"

"Yes?"

"Anything else I should do here to make sure this is all okay?"

"Not now. And again, the prosecutor might not do anything about this. He now could extradite you, if he wants to ... but that doesn't mean he will."

"If he can, he will. He wants blood. Have you heard the things he, I think his name is Perche, the things he says about me? He's French."

Clement didn't respond.

"What do you think the Secret Service would do if the international court's authorities tried to take me into custody?" Rummy asked.

Clement paused a few seconds before responding. "The Secret Service ultimately works for Trump."

Rummy nodded and frowned. His bottom lip quivered. He could feel his heartbeat thumping in his fingertips, which were pressed against his phone. "They do indeed."

A few seconds of silence went by. "Any other questions Mr. President?"

"Not now, Paul. Thank you."

"Thank you."

Rummy hung up. He was scared and numb at the same time. He needed to process this news. He then turned around to head back to the shed and saw Joyce had been standing behind him the entire conversation.

"Everything okay Don?"

"Yes hun. Everything is fine."

"I heard everything you said sweetie. They want blood? This doesn't sound fine to me."

"It's okay. Everything will be okay. This sort of thing does happen to former presidents."

"Really? The sitting president allows former presidents to be subject to international criminal courts all the time?"

"It's just a different version of the same thing, hun."

"I don't know. Trump is different. You can't deny that, can you?"

Rummy didn't respond.

"It seems different," she said.

"It will be fine," he said firmly. "I just need some time to think through my options."

Looking him in the eyes Joyce nodded softly several times and then quietly said, "Okay," before turning around and walking toward their room. Rummy watched her take a few steps. He heard her slippers ruffle against the hardwood floor. And then he looked back out the window at the mountains. He clenched both of his hands and exhaled loudly.

Throughout Rummy's life he'd consistently faced the prospect that something really bad would happen to him—from his dad's deployment in the army in World War Two, to his own service in the Navy, to the Watergate scandal, to the Ford assassination attempts, to Clarke's capture in Iraq, to the typical scares of old age. Yet the risks came and went without ever coming to fruition. Rummy understood, however, that this didn't have to be so. He wasn't immune to catastrophe. The future wouldn't necessarily look like the past.

When his head hit the pillow that night Rummy kept thinking about what Joyce had said: "Trump is different. You can't deny that, can you?" No, he couldn't deny that. Trump was indeed different. Very different. And Rummy knew that there was no iron rule—no law of physics—that protected former US officials from international courts. It was, rather, the customs and norms of historical practice, rooted in pragmatism and rationality, that insulated US officials after they left office. Those things didn't work the way they used to with Trump at the helm.

Everything will probably be okay, he thought. *Someone will talk Trump out of this. Pence maybe. Or Pompeo.* But he wasn't so sure. This all felt different. As he stared at the ceiling—wide awake—he whispered softly, "Trump is different."

Chapter 61
September 19, 2018

A month later, after he'd mostly stopped thinking about his call with Clement, Rummy was jarred out of sleep by a loud scream:

"Donald H. Rumsfeld! Open the door now!"

He sat up. Joyce sat up, too, in terror. He got up quickly and started walking toward the door. He heard fists pounding on the door. "Open the door now!"

"I'm coming!" he yelled as loud as he could.

Joyce was screaming and crying. "Don! Don! Where are you going?"

He turned back to Joyce. "Call Paul Clement right away."

Rummy reached the door and opened it. Two large officers in black uniforms with guns on their hands stepped inside. The Secret Service agents just stood there watching as the larger officer put Rummy's arms behind him and placed him in handcuffs. Rummy looked each agent in the eyes but didn't say anything. He felt deeply betrayed: the same people who had spent years protecting him simply stood there watching as he was hauled away by armed thugs. The officers walked him to a large black suburban with dark windows and huge tires. They shoved him in the back seat. Identical vehicles were in front of and behind this one. Then they slammed the door shut and got into the SUV in front of Rummy's.

Rummy looked up and saw Joyce standing in the doorway in her robe watching everything. Tears streamed down her flushed cheeks. Her husband had been at the epicenter of world affairs for decades, but he had always been on the right side of the law.

Until now.

Rummy sat in the back of the car as it sped away in the center of the three-car motorcade. The tires screeched against the pavement. Joyce could just barely make out the back of his head through the rear window. The second she lost sight of him she dashed back into the house to find a phone.

As the car accelerated into the darkness he thought about what the headlines would say. He thought about Joyce. He thought about his granddaughter Debbie. The driver and man in the front seat, both in dark suits, sat silently.

Rummy knew where he was headed.

Part Six: The Trial
September 23, 2018 – October 19, 2018

Rumsfeld Rule: "If you don't want to believe it, there is no body of evidence that cannot be ignored."

Chapter 62
September 23, 2018

Rummy sat on the edge of the cold hard bed in his jail cell looking at the gray cement floor. He was wearing a light beige full-body uniform. There were no windows, but some light was coming in between the bars making up one wall of the room. The other three walls were gray cement, just like the floor and ceiling.

Rummy had been in this jail cell for several days. Alone. This was all new, to him and to the world. A former American government official had never been held before an international tribunal before, let alone a former president. He had no idea what would happen to him.

Joyce wasn't allowed to see him until after the trial, which wasn't going to start for another week. Rummy had asked the guard for pen and paper several hours earlier. He just delivered them. Rummy started writing:

My dearest Joyce,

I write to you from a jail cell at the International Criminal Court at the Hague. After 65 years of things going right for us, everything has gone horribly, horribly wrong.

He stopped writing and looked up and stared at the wall for several seconds. He shook his head softly, squinting in the dark light, and then looked at his hand, which was shaking. The lines of his handwriting were squiggly and uneven. He exhaled and continued:

I will be put on trial in a few days, and not just for a crime I didn't commit but for a crime that doesn't exist. The French prosecutor is saying that by not sharing certain information with President Bush before we went into Iraq I somehow broke international law. Can you believe that? The whole thing is a sham.

A farce. I am being targeted for who I am—the 45th president of the United States—and not for anything I have done. In the history of the United States no former president has ever been put on trial before an international tribunal.

It was President Trump who allowed all this to happen, who allowed those thugs to arrest me from our home. All because I refused to endorse him during the campaign. I'm so sorry that you and the family have been impacted by this petty madman.

You do not need to worry, though. As painful as this experience is, it will be okay. I will be okay. We will be okay. My surroundings here at the Hague are adequate under the circumstances. I'm alone in my cell, away from other people. The food is fine, the water clean. I have the best lawyer in the world, and we are working together on my case. The jury will see through these spurious allegations. They will hear my story and see that I have committed no crime.

As I sit here with nothing to do but think, my mind is consumed with thoughts of our life together. How did I get so lucky as to spend my life with my favorite person, my best friend? I am hard to please, hard to satisfy. But this only applies to the outside world. To others. With you, I have never—not for one second—ever been anything other than deeply grateful. This is as true today, in this jail, as it was when we first met; as it was through all those busy decades of my career; and as it was when we were in Taos. I have always been so grateful for you.

I remember when we were young, so many decades ago, and just starting out in Washington. You'd wake up early with me before I went to the Capitol. You were so cute sitting in bed with your coffee. Your big smile brightening the room and filling my heart with love.

Oh, how blessed I've been to spend this life with you.

We will be together again soon. At home again with our morning coffee, our majestic mountain views, our newspapers, our family and friends, each other. This whole episode will be merely a harrowing detour before we return to our wonderful life together. This is not a wish. This is a promise.

See you soon my dear. All will be okay. I love you.
With all my heart,
Don

Chapter 63
October 16, 2018

Judge Sullivan sat in his chair several feet above everyone else in the courtroom. It was quiet. My heartbeat thumped as I sat in the gallery. I knew that this whole trial would never have happened if it wasn't for me. Seeing him in the middle of this spectacle, I questioned whether I had done the right thing.

My stomach churned.

Sullivan hit his gavel twice on the mahogany paneling. *Thwack, thwack.* "Ladies and gentleman of the jury, I want to start by thanking you for your service these last two weeks. You have patiently and carefully listened to the testimony of nearly a dozen witnesses, including members of the Bush administration, Iraqi civilians, and the defendant. It is now time for closing arguments, where each side will summarize their case and explain why you should decide this matter in their favor. Each side will have 30 minutes of argument."

Sullivan then turned to Perche. He nodded at the prosecutor and said, "Mr. Perche, you have the floor."

Perche rose from his chair about fifteen feet to Rummy's left. Tall and muscular, his broad shoulders stretched outward as he took several steps into the center of the courtroom. Then he turned to his right, toward the jury. He was wearing a dark blue suit and red tie. His full head of brown hair glistened with gel under the lights beaming down from the high ceiling.

Watching Perche sent a powerful wave of nausea through Rummy's stomach. His lips parched, he swallowed what little saliva was in his mouth. Too nervous to eat breakfast that morning, his stomach growled quietly.

Every eye in the grand courtroom—packed with spectators—was fixed on Perche. Just the way he liked it. A euphoric mix of dopamine and adrenaline coursed through his veins. He had the look of a man who was doing what he was put on this earth to do. "Your Honor, ladies and gentlemen of the jury," Perche began, "thank you for your service in this highly consequential preceding." He was walking slowly as he spoke. His large hands were empty of notes and moved about swiftly and confidently as he spoke. When his voice wasn't filling the air, the clanking of his black shoes against the hardwood floor echoed softly throughout the room.

"International law prohibits military leaders from ordering troops to commit murder, to torture prisoners, to take hostages, and to attack the civilian population. Donald H. Rumsfeld knowingly violated each of these laws while presiding over United States' forces during the disastrous, unprovoked, preemptive war in Iraq. There is no question, no argument—no debate!—that US forces committed these atrocities … and that they did so on Mr. Rumsfeld's watch. No one here disputes the tragic death toll in Iraq. No one here disputes the torture of Iraqi prisoners by American soldiers at Abu Ghraib prison and elsewhere. The only open question is why … why did all these terrible things happen?"

Rummy sat still, watching. He didn't move his mouth or shake his head. In his mind he kept saying over and over again: *This is all wrong, this is all so wrong.*

Joyce was about ten feet behind him in the front row, sitting upright. While the occasional tear fell down her cheeks, her face was stoic. She just watched as Perche went on. And on. His gaze shifted back and forth from Rummy to the jury as he spoke.

"The answer to this question—to this question of why all these terrible things happened—is sitting right here in this room." He pointed his finger at Rummy. "The answer is Donald Rumsfeld." His voice rose sharply as he continued: "The evidence presented at trial could not have been clearer: Donald H. Rumsfeld lied to President Bush; he lied to America's military generals; he lied to the American people; and he lied to the international community. He lied about the central basis for the United States' invasion of Iraq in March of 2003. Mr. Rumsfeld knew Iraq didn't have weapons of mass destruction—he admitted this while sitting in that chair yesterday," Perche howled, pointing at the witness stand, his French accent thick, his voice booming.

"He knew Iraq didn't have WMDs. And he hid this all-important fact! He didn't just hide it, though," Perche continued, now looking at Rummy and taking several steps toward him. "He said the opposite. He said Iraq did have WMDs. With eyes wide open to the truth … he lied."

Joyce put her hand over her mouth as Perche looked at Rummy. A tear fell gently down her left cheek.

"He lied to his country. He lied to the whole world." Then Perche turned to the jury box. "He lied to you, ladies and gentlemen of the jury. Donald Rumsfeld lied to you."

Sitting next to Rummy, Paul Clement straightened his tie and softly shook his head.

"And what followed from his lies? What were the consequences of his lies? A catastrophic war where thousands of innocent civilians were killed. The elderly. The weak. The innocent. Women. Children. Innocent people like you and me. Innocent people who played no role in Saddam Hussein's regime, who did no wrong, who simply had the misfortune of living in the country Donald Rumsfeld singled out to destroy."

Every eyeball in the room followed Perche as he strode confidently from one side of the floor to the other. "This man!" Perche screamed, raising his right hand toward the ceiling and then jerking his arm down violently and pointing his index finger right between Rummy's eyes. "This man—Donald Rumsfeld—has blood on his hands."

He paused again for a few seconds, staring at Rummy. "Donald Rumsfeld lied. And thousands of people died." Then he looked back at the jury. "His lies were not just a small violation of the law. They weren't just empty words. They were a high crime against humanity, under any standard of the law. The international order cannot stand having statesmen lie and cheat and steal and mislead their countries into brutal wars that lead to carnage and destruction. It cannot stand such murderous machinations. If we allow this now it will be a blueprint, a license, an invitation, for deceitful men to trick their countries into wars … again and again. Donald Rumsfeld's victims in Iraq have already died. You must find him guilty so that other innocent people don't die in the future at the hands of other sadistic and powerful men."

Perche stood motionless, staring at the jury for five seconds before continuing. "The law is very clear that war must be just and the premises must be real and accurate and the violence must be proportionate to the cause. Wars cannot be rooted in mirages. Iraq never had weapons of mass destruction and all the evidence showed this and the most powerful evidence of all—Iraq's leaders' own words—established categorically that this was true. You heard Mr. Rumsfeld read the transcript of the taped conversation between Saddam Hussein's son Qusay and Iraq's senior leader Tariq Aziz. You heard their own words. They couldn't have been more clear. Iraq did not have WMDs. And they decided not to restart their WMDs program. Yet Mr. Rumsfeld hid the tape from George W. Bush, the president of the United States. He buried it. He erased it from history. He told the world Iraq did have WMDs when he knew they didn't." Perche's eyes danced from one juror to the next, landing on each of them. "Donald Rumsfeld lied. And thousands of people died."

Then he took a few steps back to the podium and looked at his notes briefly before restarting his slow walk around the courtroom floor. "The prosecution agrees with His Honor's earlier ruling that the death penalty is not something that should be allowed. We do not seek that punishment here. But we think it is abundantly clear that Mr. Rumsfeld must spend the rest of his days behind bars. He should spend the rest of his days thinking about what he did ... and what he did not do ... and the severe consequences of his actions and inactions. Anyone who takes the reins of power and authority, who has the potential to harm thousands of people and impact the world order and change the shape of history, must know that they cannot spew lies that lead to the destruction of a whole country. We must send a message to the world that these are actions that will be punished. If he is acquitted in this courtroom, it will tell heads of state and military leaders all over the world that lying and deceiving is a valid basis for entering into war. This must not happen." He clapped his hands together twice. "This must ... not ... happen!"

He turned from the jury to Rummy. Then back to the jury.

"Donald Rumsfeld lied. And thousands of people died. Your duty to both the innocent victims, his victims, and to humanity—to prevent more victims in the future—is to hold him accountable, to find him guilty, to tell the world that lying your way into war is a crime. That is the message that we, that you, must send to the world."

Standing in the middle of the courtroom Perche again slowly looked each juror in the eye before turning up to Sullivan and nodding.

"Thank you, Mr. Perche," Sullivan said. "Mr. Clement, you're up."

"Thank you, Your Honor," Rummy's lawyer said as he stood. He was a few inches shorter than Perche. His brown hair thin and balding, Clement had a pale complexion, intense green eyes, and the soft physique of a man who'd spent his life sitting behind a desk reading the law.

"This trial has conclusively established what we have known from the beginning," Clement began, "that the prosecution of Donald H. Rumsfeld is an unfortunate and unprecedented spectacle that never should have been allowed in the first place. This case was brought without any legal basis and for all the wrong reasons."

Clement spoke much softer than Perche, and slower too. He was confident, though, in command. Like Perche, he didn't hold notes or anything else in his hands. Peering through his glasses, his eyes moved from one juror to the next, rarely leaving the jury box. Like Perche, he slowly walked around the courtroom floor.

"In the history of international law, no leader of a military has ever stood trial, let alone been convicted, for decisions about what evidence to present, or not present, to the head of state. There's a darn good reason for that: doing so makes no sense. The international legal order would descend into anarchy if military leaders were subject to international criminal prosecution based on these highly complicated and fact-specific decisions."

His voice rose and he looked Perche in the eyes: "For an outsider from a different country to second guess these intricate judgements fifteen years later—based on a sliver of the relevant facts—is absurd. Yet that is exactly what has happened here. Donald Rumsfeld has been put on trial because of decisions he made, in good faith, as the United States secretary of defense. He's been thrown in jail and subject to trial for classified communications he had with the president of the United States about matters of war and peace. There is no international law—or law anywhere—that prohibits anything Mr. Rumsfeld did or didn't do. He was his country's military leader at a time of war when this alleged crime took place. It was less than two years after America was attacked on its own soil by terrorists and more than 3,000 of its citizens were killed. He was in the building when the Pentagon was struck by a plane and helped save multiple victims. This happened on his watch as secretary of defense. He was responsible for the defense of his country, and it was up to him what information to share with the president. He made decisions every day about what information was relevant, and what information was not; what was helpful to the president, and what was not; what might confuse the president, and what might help him make the right decisions. Being a trusted and discerning filter of information was a core part of his job. And the chain of command would have been ground to a halt if Mr. Rumsfeld flooded the president's desk with every piece of information he received."

Clement paused and adjusted his glasses. Then he looked at Rummy. They nodded at each other. Rummy couldn't tell how the jury was receiving his lawyer's presentation. Perche was impressive in a traditional sense. Clement less so. But Rummy at least found his attorney's demeanor endearing, far more likable than his opponent.

"Moreover, the prosecution asserts that President Bush's decision the wage war was based on Mr. Rumsfeld's lies and omissions. This is false. It is Mr. Perche who has lied. Mr. Rumsfeld was the secretary of defense, he was not the president of the United States. Any questions about the legality of the campaign lie at the feet of the president, not his underlings. And again, there is no law that suggests communications between the head of state and his deputy can be deemed illegal. Just because Mr. Perche says there is, doesn't make it so. Why didn't Mr. Perche show you an order to torture written by Mr. Rumsfeld? Or an order to murder, or to target civilians? Simple. It is because none exist. Not a shred of evidence presented at this trial suggests Mr. Rumsfeld did any of these things."

Rummy was nodding softly. Clement's voice was rising.

"To the contrary! The evidence showed that Mr. Rumsfeld took every precaution he could with respect to innocent Iraqis.

His goal was to remove Saddam Hussein—a maniacal tyrant—from power, and to do so as humanely as possible. As part of achieving this goal, he made judgments about what to tell the president and what not to, what was relevant and what was not, what was helpful and what was not—as is the prerogative of every senior military leader in every country. These judgments should not be second-guessed now, over a decade later."

Clement stopped in the middle of the courtroom. He looked at the jury. Then at Sullivan; then Perche; then Rummy. The only sounds in the room were the inhales and exhales of the people and the scribbles of the press. Then he resumed his slow-paced stroll and continued:

"Let's take a step back and look at who Donald H. Rumsfeld really is. He's a man who dedicated his life to his country. He served in Congress beginning at age 29 and then as chief of staff to President Gerald R. Ford, helping the country move past Richard Nixon's Watergate scandal. He served as the youngest secretary of defense ever, and then again as the oldest secretary of defense ever. Then he rose to be vice president of the United States and, eventually, to be his nation's 45th president. When he wasn't in government, he was building businesses and helping his industries grow and prosper. And he still served his country as a private citizen in numerous ways, serving as President Reagan's Special Envoy to the Middle East—where he met Saddam Hussein face to face and observed firsthand the dictator's malevolence—and as the head of numerous important government commissions."

Rummy almost smiled. Despite all the stress of the occasion he still liked the sound of his biography stated out loud.

"Donald Rumsfeld was a loyal public servant who contributed to his country and the world on a grand scale for many decades. This unprecedented trial isn't just fundamentally flawed on the law, it is fundamentally immoral. It seeks to upend the international legal system, usurping power away from legitimate government officials and placing it into the hands of ambitious prosecutors. And it has targeted a good man. Mr. Rumsfeld didn't lie and cause thousands of people to die. Mr. Perche is lying to you now. Donald Rumsfeld simply did his job … as secretary of defense … at a pivotal time for his nation. He should be acquitted and allowed to go home."

Clement turned to Sullivan and nodded. "Thank you, Your Honor."

"Thank you, Mr. Clement," Judge Sullivan said. "You may be seated."

Chapter 64

After Clement sat down, all eyes turned to Sullivan ... just the way he liked it. He turned to the jury: "Ladies and gentlemen of the jury. Thank you for your service. You have observed the full trial and heard closing arguments from both sides. The proceedings are now in your hands. The bailiff will escort you to the jury room, where you will be provided with printed versions of the jury instructions. You will then deliberate and render your verdict. I have structured the instructions so that you need to answer only a single question: Did Donald H. Rumsfeld commit a crime against humanity by failing to disclose key evidence regarding Iraq's weapons-of-mass-destruction program to President George W. Bush before the United States invaded Iraq?"

Sullivan then looked at the bailiff and nodded. The bailiff lifted a metal latch and opened the gate to the jury box and motioned for the jurors to follow him. All eight jurors stood and walked in a procession out of the jury box and down the center aisle in between the two sides of the gallery and out of the courtroom.

Everyone else sat quietly and watched them leave.

Rummy wiped some sweat off his forehead. He was starving and exhausted. He turned around and mustered up a smile for Joyce. I thought he might have seen me, but wasn't sure. Joyce's cheeks were red and puffy, he could tell she'd been crying. She could tell underneath his smile he was a nervous wreck. Rummy looked over at Perche, who was speaking rapidly in French to several underlings. Members of the gallery also began talking. Slowly at first. Then faster. Joyce overheard someone with a European accent (she wasn't sure which country) say, "Justice will soon be done."

Then Sullivan's baritone voice overtook the cacophony. "The bailiff will now take the defendant to his cell. Today's proceedings are adjourned." He hammered his gavel twice. *Thwack, thwack.*

Chapter 65

By the time Rummy got back to his cell it was almost dinner time. Clement would be visiting him the next day. But Joyce still wasn't allowed to see him. His head hit the pillow that night, but his eyes never closed.

Chapter 66
October 17, 2018

The first full day of waiting moved slowly. Rummy was finally able to hold down some food at breakfast. Half a banana. Busy tending to other clients, Clement didn't come to see him until the afternoon.

"What do we do now?" Rummy asked Clement, who stood in the cell while Rummy sat on the bed.

"Well, Mr. President, we wait."

"That's all?"

"That's all."

"I still can't believe … I still can't believe I'm on trial for this … for what I chose to say or not say to the president. It's such bullshit … such trumped-up bullshit."

"I agree, there's no doubt about it. Perche has created a monster out of a molehill. But all he really had to do was get to the jury. Then it's a toss-up."

A flash of anger shot through Rummy's body hearing those words—a toss-up—describe the balance on which his future freedom hung. "What do you think the jury will do? What's your best guess?"

"Impossible to know. They didn't telegraph much. But they've already been deliberating for half a day, which means they're taking this seriously and aren't making a snap decision. That's good."

"Why is that good?"

"A snap decision is more likely rooted in animus than a deliberate one."

Rummy sighed. "Do they all have to agree?"

"Well, yes, for a verdict. A verdict of guilty or not guilty must be unanimous. If they don't all agree then there's a hung jury and then it would be up to Perche to decide whether to bring another trial."

Rummy's stomach contracted sharply. "Another full trial?"

Clement saw the horror in his eyes. "That's right, Mr. President."

"But if they do agree, then what?"

"Well, if they find you not guilty then you go home. If they find you guilty then Sullivan sets the sentence."

Rummy's jaw tightened. "Sullivan would set the sentence?"

"That's right."

Chapter 67
October 18, 2018

The second day of waiting was worse. Every time Rummy heard someone walking toward his cell, he got nervous that it was Clement coming to tell him the jury had reached a verdict. But it was always just the prison staff. He had no visitors that day.

He was alone. A desperate sense of powerlessness hung over him. It reminded him of something he had shoved deep into his subconscious since he was a child: the feeling he had when his father was deployed during World War Two. He was only 9 at the time. Day after day, week after week, month after month, Rummy desperately yearned for his father. But he had no control over the situation. No way to bring him back home. When he finally did come home, he'd been deployed for two years. Sitting in this jail cell at the Hague, Rummy thought about how so much of his time since then had been spent trying to control everything around him. It was, in some ways, the theme of his life: trying to control as much of the world as he could. And now he sat powerless in a jail cell. This brutal irony consumed his thoughts for most of the day, including when his head hit the pillow. Somehow he managed a few hours of sleep.

Chapter 68
October 19, 2018

When he woke up the next day, Rummy immediately thought of something Perche had said in closing argument: "If he is acquitted in this courtroom it will tell heads of state and military leaders all over the world that lying and deceiving is a valid basis for entering into war."

What a canard, Rummy thought. *Total bullshit. I didn't lie about anything to anyone. I was too careful with my words for that. And if nasty lawyers like Perche start criminalizing the considered judgments of statesmen then who in their right mind would ever serve their country?*

Rummy ate his full banana and braced for another day alone. Another day of waiting. But at 11 a.m. it finally happened: the footsteps were Clement's. He had come to tell Rummy that the verdict was in. "Judge Sullivan said court would resume for the rendering of the verdict in 30 minutes."

"A verdict?"

"That's right, a verdict. There's no hung jury, so this will be decided one way or the other."

"Guilty or innocent?" Rummy asked.

"That's right." Clement answered.

"Okay, thank you. Anything I need to do now?"

"Nope. Just be ready to go in about twenty minutes. I will be right back."

Chapter 69

The bailiff entered first. The jury followed.

The eight jurors walked in a line into the jury box and took their seats. Their faces were blank. Rummy tried to tease out some meaning in their appearances. But no one tipped their hand. Sitting there, watching these strangers who held his fate in their hands, Rummy thought about his shed in Taos. He craved the feeling of squeezing his axe in his hands and chopping wood, of using force to split the stumps in two. It was a powerful catharsis for him, a release of the well of stress and anxiety that had filled inside of him his whole life whenever he sat still. He wondered if he would ever be able to chop wood again.

Sullivan got right to the point: "Was a foreperson appointed by the jury? If so, please stand."

"I was, Your Honor," said a tall, slim man from South Africa said as he rose. A young adult with kind features and thick brown hair, he was wearing beige slacks and a white sweater. His eyes were soft, his voice timid.

"And has the jury completed its deliberations regarding whether the defendant is guilty of the crime alleged?"

"Yes, we have."

"And what is your verdict?"

Here we go, Rummy thought, *all the marbles*.

The man held up a piece of paper and read the words aloud: "We the jury find the defendant Donald H. Rumsfeld guilty of the crimes alleged."

Rummy didn't move. He was numb.

Joyce started to cry.

Perche pumped his fist.

Clement looked down and shook his head.

I sat completely still, processing what I'd just heard. *We the jury find the defendant Donald H. Rumsfeld guilty of the crimes alleged.* It felt surreal.

The crowd was a loud mix of cheers, jeers, and gasps.

Sullivan knocked his gavel against his desk twice. *Thwack. Thwack.* "Order in the court. Everyone be quiet." The entire room went silent.

After a few seconds, Sullivan sat up straight in his chair and cleared his throat. Not a strand of his silver hair was out of place. "Ladies and gentlemen of the jury, on behalf of the entire international community of nations, I want to say thank you. It is essential that these trials are conducted with integrity and professionalism, so that justice may be done. And you have conducted yourselves in an exemplary manner from the outset of this proceeding."

Then he turned to Perche and Clement, who both rose. "Counsel, as you know, under the rules of this court the jury decides whether or not a crime has been committed but the sentencing function is reserved for the court. I decide the length of the sentence. To help me with this process, tomorrow I would like to hear directly from the defendant." He looked at Rummy. "Mr. Rumsfeld, please come tomorrow prepared to explain to me what you think your sentence should be in light of the jury's verdict."

Rummy nodded.

"Thank you, Your Honor," said Clement.

Then Sullivan picked up his gavel and said, "Today's proceedings are adjourned. The bailiff shall escort Mr. Rumsfeld to his cell."

As Rummy walked past Joyce, he looked her in the eyes and said, "I love you."

She reached out to touch him, but he was several inches too far away. "I love you too."

Chapter 70

Back in his cell a few hours later Rummy was sitting on his bed with a yellow notepad on his lap and a pen in his hand, which was shaking. His numbness had worn off and his psyche had been overtaken by a sense of impending doom. He was trying hard to ignore the jury's verdict—the fact that he was just convicted for war crimes and billions of people around the world already knew about it—and focus on what he would tell Sullivan the next day. Clement had just left. He implored Rummy not to argue about the verdict but rather to take responsibility for what happened and to show contrition. "Sullivan is going to want you to say sorry, to admit what you did was wrong. That's how you can reduce your sentence. If you contest what the jury did he will only get angry and impose a stiffer sentence." Rummy was trying hard to follow his lawyer's advice.

I'm sorry for the pain I caused, he wrote. And then he drew a line through the text.

I apologize to the international community for what I've done. I accept responsibility for—. Again, he struck the words. He looked up at the ceiling, the dark gray slab of concrete, and inhaled deeply. Then he threw the notepad against the wall. Then the pen. He was squinting, shaking his head slowly. His eyes were wet and bloodshot.

He thought about his newspapers—those papers he missed so much. *What would they say tomorrow?* He was sure to be the lead story in every major paper in the world. The headlines would be brutal. *Rumsfeld Convicted. International Court Finds Rumsfeld Guilty. Former US President Convicted For War Crimes.*

Then he thought about what he knew. *What are the known knowns?* he asked himself. *I've been convicted. The jury sided with Perche. What are the known unknowns? What did Sullivan think? What would the judge's decision be on my sentence? And what are the unknown unknowns?* He couldn't think of anything in the latter category.

Being in a jail cell dramatically restricted the number of things that might happen to him.

His fate rested solely in category two, the known unknown. *What would the judge rule?*

Chapter 71
October 20, 2018

Just like every day of the trial so far, there wasn't a single empty seat in the gallery. I was sandwiched between an older, heavy set Moroccan man and a thin young woman from France—both members of the press.

The jury box was empty. Their work was done.

Joyce was in her same seat, in the front row right behind Rummy's chair. Her somber eyes were fixed on the back of Rummy's head. Perche was speaking softly to his team. He had a serious look on his face.

Judge Sullivan entered the room. His puffy red face and silver hair were popping out above the black robe draping his body. He looked huge as he lumbered up the steps to take his seat. Seeing the judge enter, Rummy's hands clenched and his jaw tightened. *This overweight EU bureaucrat holds my liberty in his hands*, Rummy thought. *How on earth did this happen?* He still didn't know what he would say to the judge. All he knew was that apologizing for something he didn't do wasn't in the cards, despite Clement's advice. He simply couldn't do it.

Sullivan began: "Mr. Rumsfeld, you have the floor."

"Thank you, Your Honor. May I stand at the podium?"

"Yes, you may."

As Rummy rose from his chair everyone else in the room—the judge, the lawyers, the overflowing gallery—sat still, seemingly frozen in time. He slowly walked the dozen or so steps to the podium in the middle of the courtroom. Joyce had seen her husband walk to podiums dozens of times before. But never like this.

He was more numb than nervous, but his head was clear. A tremendous amount of adrenaline was pumping through him, but he was used to that. He'd always been able to keep a straight face under pressure. This was no different. "Your Honor, thank you for letting me speak," he began. "I'm not sure what to say, really."

It was the first time Joyce had ever heard her husband utter that sentence.

"All I can do," he continued, "is explain to you that I did the best I could with the information I had, all in the honest and true service of my country. I was nominated by the president of the United States and confirmed by the United States Senate to be secretary of defense and my solemn obligation was to defend my country the best I knew how. That was my job. That was my focus. As secretary of defense, I was flooded with a blizzard of information relating to our national security. Some of it was reliable. Much of it wasn't. Some of it was clearly, obviously misinformation. Some of it was more subtle and complicated. The potential for ambiguity to confuse President Bush's decision making was immense. An essential part of my job, therefore, was to filter information, to distill the blizzard of facts and data and intelligence into something coherent and intelligible. Something actionable. Something the president could rely on."

Rummy's hands rested on the podium. They were shaking. But his voice was steady.

"I did the best I could. Sometimes I got it right; sometimes I got it wrong. It was always a matter of exercising judgment, and it was always—always—with the right intentions. I'm not a murderer, Your Honor. I wasn't targeting civilians. I wasn't ordering that people be tortured." He paused and his bottom lip quivered. Then he pounded the podium with his right fist. "And I'm not a war criminal."

He turned around and looked at Joyce for several seconds. Then he turned back to Sullivan.

"In retrospect perhaps Vice President Cheney and I should have told the president about the tape; perhaps we should have let him decide for himself what weight to give it. But the crush of information swirling around us—and the honest belief that Iraq did in fact have weapons of mass destruction—led us to the conclusion we reached. We honestly thought it would do more harm than good to share the tape with the president."

Perche was sitting with his arms crossed. He shook his head every few seconds. He kept looking up at Sullivan, trying to catch the judge's eye, but Sullivan was focused on Rummy.

"At the time we discovered the tape of Qusay and Aziz we were genuinely concerned about Iraq. Saddam had—"

"Who's we? Mr. Rumsfeld," Sullivan interjected.

"I'm referring to me and Vice President Cheney, Your Honor."

"Understood. Please continue."

"Not only had Saddam used WMDs before, but America had been hit hard on September 11th. On my watch. We felt immense concern … immense fear, Your Honor … that something else would happen to America, that Saddam would harm our country. I barely slept for weeks after the attack. As is true with all nations, our liberty depends on our defense. Saddam had tried to harm America in numerous ways before. He was shooting at our planes. He was violating UN sanctions. He tried to assassinate the former president, George Herbert Walker Bush, the president's father. If something had a one percent chance of harming our country, we had a solemn duty to do everything in our power to drive that probability down to zero. That was our job. We were charged with defending the United States and we were worried this madman would harm our nation like he had harmed other nations, like he had harmed his own people." Neither Sullivan nor Rummy blinked as they stared each other in the eyes. "Never—not once—did we intentionally deceive the president or lie to the president. We simply did the best we could with what we—"

Sullivan intervened: "What did you think would have happened if you had shown the tape to President Bush?"

"The honest answer was that we were concerned he was giving too much weight to the actual, present existence of weapons of mass destruction in Iraq—as opposed to Saddam's capacity and intent to manufacture and use them—and that this tape would cause him to make an error in judgment about whether to seek regime change."

"But he was the president, it was his judgment to make, right?"

"Yes, Your Honor, that's right. The American people elected him, not me, and not Vice President Cheney."

"So you admit that it was a mistake?"

"Your Honor I admit that in retrospect maybe it was a mistake. Maybe we should have told him."

"If you had told him and if, as a result, he didn't invade Iraq then many thousands of people wouldn't have died, isn't that right?" Sullivan then looked at Perche, whose cheeks rose into a bright smile.

"That may be true."

"May be true?"

"It would be true, Your Honor. But it would also be true that Saddam would have stayed in power and continued to threaten the United States and his neighbors and continued to brutalize his people. It's not as simple as—"

"So ... Mr. Rumsfeld ... was it or was it not a mistake not to tell President Bush about the tape?"

Clement sat stone-faced but he desperately wanted Rummy to show contrition and admit it was a mistake. Rummy just couldn't do it. "I do not think it was a mistake that violated the law. I do not think it was a mistake that means I should spend the rest of my life in jail. The secretary of defense receives a lot of very fast pitches, Your Honor, and sometimes they swing and miss. Did I make a mistake? Perhaps. But I did not break the law. I did not commit a war crime. I was doing my job the best I could."

Sullivan shook his head slightly two times and leaned back deep into his chair. "Thank you, Mr. Rumsfeld. You have given me plenty to think about." He looked out into the crowd. "I need some time to make my decision. I will issue Mr. Rumsfeld's sentence tomorrow morning at 9 a.m. sharp. After which these proceedings will close … and the world can move on."

Thwack, thwack. The sound of his gavel pummeling the wood reverberated around the courtroom.

Chapter 72

That night Rummy rotated from pacing his cell to sitting on his bed. Again and again. Sleep wasn't going to happen. He didn't even try.

Chapter 73
October 21, 2018

Judge Sullivan surveyed the overflowing courtroom gallery from his chair with pride. He'd spent the morning doing two things: thinking about what Rummy's sentence would be and reading his own name in various newspapers from around the world. Every head in the room was tilted upward and every eyeball was fixed on him. He bathed in the moment for a few seconds. Then he homed in on Rummy.

"It is now time for me to issue the final ruling in this case, namely, the length of the defendant's sentence." He exhaled audibly and shuffled his papers. "Mr. Rumsfeld, you should have told President Bush about the tape. Period. Full stop. I have no doubt about that. The tape was of two Iraqi senior leaders talking about perhaps the most important question underlying whether the United States should invade another sovereign nation—whether Iraq had weapons of mass destruction. You should have let the man elected by the people make the judgment about how much weight to give the tape."

Every person in the packed courtroom sat mesmerized. History was unfolding—bloody and raw—before them. Sullivan's voice boomed:

"But you didn't. And, in that way, you lied. You did. Mr. Perche is correct. Your lie led to the deaths of thousands of Iraqi civilians."

Perche smiled at hearing his own words emanate from the judge's mouth. He could picture the quotation in the papers already.

"The jury was right to convict you."

The stress and fear inside Rummy's head rose so high as the judge condemned his behavior that his vision started to blur. Perche's smile grew bigger. He leaned back in his chair and clenched and softly pumped his right fist.

"Nonetheless ... I am going to sentence you to time served."

Energy jumped back into Rummy's bloodstream. His nervous system stabilized.

Joyce looked up, a beaming smile breaking through on her face for the first time in weeks.

Clement softly pumped his right fist.

Perche looked shaken and disoriented.

Gasps followed by unruly boos, hisses, and sneers exploded from the gallery. The man sitting next to me (a member of the press, I think) cursed in German under his breath.

"Quiet now," Sullivan said. He picked up his gavel but when the crowd settled he put it back down. "You are 85 years old, Mr. Rumsfeld. You won't be in that cell for your final days. You get to go home now. But you will have to live with your choices in life. Those that were examined here ... and those that weren't. You can surround yourself with luxuries and with people who admire and even love you, but you can't erase your past decisions. You will have to live with them. Every day. When your head hits the pillow at night you will have to contend with the faces of all the Iraqis ... the men ... the women ... the children ... all the Iraqis who died because you lied."

Sullivan paused for a few seconds, bearing down on Rummy.

"You will be able to go home soon, Mr. Rumsfeld. But you can't change what is in your own mind. You know what you knew and what you did not know, what was right and what was wrong. Deep down you will always know."

Rummy nodded at the judge.

Sullivan cleared his throat before continuing. "As I've sat through this trial I've been stunned by two things. The first is the brilliance of your mind and your prodigious capacity to accomplish things." Looking over at Perche, he said, "You're the smartest person in this room." Perche was slumping in his chair and his frown stayed frozen in place. "But you have a blind spot Mr. Rumsfeld. You get everything right except one thing. And that's yourself. You overestimate what you can do. You've done so much in your life and you confuse that with the ability to do anything. But humans can't do anything. We have limits. All of us. Even you. You thought you could make Iraq work. You thought you could transform that country into something it's not and something it can't be. You don't do quagmires, you said. But Iraq is way too big and complicated for anyone to force into their desired mold. Even you Mr. Rumsfeld ... even you. You thought it was okay to deceive your own president because to you it was a just war and because to you transforming Iraq into a democracy was something that could be done, something the United States military under your leadership could achieve. You were wrong. And thousands and thousands of innocent people died because of that war. Would President Bush have still invaded Iraq if he knew that Iraqis leaders said there were no weapons of mass destruction, if he had seen the transcript of that tape? We will never know, because you deprived us of that chance. Because of your own overconfidence that you could turn Iraq into a democracy."

Sullivan stopped and shuffled his papers again. His face reddened.

"I've thought long and hard about this. I barely slept last night. Most people outside America want me to put you in jail for years. Many people inside America want me to as well. But I will not. Just as Mr. Perche is correct, so is Mr. Clement. An international court should be wary to second-guess the work of a statesman within his own country. If I put the former president of the United States in jail, then what follows from that? Prosecutors would set their sights on the leaders of other countries. This courtroom would descend into merely another front in the world's endless wars. The resulting international instability would be highly damaging." Looking over at Perche again, he said, "the fate of history belongs to nations' heads of state, not ambitious prosecutors." Then he turned back to Rummy. "So I am going to let you go Mr. Rumsfeld. I'm going to let you go home. Not for your sake ... but for the world's. I do think, however, that this outcome is even worse than jail for you. You're an old man now. And living out your days at the Hague wouldn't be so bad. You'd be safe. Well fed. We'd allow visitors. Here, your mind would be consumed with thoughts about what happened to you. The injustice to you. And you'd be a hero to many. But now you will go home where you will be free to think about what you've done, about the decisions you've made. About the consequences of those decisions. About how you—just one man—impacted the whole course of history. Your country went to war and you hid important evidence from your president and you presided over a failed attempt to transform Iraq into a democracy, which was the whole point of the invasion. You were wrong about what you could do. You've spent a lifetime being right about everything. Everything!" The judge slammed down his fist. "But you were wrong about one thing. You were wrong about yourself. You judged everything else in the world with precision. But you misjudged yourself."

Sullivan paused for several seconds before continuing. "You will now return to your cell here for the last time. Someone will come get you later today to process your release."

"Understood, Your Honor," Rummy said softly.

"This proceeding is adjourned." He pounded the gavel against the wood. *Thwack, thwack.*

Rummy stood up. He looked Clement in the eyes and said, "Thank you," shaking his hand. Then he turned to the first row and saw Joyce. Their eyes met. She was crying. She smiled when she saw him look at her. He smiled too. A tear meandered down his left cheek. He wiped it away.

A security guard came and motioned for Rummy to head toward the door. They walked out of the courtroom together.

Chapter 74

About two hours later Rummy was sitting in a gray steel chair in a new cell. It was different from the previous one: smaller, darker. There was just a door with a small window in the middle of it—everything else was cement walls. A single bulb in the middle of the ceiling emitted only a dim glow that left the room mostly dark.

His head was down. He was looking at his shadow on the floor. He was relieved that he was going to go home but was still decompressing from the searing intensity of the preceding weeks. He was thinking about my testimony from the third day of trial, almost two weeks earlier, replaying it in his mind. Perche, with his snooty confidence, was examining me from the podium:

"How did you find out about the tape of Qusay and Aziz saying Iraq didn't have weapons of mass destruction?" he asked.

"James Jenkins came to my office and told me." I felt uneasy sitting in the witness box, but I couldn't tell if my nervousness showed.

Rummy's head shot back when he heard me say James Jenkins' name. He had no idea over all these years that his loyal deputy and close friend outed him about the tape. All those hours they'd spent together—working at the Pentagon and the White House and on Rummy's memoirs—and Jenkins had never said a word.

"When was this?"

I fidgeted in the chair and straightened out my red dress across my lap. "In late 2003, some months after the Iraq invasion."

"What did Mr. Jenkins say?"

"He said that in 2002 Mr. Rumsfeld ordered him to put together a team of Defense Department intelligence agents to go to Iraq and find weapons of mass destruction. That Mr. Rumsfeld said the CIA wasn't doing its job, so DOD had to step in. The DOD had to find the evidence of WMDs that would support the invasion."

"What else did Mr. Jenkins tell you?"

"He said in late 2002, months before we invaded Iraq, the DOD team on the ground secured a tape of Saddam's son Qusay and Iraqi senior leader Tariq Aziz both clearly saying that Iraq did not have WMDs." I paused a few seconds before continuing, looking at Rummy. Then at Joyce. I had met her several times over the years and always found her very bright and likable. "Then he told me Mr. Rumsfeld ordered him to destroy the tape and its transcript."

"In your opinion, why did he come to you and tell you this?" Perche asked.

I paused, seeing every member of the jury sitting on the edge of their seats. Several of them were taking notes. "I'm not entirely sure. His conscience, I suppose."

"What do you mean?"

"I assume that Mr. Jenkins felt bad about what he'd done, about hiding the tape, destroying the tape, about how President Bush went to war without knowing about the tape."

"Why would he feel bad? Please explain."

"Well, because the tape was key evidence relevant to our decision of whether or not to invade Iraq. Whether or not Iraq actually had WMDs was an important question—the key question—and the tape, obviously, the tape was very relevant to the answer. I think all this weighed heavily on Mr. Jenkins and he felt obligated to tell me."

"And what did you do after Mr. Jenkins told you Mr. Rumsfeld ordered him to destroy the tape?"

"I told President Bush."

"Why did you tell the president?"

"He was my boss and, more importantly, the president. He had a right to know."

"Why did he have a right to know?"

"Well, Mr. Perche, it's pretty obvious, isn't it? The president made the ultimate call on Iraq without having a big piece of evidence."

"What did President Bush say when you told him what Mr. Rumsfeld had done?"

I waited a few seconds before answering. I always try to be careful with my words when speaking about President Bush publicly, especially with the whole world watching. We are still close friends.

"He was very angry. The most angry I ever saw him actually. Iraq already wasn't going well—the insurgency was gaining steam every day at the time. This just made things worse. His relationship with Mr. Rumsfeld was never the same after this. He asked me to confront Mr. Rumsfeld, to have him explain himself."

"Did you?"

"Yes, I did."

"What happened?"

"I went to his office at the Pentagon and confronted him, told him someone told me about the tape. I didn't mention Mr. Jenkins by name; I had promised him I wouldn't. Then I told Rummy ... I mean Mr. Rumsfeld ... I told him I knew the tape was destroyed."

"How did Mr. Rumsfeld react?" Perche asked.

"Well, it was really the only time I ever saw him flustered. He didn't know what to say. At first, he just stared at me. He was standing at his desk. I saw his hands starting to shake. Then he asked who told me. I refused to tell him, but he kept asking—he was very focused on finding out who told me. After it was clear that I wouldn't tell him, he mumbled a few things and said he would need to check with his team and get back to me."

"That's it?"

"That's it."

"Did you tell anyone else about the destruction of the tape?"

"Yes, I told Secretary Powell."

"Why Secretary Powell?"

"He also had a right to know, obviously. He was secretary of state. He gave that huge speech at the UN. He went before the whole world and advocated for something he might not have, if he had known all the facts."

"And did he confront Mr. Rumsfeld?" Perche asked.

"Not to my knowledge. I think his deputy Mr. Armitage did. There was a big screaming fight at the Pentagon between Rumsfeld and Armitage, apparently. But I never heard the full story."

"What do you think President Bush would have done differently if he'd known about the tape?"

"Going into Iraq was a very close call, Mr. Perche. There was lots of debate within the administration, lots of thoughtful analysis. The key factor was WMDs. It really was. President Bush determined that Iraq had them, based on what he knew. This is what he thought, what he told the American people. But he didn't know about the tape. Ultimately, I think the tape would have changed his mind and tipped the scales against the invasion, if the president had known."

Perche raised his voice. "So, if President Bush had known about the tape that Mr. Rumsfeld destroyed then the United States would not have invaded Iraq?"

"That's my opinion, yes."

"Thank you, Ms. Rice, for your testimony."

Rummy was now pacing the floor in the cell. Grinding his teeth. Thinking. Remembering. He could feel his heartbeat in his cheeks. My testimony was the hardest part of the trial for him to watch, worse even than Perche's closing argument. Then Rummy replayed in his mind Paul Clement cross examining me.

"Thank you, Secretary Rice, for your testimony today."

"You're welcome," I said.

"You were President Bush's national security advisor from 2001 to 2005, is that right?"

"Yes."

"And his secretary of state from 2005 to 2008, correct?"

"I actually served as secretary of state until January 2009."

Clement paused before continuing. "Okay, thank you. You're friends with the current United States Secretary of State Mike Pompeo, isn't that right?"

"Yes."

"You spoke with him about this matter, isn't that right?"

"It is."

"He called you?"

"Yes," I said, "as a former Republican secretary of state, I speak with him from time to time."

"When was your call with him about this matter?"

"I think it was in August of this year."

"What did he say?"

"He said President Trump was considering letting Mr. Perche extradite John Bolton and put him on trial here at the Hague."

"This was after Trump had fired Bolton as his national security advisor, correct?" Clement asked.

"That's right," I said.

"What else did Secretary Pompeo say?"

"He asked my opinion about it, whether it was a good idea."

"What did you say?"

"I said it was a bad idea. A very bad idea."

"Why?"

"It would open the floodgates, Mr. Clement. The United States shouldn't allow prosecutors from other countries to put our own officials on trial. It would generate lots of abuse and malicious prosecutions for improper purposes. No one serious would ever want to serve in a senior position if they thought they could be prosecuted by a foreign rival."

"Did you say anything else?"

"I reminded him that Mr. Rumsfeld faced the same charges as Mr. Bolton."

"Why?"

I paused and adjusted my skirt. "Not sure … just seemed relevant."

"Excuse me, Secretary Rice. You aren't sure. It just seemed relevant?"

"That's right."

"Hm," Clement said, glancing over at the jury and then turning back to me. "Okay, well, then what did Secretary Pompeo say?"

"He asked what I thought about Mr. Rumsfeld, about letting the case go forward with him. I said it was a bad idea … for the same reasons. If not more so. Mr. Rumsfeld, after all, is a former president."

"That was it?"

"Yes, that was about it during our first call."

Clement paused briefly and reviewed his notes. "Was there a second call?"

"Yes, about a week later."

"What did Secretary Pompeo say in that call?"

"He called back and said Trump was going to do this, over his objection, over the objection of his entire National Security Council. Trump was going to let Mr. Perche extradite Mr. Bolton and also Mr. Rumsfeld and put them on trial. He asked my thoughts about what the case would look like. I told him that, as far as I knew, Bolton hadn't broken the law. But maybe Mr.

Rumsfeld did, I said. I told him about the tape of Qusay and Aziz ... about how Rummy ... how Mr. Rumsfeld destroyed the tape."

"Why did you tell him this?"

"If it was going to happen ... if Trump was going to do this ... allow the prosecution to happen ... well, then, I thought the world should know about the destruction of the tape. It was a significant event."

"And Mr. Pompeo told Mr. Perche about the tape, isn't that right?"

"My understanding is that Secretary Pompeo told President Trump about the tape, and President Trump ordered him to tell Mr. Perche about it."

"Why did President Trump do that?"

"From what I understand, President Trump was mad that Mr. Rumsfeld, the most-recent Republican president, refused to endorse him during the 2016 campaign."

Clement paused and reviewed his notes again before continuing. "You and Mr. Rumsfeld didn't get along when you worked together, isn't that right Secretary Rice?"

"I think that's fair."

"Why not?"

"He was ... how shall I put it ... he was difficult, condescending."

"He criticized your work as President Bush's national security advisor and secretary of state, isn't that right?"

"Yes, he did. Repeatedly. Vociferously."

"You felt like he didn't respect you, isn't that right?"

"I'd say I felt like he didn't respect me *enough*."

"And you were worried he purposely and dishonestly undercut you with President Bush, damaged your relationship with the president, isn't that right?"

I shook my head. "I wouldn't characterize it quite like that Mr. Clement."

Clement's voice was rising. "You thought he lied to President Bush about you and your work for the administration, isn't that true?"

"No, I don't think he went that far."

"How far did he go?

"He was unfair but not malicious. I actually ... Mr. Clement ... I actually have a lot of respect for Mr. Rumsfeld. We had our disagreements, often heated, but at bottom I think he's a good man. He's a good husband and father. A highly intelligent person. And his intentions were good. I never doubted his intentions. He was even courageous at times—like when he ran into the burning Pentagon on September 11th to help several people. He wanted what was best for the country and genuinely thought Iraq was a threat. But he's a complicated human being, like many people are. He got too zealous about Iraq, about invading Iraq, and it clouded his judgment. It blinded him. He thought he could do what no one else had ever done and solve the Middle East, using Iraq as a great model of democracy. And, ultimately, his zealotry caused him to do something he shouldn't have done. Something, I think, the world should know about. The world should know that he had that tape destroyed, that President Bush didn't know about it when we went into Iraq."

Clement shook his head. "But, Secretary Rice, in 2002 and 2003 you advocated for war in Iraq, right?"

"I supported the president's decision, yes."

"You did so publicly, right?"

"That's right."

"Repeatedly, right?"

"Yes."

"And you knew Qusay and Aziz were liars, didn't you?"

"I knew they could sometimes be dishonest, yes."

"Were they liars?"

"I'm not sure what you mean, Mr. Clement."

"Please answer the question directly Ms. Rice," Sullivan said. My spine stiffened when my eyes met the judge's.

"Yes, Your Honor," I said.

"Were Qusay and Aziz liars?" Clement repeated.

"Yes, that's fair to say."

"So, the tape could have been purposefully inaccurate; they could have been lying, trying to spread misinformation?"

"Yes, that's possible. But the president—"

"But Ms. Rice, you knew—"

"No, no, let me finish Mr. Clement. The president still should have known about it. The president should have judged the accuracy of the tape for himself. The American people elected him, not Mr. Rumsfeld."

Clement paused and leaned in toward me from the podium. "You feel guilty about the outcome in Iraq, and your role in it, don't you? That's what's really going on here, right? You're trying to pass the blame for Iraq to Mr. Rumsfeld, by making the tape a bigger deal than it really was, isn't that right?"

"Not at all."

"That's why you told Secretary Pompeo about the tape—so Mr. Rumsfeld could take the blame for Iraq in the eyes of history, instead of you and President Bush."

"No, that's just not true."

"This isn't about the truth, Ms. Rice, this is about your legacy."

"That's just false. The truth is—"

"This trial makes you look better. It makes Mr. Rumsfeld the sole culprit. This trial—that you manufactured by telling Secretary Pompeo about the tape—this trial is your public acquittal for your role in the Iraq war, isn't that right?"

"I just wanted the truth out there, Mr. Clement. The historical record should have the full truth about something as consequential as the Iraq war and Mr. Rumsfeld's role in the whole thing. It just should."

Clement smiled. "No further questions, Your Honor."

Rummy sat back down in his chair in the middle of the cell, still furious at me for telling Pompeo about the tape. Perche might never have found out about it otherwise. Whatever tension there was between us, whatever rivalry, he didn't think I should have gone as far as I did. At the time, I don't think I thought through the full implications of telling Pompeo about the tape. I just had this visceral urge to tell him. So I did.

And Rummy was deeply hurt that Jenkins came to me in the first place. While he never asked Jenkins about it—silence seemed prudent—he always wondered how news about the tape got to me and Armitage. He assumed it was from an agent on the ground in Iraq. He had shared one secret after another with Jenkins for years—and he never once saw a sign that his trust had been violated.

Rummy was jolted out of thought by the sound of a guard walking up the hall. He stood up and walked to the door and looked through the small window, thinking it was finally time for him to be let out. But the guard kept walking.

Rummy paced the room for several minutes and sat back down. His mind turned to what Judge Sullivan had said about him, that he would always know what he knew and what he didn't know and whether he had done anything wrong. Rummy was tired and his body ached. But his mind was clear. He knew that he had the right intentions, that Perche and others were wrong about his motivations: he didn't lie about WMDs; he thought Iraq had them or could manufacture them quickly. He didn't want to invade Iraq for sinister reasons; it wasn't for retribution or oil money or to increase America's global dominance. Iraq was a real threat to the United States and to the world order. The status quo with Saddam was just as bad as he said it was.

But this experience had caused something powerful to rise from his subconscious and burst into the epicenter of his mind. Sitting in this cell, waiting to go home, he knew that he had, in fact, committed a grievous error: he of all people had confused what he knew with what he didn't. He was too confident that Iraq had weapons of mass destruction. No one really knew either way. And, above all, he was too confident that he—that Donald H. Rumsfeld—could transform Iraq and, in turn, the Middle East.

Judge Sullivan was right. Paul O'Neill was right. I was right. Sitting in his cell, Rummy knew we were right. Then he said something he never had before—in a long, slow whisper to himself: "I was wrong."

He looked up from the floor to the gray walls around him. He remembered the meeting with Jenkins in 2002 at the Pentagon, when he found out about the tape of Qusay and Aziz. He pictured Jenkins face, his nervous and bloodshot eyes. He'd told Jenkins to destroy the tape because he couldn't let anything get in the way of the invasion, in the way of Donald Rumsfeld being the man of action who finally transformed the Middle East—the man who accomplished what everyone else had failed to do. He couldn't be just another secretary of defense. He needed to be special. He needed to be extraordinary. He got it wrong, he knew, because he twisted the question about Iraq into a question about himself—and the second he did that, his judgment collapsed. He got everything in the world right except for himself. Everything in his field of vision was clear except for one thing: his own self-image.

He looked back down at the floor. His eyes began to water, and his breathing slowed. The room was quiet. He sat motionless in the chair digesting, absorbing, accepting this fact. He got everything in the world right ... except for himself.

Suddenly he heard the keys ram into the lock in the door. It startled him. He looked up. The key turned with a heavy clank. The door opened and a flood of bright light slowly entered the dark room. He squinted in the glare and looked down at the floor. The guard took several steps back as he opened the door and pulled the key out from the lock. His key chain rustled, and he stepped aside.

Then Rummy looked back up.

And a dark silhouette appeared and took two steps toward him, surrounded by light. Rummy's eyes adjusted and the figure slowly came into view. It was Joyce.

His whole body relaxed for the first time in weeks.

"Time to go home," she said.

Acknowledgements

A number of people helped make this book happen. Among them: Andrew Eck, Lara Terco, Lissa Warren, Daniel Edelman, Michael McKinley, Erik Fleming, Angie Boyter, and Zeljka Kojik.

Thank you all.

Also By William Cooper

Fiction
A Quiet Life

Nonfiction
How America Works ... And Why It Doesn't

Contact

Website
will-cooper.com

Bluesky
wcooperbooks.bsky.social

Author Newsletter
democracyinamerica.substack.com

Made in the USA
Middletown, DE
26 September 2025